ENVY ON 30A

Deborah Rine

Envy on 30A is a work of fiction. The characters, incidents and dialogue are drawn from the author's imagination and are not to be construed as real. Any resemblance to actual events or persons, living or dead, is entirely coincidental.

ISBN- 9781731038609

This book is dedicated to the fine people along Highway 30A who have given of their time, abundance and heart to the survivors of Hurricane Michael.

Books by Deborah Rine

Banner Bluff Mystery Series:
THE LAKE
FACE BLIND
DIVERGENT DEATHS

Contemporary Novel:
RAW GUILT

Emerald Coast Mystery Series:
THE GIRL ON 30A

Deborah Rine can be contacted at:
    www.deborah-rine-author.com
    http://dcrine.blogspot.com/
    Facebook and Twitter

For where there is envy and selfish ambition, there will also be disorder and wickedness of every kind.
—James 3:1

Prologue

The news stations reported the crowds along the funeral route were in the thousands. Women dressed in shades of pink flocked around the Great God of Forgiveness Cathedral. From a helicopter it looked like a field of wild roses. Proceeding the hearse was the Texas marching band and a parade of pink-frocked choral groups, their voices raised in song.

Pastor Ron Bates stood on the wide marble steps of the cathedral. His handsome face bore an expression of deep sadness, real or feigned. When the hearse stopped in front of the church, eight pallbearers stepped to the back of the vehicle and slowly pulled the casket out. White platinum and gold, it weighed over five hundred pounds. Before the pallbearers could ascend the stairs with the heavy load, a woman broke through the police barricade and threw herself onto the coffin. In her hand was a bouquet of pink roses.

It was as though a dam burst. Throngs of mourners surged forward, wanting to touch the casket of their beloved idol. The police lost control. Shots were fired, people were trampled. Later, the media reported cases of police brutality and general mayhem.

Chapter 1
Wednesday Afternoon

Morgan looked across her desk at the Russo family, who were seated in a semi-circle on the elegant Louis XV fauteuil chairs. Daughter Gabriella was aglow. Dark curls had escaped her pony tail and framed her pretty, round face. Morgan could guess her thoughts. She was imagining herself on the beach, dressed in a flowing white gown, her soon-to-be husband gazing into her eyes in adoration.

Gabriella's mother, Lena, was aglow as well. Probably imagining herself in that blue silk dress she'd mentioned seeing at Dolce & Gabbana. "It's expensive, but worth it," she'd said during yet another consultation yesterday. "And I can always lose twenty pounds before the wedding. There's plenty of time."

Gabriella's father, Marco, was not aglow. He was sweating profusely. They had just gone over the approximate cost of everything, including venue, flowers, band, tent and all the miscellaneous details that make up a fabulous wedding at the Magnolia Resort and Spa.

Marco Russo pushed back his chair and stood up. "We're out of here. This wedding is ridiculously expensive." He looked over at Morgan. "I'm sorry we've taken up so much of your time, but I can't afford to spend that much money on a one-day extravaganza."

Gabriella burst into tears. "Daddy, this is my wedding day. It has to be perfect."

Lena looked up at her husband and sputtered, "Marco, what are you saying? This is the most important day of your daughter's life."

"Most important day of her life? Give me a break. With that five hundred thousand dollars, I could buy her a nice condo up on Silver Hill."

"*Da*...ddy," Gabriella cried. "I told all my friends this is where the wedding would be. We can't back out now."

"Yes, we can, and we are." He turned again to Morgan. "You've done a great job selling your package but it's out of my league."

Gabriella was sobbing in her mother's arms, while Lena's dark eyes sent poison darts in her husband's direction. But Marco was not to be cowed. "Let's go, Gabby. We'll still manage a great wedding at a price I can afford."

Just then the door flew open. In a hurricane of movement, Victoria Palmer stormed across the room and over to Morgan's desk. The already charged air exploded in thunderbolts of tension and anger as Victoria leaned forward, her hands spread on the sleek surface. "This will not do. I said lavender buds and I will not accept white or dull pink. You promised. You need to deliver." Victoria's face was flushed, and her violet-blue eyes flashed. Jet-black hair fell in waves around her flawless face with its rosebud lips and perfect nose. Right now, the rosebud lips were twisted in a snarl.

The Russos stood there, mouths agape and eyes wide. All three recognized Victoria Palmer. The social media queen wore jean short-shorts and a simple, white V-neck tee and yet she looked ravishing. Morgan had to admit the girl had fabulous style. Right now, Mr. Russo was probably enjoying the view of Victoria's frequently photographed, well-known rump.

Morgan stood up. "Hello, Victoria. Let me introduce the Russos."

Victoria spun around and produced one of her fabulous smiles. "I'm so sorry to have barged in like this."

"No problem, we were just leaving," Mr. Russo said as he dragged his daughter and wife towards the door. Reluctantly, Gabriella and her mother followed his lead. Lena's arm was wrapped around her daughter's shoulders. Gabriella hiccupped between sobs. Neither of them looked back. Marco held the door open, ushered them through and shut it firmly behind them.

Victoria chuckled. "Can you imagine that girl in a wedding dress? She'd look like an over-stuffed bratwurst."

Morgan chose not to answer the unkind comment.

"Anyway, Morgan, you have to do something about the flowers."

"I'll look into it."

"Don't 'look into it'. Get what I want." Victoria formed an imaginary gun with her hand and pointed it at Morgan. Then she turned and left, slamming the door behind her.

Suddenly the office seemed incredibly quiet. Morgan felt as though she'd been through a tsunami of emotions. She'd had a feeling from the start that the Russos were not typical Magnolia clients. Since they didn't own a cottage on the island, they had to pay the $30,000 surcharge. Then Gabby and her mother included a bunch of extras that increased the final price of the event. Mr. Russo hadn't been brought in until today. As Morgan outlined the expenses, she'd sensed his shock and disbelief, and disapproval. She didn't begrudge the time she'd spent. As her dad would say, "You win a few, you lose a few."

Morgan walked over to the window and pulled back the sheer curtain with her well-manicured fingers. She had a superb view of the Gulf of Mexico and the shoreline. Bright blue beach umbrellas and matching beach chairs were perfectly lined up along the shore. The sky was a robin's-egg blue, the water turquoise and the sand sugar-white. Directly below her window lay a free-form swimming pool surrounded by blue-and-white striped deck chairs and umbrellas. She could see children frolicking in the pool and Jack in his guard chair.

Morgan let the curtain fall back in place and stepped over to her desk. She closed her laptop and placed the Russo papers back in their folder. Generally, she enjoyed being the wedding planner for the Magnolia Resort and Spa. Even when she had to deal with clients like Victoria Palmer. Morgan always dressed with elegance. Today she wore a pale green dress with a string of pearls and beige heels. Her thick blonde hair was tucked in a sleek chignon at the back of her neck. It was all part of her shtick. The Magnolia exuded an aura of chic sophistication and exclusivity. The brides needed to feel they were being pampered right from the start.

The Magnolia Resort was a gated community located along Highway 30A that ran along the Gulf coast. As a presque-isle, it was surrounded by Lake Nawatchi, which opened to the waters of the

Gulf of Mexico to the east. To the west a slim isthmus along the dunes was used as a service road. Supplies, cleaning staff, wait staff and gardeners accessed the resort on a narrow two-lane road across the causeway.

Resort members and guests used an unobtrusive entrance off of 30A with a security gate. A winding road through a forest of majestic palms led to a shaded parking lot. No cars were allowed on the resort property. After members parked in the lot, Magnolia staff loaded suitcases and belongings onto golf carts and took them over an elegant arched bridge designed by Nico, the famous Japanese architect. On the island, members circulated in golf carts, rode bikes or walked along the intricate system of paths winding through the resort. Apart from the main building, which served as hotel and spa, the resort contained fifty cottages hidden among the tropical flora. Morgan smiled at the thought. *Cottages* was somewhat of a misnomer, considering that some could house twenty people comfortably.

Resort members came from all over the country, although there was a preponderance of southerners and Texans. They desired a quiet, idyllic getaway and privacy from their neighbors. Among the verdant gardens were gurgling brooks, sparkling waterfalls and carefully tended stretches of lush lawn. For those inclined, there were tennis courts and swimming pools. A boat house with canoes and sailfish nestled near the Nico bridge. Members joked that the Magnolia Resort was the closest thing to paradise.

***

Morgan picked up the folder for the Russo-Simon wedding and opened the door to the outer office. Itzel looked up from her computer, her brown eyes wide with surprise.

"Wow, what happened? Miss Gabriella and her mother were pretty upset." Petite and voluptuous, with jet black hair and a fabulous smile, Itzel's face was an open book. Morgan could read her every thought. She was the best assistant Morgan had ever had: efficient, energetic and great with details.

Morgan hefted the folder. "Mr. Russo thought the wedding was too expensive for his budget, so he pulled the plug."

"You couldn't cut back on something?"

"No way. You remember how the mom insisted on Wagyu fillet, Dom Pérignon champagne, mountains of white roses and the spa treatment for the entire wedding party. I presented it all to Mr. Russo. He didn't want to negotiate. He wanted out."

Itzel leaned back and crossed her arms across her chest. "Gosh, Morgan, you spent a lot of time with Gabby and her mother."

"I know. That's the way the cookie crumbles." Morgan handed her the folder. "I'm going upstairs. I don't have any more appointments today. You should head home, too. It's nearly five o'clock."

"Yeah, I think I will. I'm having dinner tonight with José."

"That should be fun."

Itzel groaned, "Yeah right, except Luis, his five-year-old nephew, is coming too. We're going to Panama City Beach, to the Pier Park amusement park."

Morgan laughed. "Doesn't sound very romantic."

She left her office, walked down a short hall and through the spacious lobby to the elevator. Her heels tapped a staccato tattoo on the red tiled floor. Decorated in red, blue and yellow, the space evoked a stylish Mexican hacienda. Curved sofas and comfortable chairs formed groupings around the high-ceilinged hall. On the far side, picture windows framed the Gulf. The entrance to the Orchid Lounge was to the left and the Sail Fish Restaurant to the right. Both locales sported beach views. Morgan could hear music and quiet voices emanating from the lounge.

She waved at Lionel, who manned the front desk. Phone to his ear, he waved back distractedly. Morgan headed toward a bank of elevators that would take her to her suite on the top floor. She called it her secret hideaway. Few people knew that her father and uncle owned the Magnolia Resorts. She had worked her way up, doing a variety of jobs in the kitchens, housekeeping, spa and the front desk. Little by little she'd learned about the resort's inner workings. Her brother ran the Magnolia near San Diego and her cousin was down in Palm Beach. Morgan could have taken an executive role as well, but instead chose to become a wedding planner. She loved the

7

creativity in designing a fabulous event. Sometimes the brides could be high-maintenance, but each new wedding brought on a new set of exciting plans. Morgan was also excellent with people and she often acted as a pseudo- therapist, nudging clients through emotional firestorms.

Morgan exited the elevator on the top floor and walked down to the last door on the right. She tapped in a code on the panel by the door, listened for a beep, and pushed the door open. A small entryway led into a sleek, modern living room decorated in white on white. A nubby carpet of different textures of white wool lay under a Roche Bobois white leather sofa and matching bucket chairs. In a corner, clear plastic chairs surrounded a glass dining table. Behind a silk-paneled screen lay an ultra-modern, minimalist kitchen. Vases filled with a mad array of vibrant flowers sat on the dining table, the glass desk and the white marble coffee table. Along with several Impressionist prints, they offered the only color in the room.

Morgan pulled off her heels, padded across the white marble floor, and opened the curtains. In the afternoon sun, the Gulf glimmered, and seagulls danced over the waves. She loved this view and never tired of seeing the white beach that stretched into the distance. Her eyes searched the horizon. Not even a wisp of a cloud. According to the Weather Channel, it would be smooth sailing throughout the weekend. It had to be. The four-day wedding extravaganza featuring Victoria Palmer and Bradley Hughes III began tomorrow. *And God forbid anything dares to ruin Victoria's perfect day.*

Chapter 2
Wednesday Evening

Morgan changed into white shorts and a white t-shirt with the pink magnolia logo on the front. At the dresser, she unpinned her bun and loosened her hair. With a silver-handled brush, she smoothed out her long, wavy mane. She dashed a little blush across her high cheekbones, touched up the color on her full lips, slipped on some flip flops, and grabbed her purse. The bag was ultra-soft white leather, a gift from her friend Claire. Tonight, Morgan was meeting Claire and another friend on the Whiskey Bravo roof terrace. It was a perfect evening to watch the sun set over the Gulf.

She took the stairs down and made her way through the lobby and out to the staff parking lot hidden from view behind a wall of fuchsia bougainvillea. Her blue Mini Cooper was parked in its usual spot near the security gate. She tapped in the code and drove through the gate, watching in the rearview as it rumbled shut behind her. A short drive on the paved two-lane road took her across the causeway. To her left lay sandy dunes and the blue Gulf. To her right, the dark waters of Lake Nawatchi.

At the end of the isthmus, Morgan turned right and took the road through the woods that followed the banks of the lake until it arrived at Highway 30A. Ten minutes later, she pulled into the parking lot at Whiskey Bravo. Upstairs on the roof terrace, she spotted Claire and Olivia deep in conversation. They both looked up as she approached.

"Hi, am I late?" Morgan slid into an empty chair.

"No, you're right on time. I came early so I could snag this table." Olivia pushed a wayward strand of unruly hair off her forehead. She was a petite bundle of energy, with dark curly hair, a pixie face and an acerbic wit.

"I have some news and I couldn't wait to get here." Claire said, blushing.

Morgan leaned forward. "What news?"

"Well..." Claire pulled her left hand out from under the table. On her finger was a classic solitaire diamond ring, lovely in its simplicity. "Ta-da...I'm engaged."

Olivia grinned. "Wow, congratulations."

"I'm so happy for you." Elated, Morgan got up and gave Claire a hug.

"Tell us all about it," Olivia said. "Was Dax down on bended knee?"

Claire looked down at the ring and then up at her friends. She was glowing with happiness. Her grey-green eyes lit up and her smile illuminated her face.

Two years ago, Claire had worked undercover with Daxton Simmons, a local FBI agent, and almost got killed by the leaders of a drug gang. For the past year, she and Dax had been living together and now Dax had popped the question. When Morgan was around them, she could feel the vibes. They were perfect together. Recently, Dax had left the FBI and now worked as chief of the Santa Rosa Beach sheriff's department.

"It was after dinner last night. During dinner he barely said a thing. I figured he was thinking about work. Anyway, I cooked, so Dax did the dishes. I went outside on the deck with my laptop. I was busy looking at sales numbers for the month. He came out and kept moving around; fussing with a plant, brushing sand off a deck chair, stuff he never does. He was kind of annoying and I finally said, 'What's up? Have you got a problem?' He hemmed and hawed, not really answering or looking at me. Then all of a sudden, he got down on one knee and said, 'Will you marry me?' Just like that." Claire laughed. "He said he had planned something special for Saturday at The Bay... that's where we had our first date, but he couldn't stand to wait four more days. Then we both started laughing." Tears shone in her eyes, though she was still smiling. "I'm so happy...we're so happy."

"Let's order champagne. We'll celebrate," Olivia said.

A few minutes later they toasted Claire with glasses of bubbly. Then they ordered some appetizers to share: crispy grouper bites with remoulade sauce, boiled shrimp with cocktail sauce and fried mac and cheese sticks with chipotle aioli.

"When is the wedding?" Olivia asked as she wiped her fingers on a napkin.

"Dax wants to get married right away. He says why wait. We want to have a small wedding, just family and close friends. But I know this will take a few weeks to organize."

"I'd be glad to help," Morgan said.

"I know you would, but…the truth is, I can't afford a wedding at the Magnolia."

"I know. I meant I could handle some of the plans. What were you thinking to do?"

"We want to get married in the Chapel at Seaside. That's where we go to church."

"I love that church. It's pristine," Olivia said.

Claire nodded and took a sip of champagne. "Then we thought we would go back to the house and have a party. See, Dax has six siblings, and several are married with children. My brother has three kids. We thought it would be easier to be at home and the kids can play on the beach and just run around during the reception."

"That sounds nice. How about if I cater the event?" Morgan said.

Claire's eyes widened. "Really?"

"Sure, it'll be my gift to you. Let's work on the menu together. And I can also get you some flowers wholesale."

"Gosh, that would be really nice." Claire reached over and squeezed Morgan's hand.

"I'll help too. I'll be Morgan's second-in-command." Olivia saluted with two fingers to her forehead.

They raised their glasses and smiled at each other.

After a sip of champagne, Olivia asked Morgan, "What have you got going this weekend? Is Grady in town?"

Morgan raised her hands in prayer. "I have got the biggest wedding I've ever organized happening over the next four days."

"Four days?" Olivia and Claire said in unison. They looked at each other and laughed.

"Yes. It's the Victoria Palmer wedding."

11

Olivia shifted to the edge of her chair. "You mean, *the* Victoria Palmer? She's a major thirst trap."

"The one and only. The bridal party is arriving tonight. They're spending Thursday together, playing volleyball on the beach, croquet on the lawn, and swimming in the pool. That night they're dining at The Red Bar in Grayton Beach. Friday, friends and family arrive. There's a big rehearsal dinner on Friday night in the Mimosa Garden. Saturday afternoon is the wedding on the beach. The reception will be in the Magnolia Park under a tent; dinner and dancing. Sunday, more entertainment and a brunch. I figure by Sunday night I'll probably be near dead from exhaustion. You guys can come over and resuscitate me."

"Oh, my God. All that and Victoria Palmer! What's she like?" Claire asked.

"I really shouldn't discuss the wedding or the bridal party." Morgan sighed and looked heavenward. "Let's just say she's used to getting her own way."

Chapter 3
Wednesday Evening

The clear sky had turned a smudged salmon pink as the sun dropped below the horizon. Now it was a velvety dark blue. Before turning in at the road to the resort, Morgan noted people camped out along 30A. *Oh, my God, Victoria's fans have already started to arrive.*

Morgan drove down the causeway between the Gulf and Lake Nawatchi. To the east she could see an almost full moon coming up. After the security gates clanged shut behind her, Morgan parked her car in her usual spot and sat for a moment. Once she got out of the car, her job would begin. She would be fully immersed in wedding events for the next four days. It would be a marathon, but she loved the excitement. When she was feeling particularly egotistical, she realized she loved the feeling of control as she manipulated the major players in the wedding. Like a puppeteer, she pulled the strings and the bride and groom performed their wedding roles. Of course, a million things could go wrong, but usually she managed to smooth feathers and nurture her clients through the difficult moments. People knew she cared. They felt comfortable around her and trusted her.

Morgan entered the main building at the back through the kitchens. Things were quiet. The hotel was nearly empty, as most of the rooms were booked for the wedding. Guests would start arriving on Thursday. Tomorrow the kitchens would be a hotbed of activity.

As she emerged from the Jasmine Bistro, she saw a tall, slim girl dressed in grey sweatpants and a grey hoodie talking with Lionel at the front desk. Lionel beckoned her over. Thin and dark-haired, he had a fabulous smile and was punctilious in performing his job.

"Ms. Lytton, this is Ms. Fairbanks. She's an attendant in the Palmer-Hughes wedding party."

Morgan held out her hand. "Welcome to the Magnolia. And please call me Morgan. I'm the wedding planner."

Light brown eyes magnified by large round glasses considered Morgan. The girl scrunched her nose and pushed her glasses up with her index finger. Morgan noted the girl's fingernails were chewed to the quick.

"Hi, I'm Mindy. Wow, this place is fabulous." She surveyed the lobby. Her brown hair was pulled back in a messy pony-tail and she wore no make-up. Morgan couldn't help but wonder how this waif was a buddy of Victoria's. The two women were total opposites.

"Let me show you to your suite, Mindy. Where's your luggage?" Morgan asked.

Mindy pointed down at a tired-looking duffle. "This is it. I've got underwear and pjs in the bag. That's about it. You know, Victoria is providing all the clothes for the four days. I mean, everything." She cocked her head and looked at Morgan with a wry smile.

"Right, I guess I did know that." Morgan bent down to pick up the duffle. It was heavier than she'd thought.

Mindy reached over and grabbed the bag from her. "And someone's going to do my make-up every day, which is a joke, since I never wear any." Together they headed for the elevator as Mindy chattered away. "Can we take the stairs, please? I always walk up. It's much better for you."

"Sure, the stairs are right here." Morgan led the way. "Where do you come from? Texas, like Victoria?"

"No, I'm from Missouri, a little town no one ever heard of. Where do you come from?"

"California, but I've been down here for a while." At the top of the stairs, Morgan pushed open the heavy fire door and led the way down the corridor to Number 208. "Here's your suite."

Mindy slipped the keycard into the slot. When the green light flashed, she pushed open the door. Several lights came on, bathing the room in a soft glow. Mindy looked around, then stepped over to the French doors and pulled open the curtain. "Shit, I'd hoped for a view on the Gulf side. But this is all right." Her view gave on the front of the hotel, where a pond and a cascading waterfall were visible surrounded by artistically lit tropical vegetation and tall palm trees.

14

Morgan felt an impulse to apologize. "Victoria decided on the rooms."

"Right, I'm sure she did." Mindy shrugged and looked around the sitting room, paying more attention this time. It was attractively decorated in white, turquoise and beige, a current Florida palette. On a side table sat an enormous basket of goodies, chosen by Victoria: red and white wine, vitamin water, crackers, wrapped cheeses, chocolates, ripe peaches and avocados. Mindy unwrapped a Ghirardelli square and popped it in her mouth. "You've got to admit, Tory does everything to the max."

Morgan nodded. Then Mindy walked into the bedroom. Morgan could hear her opening the closet doors. "Oh, my God. Check this out."

Morgan went into the room. She already knew what was in the closet: shorts, t-shirts, dresses, bathing suits and the pink bridesmaid's dress. On each item, an attached card bore a name—in this case, *Mindy*—a day, and a time. Also included was the name of the make-up artist and what time she would appear to work her magic.

Mindy shuffled through the hanging garments. She pulled out some turquoise shorts and a polo shirt, then began reading the card: "Friday morning, 8 AM. Give me a break. This is *so* Victoria." She threw the clothes on the king-sized bed, she sat down on the edge, and bounced up and down like a little kid. "I'll have to invite a guest. This bed is way too big for li'l ol' me."

***

After Mindy had settled in with a glass of red wine and her laptop, Morgan went back downstairs and over to the front desk. "Lionel, has anyone else arrived for the wedding?"

"Yes, another girl came in while you were upstairs. Let's see..." He consulted the computer. "Georgina Ralston. She went right upstairs; said she was tired and didn't want to see anyone tonight. She seemed a little frazzled." He gestured towards the Orchid Lounge. "Three guys from the wedding party went in there. They arrived together about an hour ago. Do you want their names?"

"No, I'll just go in and introduce myself, see if they have everything they need."

"Oh, and the film crew is in there too. Guy and a gal in grey hoodies."

"Okay, thanks." Morgan started to turn away, then stopped and said, "If anything comes up…anything at all, please text me immediately. I need to be on top of any potential disaster."

Lionel grinned. "I hear you. Crazy things can happen, especially at weddings."

Chapter 4
Wednesday Night

Morgan headed across the lobby and into the Orchid Lounge. "Sunny" by Bobby Hebb was playing in the background. The mustached bartender was wiping down the bar with a cloth. At one end, three tall men were in deep discussion, a redhead, a dark blond, and an African-American. All three wore cargo shorts and t-shirts. On the counter in front of them lay a plate of empty oyster shells and the detritus of a demolished spicy-wing platter. Several bottles of 30A brand beer stood on the counter. Morgan recognized the blond man as Bradley Hughes III. With that wavy hair, grey eyes and tall, slim frame, he could have made it in the movies. He was *that* handsome.

He glanced up and waved as she came in. "Morgan, how great to see you. I want you to meet my friends." Bradley was a true gentleman. He always made Morgan feel special. When she talked to him, she felt as though he was hanging on to her every word, like she was the only person in the room. Undoubtedly, this quality was useful in his job as junior partner in the mammoth law firm of Smith, Schmidt and Saunders; a.k.a The Triple S. He'd attended Talbot College along with the other members of the wedding party and graduated *summa cum laude*. Morgan had made it a point to google all the members of the bridal party. It was important to know who she was dealing with.

Brad came over, bent down and kissed her cheek. Then he took her hand and led her over to the bar. "Guys, let me introduce Morgan Lytton, our number one wedding planner. She's done a fabulous job arranging the next four days."

Morgan laughed. "Let's just say, I've facilitated things. It's your bride, Victoria, who had the vision."

"Man, if you were able to work with Tory and not get chewed up and spit out, I'd say you're Wonder Woman," said the tall red-headed man. He sported a dark red beard and had twinkling blue eyes.

"It's a pleasure to work with someone who knows exactly what they want," Morgan said lightly. She didn't want to offend Brad, talking about his wife-to-be in a derogatory manner.

The red-haired guy laughed. "Very diplomatic. I can see why you're successful." He stuck out his hand. "Carter Perry. I'm a childhood friend of Brad's. We went to high school and college together. We all played football together, too." He gestured to the striking African-American man standing beside him. "We've been talking about the fact that we wouldn't have won the Rose Bowl if it wasn't for me as running back."

"Carter, you would not have run in for that touch down if I hadn't thrown the ball... perfectly, I might add," Brad said.

The black man added, "And if I hadn't blocked the SOB who was an inch from you." He turned to Morgan. "Hi, I'm Josh Brown. I'm pleased to meet you." Josh had café-au-lait skin and warm brown eyes. Morgan liked him immediately. She knew he was a gym teacher and a football coach at a Texas high school.

"It sounds as though the Talbot Tigers never would have won without the three of you," Morgan said.

"That's for sure." Carter's smile made his face come alive. "So, what's on tap for tomorrow?"

"Up in your suite is a pamphlet with a schedule for the next four days. You'll see what you're doing—"

Josh interrupted her. "...and what we're wearing. Check out the closet. There's an outfit for each event, complete with shoes and socks."

"You're kidding." Carter made a face. "Like what...costumes?"

"Some are, but the others are really nice clothes," Josh said. "And we can take them home afterwards."

Bradley looked from one guy to the other. "Remember, Victoria is going to have this whole thing filmed for her blog, webpage and Instagram."

"So it's like we're making a movie for four days straight?" Carter grimaced. "I really wonder how this will go. Hopefully, we won't kill each other before Sunday rolls around."

"We better go upstairs and get our beauty sleep," Josh said. "I want to look my best. Maybe a Hollywood scout will see the YouTube video and want to cast me in his next movie."

"I think I'll be the next DiCaprio," Carter said.

The two of them started laughing and punched each other in the arm. Then they headed for the lobby.

Bradley reached over and touched Morgan's elbow. "Don't mind those guys. They're great friends." He watched them leave the room. Then he looked into her eyes. "Listen, I wanted to thank you in person for all you've done. This will be a wonderful wedding and we owe it all to you and the Magnolia Resort."

Morgan blushed. "You're welcome. I hope it will be the perfect beginning to a happy marriage."

Brad nodded. "Right…well, I'll see you tomorrow." Then he left.

Morgan watched him go, feeling unsettled. She couldn't put her finger on why. Just tired, probably. Before going back upstairs, she should introduce herself to the film crew. Two people in grey hoodies, Lionel had said. She glanced around and saw them watching her from across the room. She walked over to their table. "Hi, I'm Morgan Lytton, the wedding planner. You'll be filming the wedding? It's a pleasure to meet you both."

The man stood up. He was tall and skinny with long brown hair in a ponytail. His deep-set dark eyes seemed to be assessing her. "Hi, I'm Rex and this is Jill."

Morgan bent to shake Jill's hand. "Nice to meet you." Jill's blond hair was cut Dutch-boy style, straight bangs and blunt at the chin line. She had several ear piercings and a small silver ring in her nose. She was pretty but had a hardness about her.

"We'll be videotaping the wedding for Victoria's social media," Rex said.

"We work for Tory on a regular basis," Jill added.

Morgan gave them a practiced smile. "Wow, that sounds like a big job."

"We went to Talbot, too. But we're not part of the beautiful people." Jill waved toward the doorway where the groom and his two friends had departed.

Rex looked uncomfortable. "Come on, Jill. Give it a rest."

"We were the geeks," Jill said. Her words sounded a little slurred, and Morgan wondered if she'd had one too many.

"If there's anything you need, please text me and I'll help you out." Morgan extracted a card from her bag and handed it to Jill.

"Right, I'm sure you will." Jill said sarcastically, gazing at the martini glass in her hand. Then she looked up. "Sorry to be a bitch."

Dismayed, Morgan saw there were tears in her eyes.

Chapter 5
Thursday Morning

The next morning, Morgan awoke with anticipation for Day One of the Palmer-Hughes wedding. It would be a perfect day. The weather service indicated sunshine and a high of eighty-two degrees. Morgan checked her phone and saw a text from Grady. He wanted to know when they could get together. She suggested meeting at The Red Bar that night after she escorted the wedding party to the restaurant. He responded right away, saying he would be there. Morgan smiled happily. He'd been gone for two very long weeks.

After a cup of coffee, Morgan showered and dressed in a lemon-yellow sheath and white sandals. Around her neck she wore a fanciful necklace of coral and turquoise she'd bought at Beach Mania in Seaside. Victoria had tried to get her to wear the same outfit as the wedding party, but Morgan had resisted.

Downstairs, she headed for the Jasmine Bistro where the breakfast was to take place. When Morgan entered the room, she did a quick check of the setup. A long table for eight was covered with a white tablecloth, a bowl of wildflowers in the middle. Turquoise and peach striped napkins, sparkling silverware, and pitchers of orange juice decked out the table. The wait-staff stood by the doors to the kitchen with bottles of champagne in their hands. Rex and Jill were setting up on opposite sides of the room. Five members of the wedding party were standing around and talking.

Carter looked up, spotted Morgan, and greeted her. "Here comes our tour guide. Let the games begin." Dressed in salmon-pink Vineyard Vine shorts and a white polo with the little whale on the pocket, he was a handsome guy.

Morgan smiled. "Good morning, everyone. I hope you all slept well and are ready for a day of fun."

"A day of fun! Give me a break," Carter said.

21

"Come on, Carter. We *are* going to have fun. The whole gang is here. And we came here for Brad," Josh said, good-naturedly.

"Yeah, I suppose you're right, I should shut up. But I feel like I'm just window dressing for some second-rate movie."

"It *is* a movie," Mindy said.

Morgan glanced over at the girl. She looked totally different in her preppy clothes. Like the others, Mindy was wearing the required Vineyard Vine shorts, hers in turquoise, and a white polo shirt. Her hair was in a ponytail. Morgan noted her smooth complexion, rosy blush as well as the eye make-up behind her round glasses.

Near the door were the Johanssons, who Morgan hadn't met the previous evening. She remembered their first names, Lars and Jenny. With light brown hair, brown eyes and tall, lanky builds, they could have been brother and sister instead of husband and wife. They were following the repartee in uncomfortable silence. Morgan introduced herself.

"Pleased to meet you," they responded in unison. Then they turned to each other and laughed. They *were* like a set of twins, Morgan thought.

"Sorry we didn't meet you last night. We drove here from Raleigh. It was a super long drive. We just fell into bed when we got here," Jenny said.

"How many hours was the drive?" Josh asked.

"About eleven hours," Lars said. "But we wanted to stop for lunch and stuff, so it took longer."

"I drove, too. It took me about ten hours. I'm living outside Houston," Josh said.

Lars asked, "What are you doing these days, Josh?"

"Teaching PE and coaching football. I love it. Love the kids and the staff."

"I'm surprised. With your grade-point-average, you could have gone to graduate school and gone into business."

"You're right, but I love what I'm doing." Josh grinned. "What about you?"

"Jenny and I took over her dad's insurance office. We like working together." Lars turned and smiled at Jenny. "Don't we, honey."

She nodded and grinned back.

Morgan glanced over at Carter. He was rolling his eyes at Mindy. *Some interesting dynamics in this group*, Morgan thought.

Just then Victoria came in, with Brad by the hand. For a minute, it seemed as though time stood still. Victoria's presence could take over a room. She looked beautiful: glossy blue-black hair, porcelain white skin, violet-blue eyes and her Barbie-esque figure. Victoria Palmer was the dream of men and women alike. Men wanted to claim her, women wanted to *be* her. Millions followed her on social media and she had made a fortune in her line of toiletries and fashion accessories. Like the others, she wore Vineyard Vine shorts and a polo shirt but somehow, they looked better on her. The only sour note was the clouded-over expression on her perfect face. "Morgan, where is Georgie? She hasn't come down and she hasn't answered my texts. We have to get things going right now. We're supposed to start filming at eight."

Morgan grumbled inwardly but she was used to Victoria's czarina-like manner by now. Before she could say anything, Brad spoke up. "I'll go get her."

"No, I need you with me." Victoria reached up and caressed his cheek.

"I'll go check on her. No problem," Morgan said.

"Please do and hurry her down."

Morgan left the bistro and took the stairs up to Georgie's room, next door to Victoria's. She knocked, and a few seconds later the door opened. Morgan recognized one of the make-up artists. The woman looked distraught.

Morgan spoke gently to put the woman at ease. "Hi, I'm here to get Ms. Ralston."

The make-up artist gestured toward the bedroom where Georgina Ralston sat on the edge of the unmade bed, tears running down her cheeks. She'd dressed in the required shorts and polo, but her feet were bare. Morgan recognized her from the pictures and videos on

Victoria's blog. Tall and voluptuous, Georgie had Scandinavian looks: white-blond hair and ice-blue eyes along with a turned-up nose and, normally, a glorious smile. Right now, though, the poor girl was having a major meltdown.

Morgan walked over and sat down next to her on the bed. "Hi, Georgie, I'm Morgan...I'm the wedding planner. We're all waiting for you downstairs," she said gently.

After a sob and a few more sniffs, Georgie said, "I can't go down there. The whole weekend is a mistake."

"What do you mean? It's going to be fabulous. You'll have a good time."

"No, it will be pure torture. You don't know."

"Victoria has everything planned. Today, there's tennis, the beach and a great dinner. It'll be fun...like a vacation."

Georgie looked up. Tears and pain filled her eyes. "I love Brad," she burst out. "I've always loved Brad...ever since sophomore year. But Tory stole him." She gulped down another sob. Then she stood, hands clenched at her sides, her red-blotched face suddenly turning white. "Tory gets everything she wants. Sometimes I hate her."

Chapter 6
Thursday Morning

It took all her powers of persuasion, but Morgan calmed Georgie down and got her to the bistro. As they entered, the wedding party was being served mimosas, eggs benedict with slices of papaya and mango and plenty of French roast coffee. The conversation was subdued, punctuated by quiet laughter. Except for Victoria and Georgie, they seemed somewhat intimidated by the cameras.

At nine-fifteen, the group headed outside to golf carts waiting to transport them to the tennis pavilion. Another cart pulled up for Rex and Jill and their apparatus. After Morgan had seen them all off, she walked back to the bistro, where the busboys and girls were clearing the tables. She thanked them for a beautiful job. Then she went into the kitchen to compliment the sous-chef on the quality and presentation of the breakfast. Chef Pierre was in his small office. Together they went over the menu for the luncheon that would be served on the beach at one o'clock.

When she arrived at her own office, Itzel was waiting for her.

"Good morning, Itzel. How was your dinner date last night?"

"It was fun. We went to Angelina's on 30A. I love that place. José and I split a pizza and Luis wanted spaghetti. After dinner, we took Luis home. His mom came home early. So…José and I had some time alone together. We walked on the beach." Itzel smiled dreamily. "It was a beautiful sunset."

"Sounds perfect."

Itzel shook herself. It was time to get down to business. "I've got a couple of things to go through with you."

"Fire away," Morgan said.

"I got an email from the florist. They're having trouble finding enough lavender rosebuds for the table decorations and the wall hangings. They'd like to substitute more pale-pink roses."

"Tell them to keep hunting. Victoria was pretty adamant about the color scheme. She'll probably be counting the number of lavender roses."

"They've only got two days before the wedding, or really one and half, to find the flowers."

"I know, but let's push them a little."

"Okay." Itzel looked flustered. "Then there's the band. They added a rider to the initial contract. They want bottles of San Pellegrino Limonata. That's what they drink between sets."

"We can do that. No problem."

"There's a bigger issue. They want to add another break between sets since they're playing longer than usual."

Morgan shook her head. "No way! We already went through all this with the agent. They signed the contract. Tell them no."

"Gosh, what if they pull out?"

"They won't pull out. They know their music is going to be featured on Victoria Palmer's website. For them, it will be massive publicity."

"I guess you're right, but this guy was pretty insistent."

"Just call back and say yes for San Pellegrino and no for the extra break." Morgan felt a vibration in her pocket and pulled out her phone. It was Daxton Simmons, Claire's fiancé.

"Hello, Dax. Congratulations!"

"Thanks, Morgan. We're both pretty happy. Claire told me you offered to help with the big event."

"Yes, I'd love to. You guys are some of my favorite people."

"You know, our wedding will be nothing like the extravaganza you're planning for this weekend."

Morgan laughed. "You're right. Nothing could compare to Victoria Palmer's wedding."

"That's what I called about. I was checking on logistics. You'll have extra Magnolia security personnel on the island, right?"

"Yes. Along with our usual crew, we've hired a couple of retired cops."

"Okay. As of Friday afternoon, we'll have a sheriff's deputy at the entrance to the causeway and another couple of officers at the main entrance for guests. It's important to the Emerald Coast that things don't get out of hand."

"It's important to the Magnolia as well. We want to make sure no crazy fans sneak into the resort."

"Good luck, Morgan." He sounded amused, but also concerned.

"Thanks, and again congratulations."

Morgan ended the call and went into her private office, where she spent a half hour with email. There were several messages from brides-to-be, requesting information about weddings at the Magnolia. She decided to wait until Monday to respond. There was just too much going on right then.

***

A short while later Morgan walked over to the tennis courts, following the winding path through the extensive Magnolia gardens. Houses were visible, but somewhat hidden behind flowering bushes and low walls. As she approached the tennis pavilion, she heard raucous laughter and the sound of tennis balls bouncing off the clay courts.

The wedding party occupied two of the four courts. On the nearest one, Victoria and Georgina played doubles with Lars and Jenny. The game seemed pretty serious and there wasn't much talking. Jenny served a wicked ball. Georgina dived for it and barely managed to return it. On the other court, Carter was playing singles with Brad. Josh sat at the net, his feet up on the net post, laughing hysterically. Carter and Brad seemed intent on their game, but they were laughing, too.

Mindy was sitting on a bench under the shaded pavilion. Behind her on a wrought-iron table stood a pitcher of lemonade and several blue-and-green striped glasses. Mindy held a frosty glass in her hand. Morgan sat down on the bench. "Have you already played?"

"No, I don't know how to play tennis. I'm just watching." Mindy's eyes weren't on the tennis players, but on Jill and Rex, who were filming from different angles. Mindy sighed. "You know, I really don't belong here. I'm not part of the beautiful people. I just work for them."

"What do you mean?"

"I run Tory's website and the other social media. I'm her virtual assistant."

Morgan thought about the live-streaming going on right then. "Shouldn't you be working now?"

"I'm leaving it all to my crew. We've been in contact this morning and they're managing without me. If there's a problem they'll contact me. It's not actually live-streaming, the guys are cutting and splicing the action. It's delayed."

"That's great. Then you can be on vacation." Morgan got up and poured herself some lemonade. When she sat back down, she said, "You and Victoria must be good friends."

Mindy stared at the glass in her hands. "No, we've never been friends. I've always been…" She searched for the right word. "…useful to Tory…right from the beginning."

"I don't understand." Uneasy, Morgan sipped her lemonade.

Mindy slid her a glance. "Freshman year at Talbot, we were roommates. I was amazed and frightened by Tory. She was this beautiful, rich girl and I was this skinny, ignorant scholarship student." She fell silent briefly and watched as Victoria smashed a ball over the net. Victoria smiled wickedly at Jenny, who had landed on her knee trying to return it.

"Back then I would do anything to be in her good graces," Mindy went on. "She sent me out on errands, to pick up a meal, get her laundry or find a book she'd left in the lounge. I wrote papers for her and coached her on tests." She turned to look at Morgan. "Don't think Tory is stupid or lazy. No, she just had her priorities. If she didn't go to class, it was because she was hooking up with some upperclassman."

"That must have been a hard year for you," Morgan said.

"Oh, it continued beyond that. She moved into the sorority house and I was in the scholarship dorm. We all had jobs maintaining the place. I washed dishes and cleaned the bathrooms on Thursdays." Mindy drank down her lemonade and turned to place the glass on the wrought-iron table. "Anyway, Tory would text me and want something done." She lowered her voice. "Junior year she got pregnant. I found a doctor and drove her over to the next town. We spent the night in a motel after the procedure. That night she gave me five hundred dollars cash for helping her out. At first, I said no, but she insisted. She's been paying me ever since—"

A loud shout echoed from the court where the guys were playing. Josh had stopped laughing. Carter was screaming, his face red with anger. "You cheating SOB. That shot was in. I saw it. You know it was in."

"Come on Carter. It was out." Brad turned to Josh. "Wasn't that shot out?"

Josh stood up and gestured with both hands. "I wasn't watching. I don't know. But it doesn't matter. It's just one point."

"It *does* matter. You've always got to win, Brad. I'm fucking tired of it." Carter threw his tennis racket on the ground and stomped across the court and through the bushes, where he disappeared from sight.

Chapter 7
Thursday - Early Afternoon

From her balcony, Morgan watched the wedding party down on the beach. It looked as though peace had been restored. Now four of them were playing volleyball and the others were in the water, jumping waves. The girls wore colorful striped bikinis and the guys were in matching trunks. Rex and Jill, dressed in grey shorts and t-shirts, were busy working. This section of the beach had been cordoned off and Magnolia security stood guard. Beyond, clusters of onlookers held their cell phones aloft. Morgan grimaced. The next few days would be a challenge, but Victoria must be used to the attention. She probably relished it.

The luncheon would be served in a few minutes and Morgan wanted to be on hand. She went inside her apartment, pulled on her one-piece black suit and a black lace cover-up, then hurried down to the beach.

The staff had set up a tent on the sand, over a long table covered with a blue-and-white striped cloth. Two pitchers of daisies stood at each end. A parade of waiters brought out the food. There were platters of Swedish open-faced sandwiches, each one artfully assembled; shrimp on a bed of lettuce with sliced hard-boiled eggs and radish roses; smoked salmon decorated with curled lemon slices and dill; and roast beef with horseradish mayonnaise and cucumber slices. Another platter held crudités and a bowl of aioli for dipping. Along with bowls of fruit and chips, there were bottles of beer and wine. Before the wedding party served themselves, Rex took some close-ups of the food and the presentation. Morgan breathed a little easier. Everything seemed to be back on track.

***

After lunch the group stretched out on chaise lounges to chat. The guys were back to talking football. Morgan wondered if they related to each other in any other way.

Victoria and Georgina were discussing make-up. Georgie had found a new line of products that moisturized but also had an SPF of eighty. Victoria turned to Morgan. "What do you use? You've got fabulous skin."

"Pretty much Dove soap and Maybelline. But I splurge on Nuxe Huile Prodigieuse." She pronounced it with a passable French accent. "It's an absolute must when you live this close to the ocean."

"I've heard of that," Victoria said. "It's a multi-purpose dry oil."

"Right."

"Well, I think great skin boils down to great genes," Georgie said.

Jenny chimed in from down the row of chairs. "And avoiding the sun at all costs."

"It's too bad you've got such bad skin. It seems like you were always breaking out back in college," Victoria said.

Jenny blanched, and her hand shot up to cover a blemish on her chin. Mindy turned to lie on her stomach. Further away, Georgie glared in Victoria's direction. Morgan seconded the feeling but kept her face neutral. Victoria was her client, like it or not.

Victoria seemed oblivious to Jenny's discomfort and Georgie's anger. She held up her phone and looked at herself, turning her head from side to side and forming her lips into a pout.

"Hey, let's go swimming. I'm roasting," Brad shouted. He came over and pulled Victoria to her feet, kissed her on the lips and said, "Come on, beautiful, let's go swimming. Let's put on a show for your crew." He waved at Rex and Jill. Like the others, he didn't acknowledge them as fellow graduates from Talbot. The wedding party generally treated them as extraneous robots or necessary servants.

Everyone except Carter got up and dropped their phones and sunglasses on their deck chairs. The girls pulled on matching pink swim caps and raced into the waves. To Morgan's surprise, even Mindy joined in. The girl had kept herself apart since lunch, but right now looked like she was having fun.

Carter moved over and sat at the end of Morgan's deck chair. "Hey, I apologize about earlier on the tennis court. I'm usually pretty chill, but I lost it this morning."

31

"No need to apologize to me." She smiled at him. "Hopefully, it wasn't caught on film."

He gave a wry laugh. "I checked with Rex. My tirade will not go viral."

They fell quiet, watching the others plunging into the surf.

"So, uh. Do you like your job? Hanging out at other people's weddings?" Carter asked. His dark red hair glowed copper in the sun, and his blue eyes glimmered with humor.

Morgan chuckled. "I wouldn't characterize my job that way. And yes, I do like it. I like people and I enjoy the creativity involved in putting an event like this together."

"I think I would hate your job." He smiled. "But I like you."

Morgan let the compliment pass. "So, what do you do for a living?" She knew he taught at UCLA, but the question always broke the ice.

"I'm a biochemist and a professor. UCLA."

"I can't imagine doing *your* job...or getting through the long years of studying."

"It was a grind getting my PhD, but I loved the research. I'm still fascinated by what I've learned and amazed at what I don't know." His grin widened. "I'm actually a nerd."

He had a nice smile, Morgan decided. "When did all of you meet?" She gestured to the others, who were tossing around a beach ball beyond the breakers.

"In a science class at Talbot, believe it or not. We'd all done well on our AP chemistry and biology exams, so we were placed in a higher-level biology class. There was a large lecture class and then they divided us up for the labs. We had this Indian guy with an amazing name...Madhavadity Balakrishnan." He pronounced it carefully. "We called him Krishna. He had a mean accent, but he was a brilliant guy. Anyway, the eight of us were in the same lab sessions. We got in the habit of going out after class. It was fun until the accident—" Carter broke off and stared out at the waves. Then he stood. "Where's Georgie? I don't see her."

Morgan stood too and gazed out at the water. She counted six heads in the surf. Heart pounding, she reached for her cell phone.

Victoria had nixed a life guard. Now Morgan wished she had insisted. "I'm calling 9-1-1."

Carter yelled, "Where's Georgie?" and dashed toward the surf. He jumped over the low waves and plunged into the rolling water beyond.

The emergency dispatcher responded, and Morgan told the woman what had happened and where they were. As she signed off, she glanced over at Rex and Jill. They were filming the whole thing. Sick with anxiety, Morgan wondered how they could remain so calm.

She looked out at the water again and saw Carter plunging back through the waves, a body in his arms. When he reached the shore, he laid Georgie on the sand and began CPR, pressing rhythmically on her chest. The others came out of the water and formed a circle around Carter and Georgie. Morgan hurried to join them as Carter kept performing CPR. After another tense minute, Georgie sucked in air. He turned her on her side, and she vomited water and lunch. Victoria stepped back, looking repulsed. As Rex approached, she shouted, "Don't film this. It's disgusting."

Georgie tried to sit up. Carter steadied her, grasping her shoulders. Morgan gazed around the circle of people. They all wore shocked expressions. Georgie looked spaced-out.

Carter crouched down next to her. "What happened?"

Georgie gazed up at the faces staring down at her. "I don't know exactly. It felt like someone was pushing me down. I couldn't breathe." Her voice rasped. Abruptly, she turned her head and vomited up more water and bile.

Chapter 8
Thursday Evening

Morgan turned to look at the wedding party seated behind her in the Magnolia Resorts van. They all wore the same outfit, jeans and red t-shirts with the Talbot logo written in white. Morgan was the odd woman out, wearing her favorite blue sundress since she was meeting Grady after she herded the wedding party to their destination. The color enhanced the blue of her eyes—and right now she needed a pick-me-up, even a minor one.

Behind her, the group chatted happily, the day's unpleasant moments apparently forgotten. Mentally, Morgan went through the day. She remembered Georgie's revealing comment about hating Victoria and secretly loving Brad. Victoria really did seem to have everything, Morgan thought, and not much consideration for her friends. That alone must make it difficult to hang out with her, never mind the love triangle. Watching them now, though, Morgan wondered how seriously to take that claim. Georgie and Victoria were giggling as if sharing some private joke. How could Georgie act that way if her feelings for Brad were real?

Then there was Carter's anger; throwing his racket and storming off the tennis court. He'd apologized but she wondered what was behind his rage. It had been way over the top. Right now, he and Josh had their heads together as if engaged in a serious discussion.

The near-drowning at the beach came back to her, suddenly and vividly. Georgie had said she felt as though someone was holding her down. Could that really have happened? Who would want to drown Georgie? Morgan scanned the faces in the seats behind her. Mindy and Jenny sat next to each other, Jenny waving her hands around, her face vivacious. She glanced back at Victoria, then said something to Mindy. The two of them burst into laughter. Morgan remembered what Mindy had said about her relationship with Victoria back in college, when Victoria needed a gofer and Mindy needed the money. Things hadn't changed much since.

Behind Morgan, Brad was talking to Lars. Apparently, the insurance firm was involved in a lawsuit. Lars asked several questions and Brad answered them patiently. Morgan had yet to talk to Lars and Jenny. She would make a point of doing that tomorrow.

In the back of the van, Rex and Jill sat armed with their various cameras. In black hoodies and black jeans, they stared out at the Western Lake and the low dunes flashing by. Their faces gave nothing away.

Morgan shook herself. They'd be at The Red Bar soon, where she could unload her charges and get them settled. Then she'd meet Grady and spend the rest of the evening *not* thinking about anything to do with Victoria Palmer's wedding.

***

The Red Bar was a favorite of locals and tourists alike. Red lights strung around the painted red walls gave the place a funky vibe. French posters from the nineteenth century and celebrity photos covered the walls and the ceiling. Hangings and curios added to the eclectic décor. The Red Bar Jazz Band was playing in a corner. Couples lounged on sofas around the small stage, listening to the music.

Morgan found a large table in the middle of the dining room for the wedding party. Undoubtedly many patrons recognized Victoria and Georgie from Victoria's website, but they were polite enough not to bother the group. Henry, the waiter, arrived with a large chalkboard, the menu of the night printed on it in curly script. Morgan recognized several Red Bar favorites: the famous crab cakes, popular panné chicken and delicious stuffed eggplant.

Morgan bent down and whispered to Victoria, "I'm going to leave you in Henry's capable hands. The van will be waiting outside. I'll see you tomorrow morning."

"Okay. Remember, we've got the shopping trip," Victoria said.

"Right. I'll be there."

Carter had seated himself beside Victoria. He looked up at Morgan. "Where are you off to? Stick around. It wouldn't be a party without you."

35

"I've got a date. See you tomorrow." Morgan waved and went into the room next door. The place was hopping. People were standing at the bar and seated in booths. At first, she didn't see Grady. Then she spotted him, seated in a booth with his back to her. She walked over and laid a hand on his shoulder. "Hello, handsome."

Grady stood up, and in one smooth movement she was in his arms. He kissed her lips and then held her close as he whispered in her ear, "Man, I've missed you. Two weeks is too long." He hugged her again.

Grady epitomized the expression *tall, dark and handsome.* He had thick wavy hair, almost black, and ruddy skin. His chocolate brown eyes sparkled with intelligence and geniality. He and Morgan had been an item for a couple of years. It mostly worked out, except Grady captained a charter fishing boat and was gone for weeks at a time. After graduating from MIT, he'd developed an app that just about every grocery store in the country used to manage their inventory. He'd made billions, sold the software, and come back to the Emerald Coast where he grew up and bought his dream boat, the *Black Lion.* He loved being out on the water. Morgan, on the other hand, was frightened of the ocean's power. She'd never been out on his boat and wasn't eager for the chance. They argued about it sometimes, which bothered Morgan, but she couldn't just set her fears aside.

Morgan slid into the booth and Grady slid in next to her. They sat hip to hip, holding hands. Grady had already started on a 30A beer. When the waiter came, Morgan ordered a glass of pinot grigio.

"How's the latest wedding going?" Grady asked.

"They're right next door. I settled them at their table and now they're on their own." She laughed. "This is the Victoria Palmer wedding."

Grady looked baffled.

"Come on, Grady, you must know who Victoria Palmer is? She's better known than the Kardashians."

He shrugged. "I've heard the names, but I don't know who these people are."

"Victoria is a social media celebrity. She's gorgeous and has cleverly built a name for herself. She has millions of followers and sells them all kinds of stuff—cosmetics, clothes, accessories. It's a lifestyle, really."

He nudged her leg with his. "Nowhere as gorgeous as you, my dear."

She looked into his eyes and kissed him quickly. The waiter arrived with her wine, and between sips Morgan told Grady all about the over-the-top wedding. "This is the most anyone has ever spent at the Magnolia...over seven million dollars. The wedding party is here for four days. Tomorrow the other guests start arriving from around the country."

Grady looked thunderstruck. "Seven million dollars...how do they reach that figure?"

"Massive amounts of flowers, fabulous food, amazing band, a big crowd. The whole shebang is being filmed and photographed for her online fans. It's out-of-sight." Morgan glanced around at the people nearby, making sure none were in earshot. She didn't make a practice of revealing wedding information, especially of famous clients like Victoria Palmer.

The waiter approached again, and they ordered the blackened grouper on a grits cake. While they ate, Grady talked a little about his latest trip. Then they discussed a book they'd both read: *The Store* by James Patterson. "To me, this is Amazon taking over the world," Morgan said. "Already, Amazon wields a lot of power."

"As do Facebook and Google."

"Right, but they remain in the cloud or as an intangible. 'The Store' in the book, or Amazon in real life, has a presence everywhere. They *do* know what people read, what they buy, where they live, all of that. With Alexa, Amazon is right there in your house watching everything you do. Amazon can satisfy just about your every need and desire."

Grady raised his eyebrows and leered at her. "Not *my* every need and desire." Then he turned serious. "Already we live in a society where there are hidden cameras and video streaming. Big Brother is watching us. That's why it's good to go out on the open sea where you can be your own master."

She ate the last bite of grouper. "Couldn't a satellite record what you're up to out there in the Gulf?"

"I suppose. I guess we're doomed." Grady took her hand. "Let's get out of here and go to my place."

As they left, Morgan glanced through the opening into the dining room. Carter looked over at her. He winked

Chapter 9
Thursday Night

At Grady's house, they poured glasses of wine and went out on the deck that overlooked the beach. Under the moonlight, the crests of the waves rippled like flowing white lace. They shared a chaise, squeezed close together. Grady nibbled on her earlobe. "I've missed you," he whispered.

"Likewise." Morgan turned her head and they kissed, long and sweet.

Then he said, "What if you moved in here? Then we could be together more."

Morgan pulled back and looked at him. "We've had this discussion before. You're gone a lot. I'd be alone here in this big house."

"Maybe I'd stay ashore longer, if you were around."

"Maybe...but the problem is, you live too far from Magnolia. With the traffic on 30A, it would take me ages to get there. I couldn't do my job."

He nuzzled her neck, "Maybe you could stop working. If you were mine, you wouldn't need to work."

"What do you mean, if I were *yours*?" Morgan wondered if this was a quasi-proposal, Grady-style.

"You know..."

Morgan felt frustrated. What was he saying? She started to move away but he pulled her back. "Okay, let's not talk about this now," he mumbled. As his lips sought hers and his hands moved up her bare leg, she felt her annoyance melt away. Her hunger for him took over.

Later, they moved into his bedroom and made deep, slow love. Then they fell asleep wrapped in each other's arms. At two AM, Morgan awoke. She had to get back to the resort tonight. She couldn't sleep over with everything to do in the morning. Gently, she shook Grady's shoulder. "Hey, I've got to get back," she whispered. He didn't react. She wrapped her arms around him and said, more loudly, "Grady, I've got to go home. You've got to drive me."

He snorted, then jolted awake and blinked. "You're sure you can't stay?"

"Tomorrow is a full day. I've got to get back."

"Okay," he mumbled. He reached for her, but she was already rolling away. As Morgan pulled on her dress, Grady slipped out of bed and grabbed some shorts and a t-shirt. Clothed once more, they walked down the stairs, through the kitchen and out to the garage, both of them half-asleep.

In the Porsche, Grady tuned the radio to a jazz station. The music filled the car as they drove. There was practically no traffic; they only passed one pickup. He reached over and patted her thigh. She covered his hand with hers. They smiled at each other.

Halfway to the resort, Grady turned down the music and cleared his throat. "I forgot to tell you something." He cleared his throat again, eyes on the road. "I'm leaving tomorrow afternoon."

"Leaving?" Morgan sat up straight.

"These guys came down from Chicago. People I used to know in the business. Anyway, they chartered the boat for a week starting tomorrow." He looked over at her. In the darkness, she couldn't see his expression, which meant he couldn't see hers.

She felt annoyed again. "I thought we'd decided to spend some time together next week? We were going to Fairhope for a couple of days. My wedding for next weekend is not a big deal. I was going to take off Monday through Thursday." Was she whining? She hated the tone of her voice.

"I'm sorry, babe. You're right, but I've known these guys for a long time."

Morgan pulled her hand away and stared out the window across the Western Lake and at the dunes in the distance. She was thinking, *you've known me for a while too.*

"We'll plan on that trip in a couple of weeks, I promise."

Morgan sighed. "Okay." Under her breath, she said, "Whatever."

They were silent as they rode through Watercolor, Seaside, and towards the resort. Miles Davis's "Blue on Green" filled the void. Finally, Grady drove down the causeway and pulled up outside the employee gate. She opened the car door and started to get out. "Thanks for the ride."

"Morgan don't be upset." Grady got out and came around the car, taking her in his arms. "I'm really sorry about next week. I'll make it up to you."

Morgan remained rigid in his embrace. *That stupid boat.*

"Come on, give me a kiss goodbye. I'll miss you."

Morgan felt an irrational giggle rise in her throat. "You are not going to miss me...not while you're out riding the waves, drinking beer and fishing with your buddies." Now she was laughing. Grady laughed too, probably relieved. They kissed good bye and then she punched in the entrance code to the gate.

In the lobby she waved to Marco, the clerk on duty at the reservation desk, and started for the elevator. Then, she thought about Mindy's health advice and decided to take the stairs. On a whim, at the second-floor landing, she opened the fire door and glanced down the hall. This was the floor where Victoria, Georgie, Mindy, and the Johanssons had rooms.

In the dim light, she saw a tall figure in a dark hoodie walking toward the stairwell at the other end of the hallway. Who was it, and which room had they just come out of? She peered down the hall, trying to identify the disappearing figure, but the person vanished through the far door with Morgan none the wiser.

Never mind. If someone wanted to wander around in the wee hours, that was their business. She shut the fire door and hurried up the staircase to her apartment.

Chapter 10
Friday Morning

Morgan woke abruptly and glanced at the alarm clock. Eight AM. She'd overslept. As she slipped out of bed, she went over the wedding events scheduled for the day. There were a multitude of details to oversee.

Morgan dressed quickly in navy shorts and a French navy-and-white striped shirt. She had agreed to accompany Victoria and her bridesmaids on a bike ride to Seaside, where the girls would do some shopping and have lunch. The groomsmen were headed off to the Magnolia Golf Course on the other side of Highway 98. Morgan figured the two events would be filmed for the entire world to see. In the afternoon they would reunite for high tea at the Eden Gardens, and that night there was a Texas barbeque.

Just before she left her apartment, she logged on to the Weather Channel. The wedding plans depended on sunshine and cool breezes. Friday looked perfect, as did Saturday. Far to the south in the Gulf of Mexico, a storm was brewing. Luckily, it looked as though it probably wouldn't hit the Emerald Coast, and even if it did, it wouldn't arrive until Sunday morning. The Sunday morning brunch was scheduled indoors in the large Magnolia ballroom, so by then the storm would cause no problems.

As Morgan rushed down the stairs, she thought again about the figure in the hoodie she'd seen the previous evening headed down the second-floor hallway. Who could it have been? She had a sense it was a man. Probably Brad. Victoria had a suite right about where she'd first seen the figure. But had she seen him come out of a room, or had she just assumed it? Oh well, it didn't matter who was sleeping with whom. It was absolutely none of her business.

Morgan was dying for coffee, but before she went into the Orchid Room where the breakfast buffet was laid out, she stopped by the front desk to check in with Katarina. The morning clerk was almost-anorexic thin, with dark blonde hair and large grey eyes. With her

42

sloping shoulders and long neck, she reminded Morgan of an exotic bird. She'd been hired several months ago and seemed to be working out. From Katarina, Morgan learned that several wedding guests had arrived the previous evening.

"Today, there will be an onslaught," Morgan said. "Remember, every guest gets a welcome brochure and a map. We don't want anyone to get lost."

Katarina nodded.

"Oh, and please contact Marina to remind her again that all rooms should get a welcome basket of goodies."

"Will do." Katarina smiled as she reached for the phone.

Morgan passed the door to the Jasmine Bistro and went around the corner to the kitchens. She pushed open the double doors and found herself in a whirlwind of activity. On the far side of the room, over the hubbub, she heard loud voices raised in argument.

She wound her way around the stainless-steel tables, carts and Vulcan stoves. Cooks, kitchen porters and pastry chefs were hard at work. In the small office at the rear, she found Chef Pierre and another man in jeans, cowboy boots, a red-plaid shirt and a soiled apron. His was the angry voice she'd heard, with a pronounced Texas twang. "We always put mustard in the potato salad. And it's got to be yellow American mustard. None of that French Gray Poupee stuff."

Chef Pierre pursed his lips in disgust. "I don't think we even have enough of that *moutarde* in my kitchen."

"I'll get my boys to whip up the potato salad. If you've got the potatoes and some onions, we'll do the job right."

Morgan stepped into the small room between the two quarrelling men. With a sweet smile, she said, "Good morning, gentlemen. Let's see." She turned toward the Texan. "You must be Chef Robinson. Welcome to the Magnolia. I do so hope you and Chef Pierre will be able to work together. I know Mr. Palmer would not like to hear of any issues that might ruin his daughter's big day." She knew neither of them wanted to incur the wrath of Victoria's father, let alone Victoria herself.

Robinson calmed a bit. "No, ma'am, I'm just here to instruct this here cook on how we make things in Texas. I mean, this is a Texas barbeque, right?"

"I'm sure Chef Pierre is eager to follow your instructions, but he might have an idea or two himself. Remember we're all on the same side here, working to provide a beautiful feast for the Palmer-Hughes rehearsal dinner," Morgan said.

Chef Pierre rolled his eyes toward heaven. He undoubtedly felt this redneck should not be instructing him in *cuisine*.

Morgan turned back to Chef Robinson. "Is there anything else I can help you with?"

"No, ma'am, we got the smoker goin'. The brisket has been cookin' for a while now. It should be perfect by tonight."

"Wonderful. Chef Pierre will help you with anything else you might need. Thank you, gentlemen." Problem solved for the moment, Morgan turned and made her way back through the kitchen. She stopped and talked to the head pastry chef to verify the plans for the afternoon tea. He assured her everything would be ready for transport to the Eden Gardens at the right time.

In the Jasmine Bistro, Morgan found Brad, Carter and Josh having breakfast at one end of the table. Mindy and Georgie were sitting at the other end. This morning there was a buffet of eggs, bacon, sausage, pancakes, and fruit and a large pitcher of a poisonous-looking green liquid. The meal was not being videoed, so Rex and Jill were eating at a side table.

Morgan got herself a cup of coffee and some scrambled eggs, then sat down across from Mindy and Georgie. From the other end of the table, Carter addressed her. "Good morning, Morgan, did you have fun last night?"

Morgan thought it was none of his business, but she answered sweetly, "Lovely, simply lovely."

Carter cut into his stack of pancakes. "We missed you last night. Maybe you could have put out the fire and smoothed the ruffled feathers."

"Hmm." Curious though she was, something told Morgan she shouldn't pursue the matter. She sipped her coffee. It was black and strong, just the way she liked it. She picked up her fork.

As she dug into her eggs, Georgie bent over the table and whispered, "Tory went after Lars and Jenny. They got really upset and Ubered it back to the resort."

"You don't have to whisper, Georgie, we were all there," Carter said.

"Let's let sleeping dogs lie," Brad said. "Victoria had one too many. I know she feels terrible about what she said."

"Maybe Jenny and Lars will go home this morning and not stay for the wedding." Georgie carefully sliced a link of sausage into small coins.

Just then the door swung open and Victoria, Jenny and Lars walked in. Victoria had one arm around Jenny's shoulders and the other through Lars's arm. "Hi, everyone, sorry we're late. We just had a discussion and I apologized. We're good. Right, Lars? Right, Jenny?"

Jenny and Lars nodded, but their expressions said otherwise. Chances were Victoria had beaten them down, Morgan thought.

Victoria laughed. She seemed to fill the room with her presence. "My, look at all this delicious food." She went down the buffet, surveying the breakfast selections. Then she took a large water glass and filled it with the green concoction in the pitcher. As she was about to sit down, she looked over at Georgie's plate, laden with pancakes and sausage. Victoria frowned, her perfect eyebrows sweeping up like blackbird wings. Georgie turned bright red. She pushed away the plate and accepted the glass of green smoothie Victoria handed her.

Chapter 11
Friday Morning

At ten, the guys left in a golf cart. They all matched in light blue Peter Millar golf shirts and white shorts. Rex and another photographer were installed in a second golf cart with their equipment.

The Magnolia bicycle manager had brought around five shiny blue bikes. Victoria and her contingent were dressed today in black and yellow biker gear. The slim-fitting tops and tight shorts looked fabulous on Victoria and Georgie with their perfect figures. Surprisingly, Mindy and Jenny looked great too. As they started out, Morgan thought the bride and her bridesmaids looked like four hornets buzzing along the Magnolia paths. There was a lot of laughter. Clearly none of them had been on a bike for years and it took them a while to gain confidence.

Morgan rode in the rear, far behind the girls. She didn't want to appear in the photos. Jill and another photographer were placed to take pictures of them coming over the crest of the Japanese bridge. In the Magnolia parking lot, they would meet up with Victoria's security detail. Then, as the bridesmaids rode along the bike path on 30A, one security guy would ride in front and another would bring up the rear. Jill would photograph the bridal party periodically from the back of a pickup truck.

Once they were on the bike path, Mindy slowed down and came parallel with Morgan. "Gosh, I haven't ridden a bike since forever. This is actually fun."

"I could ride all the time, but I never do. It is great exercise, though," Morgan said.

"Yeah, I know. Tory always bugs me about exercising. She's a maniac about it. She's got to keep her figure perfect for the camera." Mindy grinned from under the rim of her black-and-yellow striped helmet.

Morgan grinned back. "I think you all look great."

"You probably think we're pretty pathetic hanging around Tory. It's like she's controlling all of us."

"I really haven't thought about it," Morgan lied.

The white pickup with Jill went by, cameras aimed at the three girls up ahead. Mindy nodded toward the truck. "Even Rex and Jill. They depend on Tory for their livelihood. And look at me, I've yet to break away."

"Do you like the job?"

Mindy thought about it. "Yes, I do."

"Well, think of it that way. You've got a well-paying job you like. Maybe you're not always in agreement with Victoria…but few people love their boss. You know what I mean?"

The girl didn't respond. When Morgan glanced over at her, she said, "So do you want to know what happened last night?"

Morgan didn't answer. They passed a middle-aged couple going the other way.

Mindy continued. "We'd all had a couple of drinks. Everything was great. Then Jenny said she and Lars were trying to have a baby and it wasn't working. Georgie said, 'Be patient. It'll happen.' Then Tory blurted out, really loud, 'I know, that's because Lars can't get it up. He's got that tiny little dick.' After that, there was this uncomfortable silence. The guys were looking every which way. Lars turned beet red and said, 'Jenny, let's go.' And they left, just like that." Mindy shrugged. "We all know Tory dated Lars sophomore year. So she probably slept with him and knew what she was talking about."

Listening to her, Morgan felt the girl was relishing every minute of the story. There was something perverse in her manner. Did she want Morgan to know what a jerk Victoria was? Or did she enjoy the embarrassment Jenny and Lars had experienced?

For the first time since signing the contract to plan this wedding, Morgan wondered what on earth she'd gotten herself into.

***

In Seaside, they stopped for iced coffee at Amavida and sat out on the terrace chatting. A couple of teenage girls approached

47

Victoria and she graciously signed their copies of *Victoria Palmer, America's Princess*. They weren't the only ones. For fifteen minutes, women and girls presented books, napkins and restaurant receipts for Victoria to sign. She also took selfies with them and was photographed by the crowd. Eventually Victoria had enough, and her security guards stepped in.

As a group, they made their way from store to store. In La Vie Est Belle, Victoria bought each of the bridesmaids a pearl and leather necklace. They wandered in and out of Déjà Vu and Mercantile. Jenny insisted on going into Sundog Books. She ended up buying a copy of *The Girl on 30A* and some hand-painted postcards of the area. All the while, Jill and her assistant took photos and video. Morgan hung back and followed along.

At noon, they crossed 30A and checked out the restaurants along the beach. They had a myriad of possibilities: hamburgers at Pickle's, tacos or pizza at Bud and Alley's, seafood at several places. They ended up choosing The Shrimp Shack, or rather, Victoria did. The view from the pavilion was ideal: sea and sand. They shared platters of boiled shrimp, royal reds, and corn-on-the-cob. Morgan noted Victoria and Georgie only picked at their food. As they ate, they discussed their college days.

"Remember that weird girl who joined the sorority? What was her name—Katy or Kathy?" Georgie asked.

"Yeah, whatever happened to her?" Jenny pulled the shell off a shrimp and dipped it in sauce.

"She left school. Don't you remember?" Georgie said. Mindy snagged another shrimp, apparently oblivious to the conversation. She hadn't been in the sorority, Morgan remembered.

"She couldn't take a joke. Someone put a frog in her bed and she made a big stink to the housemother." Victoria snickered. "Then someone put Glad Wrap over the toilet seat in her bathroom. She screamed like crazy. Everyone up and down the hall laughed."

Jenny wiped her hands on her napkin. "I think that was mean."

Victoria sipped her Perrier with lemon. "You all thought it was funny at the time." She looked up and held out her glass as Jill photographed her with the white sand and blue water behind her. "After the last prank, she left school."

"What was the last straw?" Georgie asked.

"Don't you remember? We stole her 38D bras and hung them out the window with a big sign that said. "How is Kati holding up?" It was Kati with an I. She pulled out of school after that."

Jenny pushed away her plate. "I can't believe I thought that was funny."

Victoria giggled. "Oh, girls will be girls."

Chapter 12
Friday Afternoon

Back at the resort, Morgan changed into a silk organza flowered-print dress with a full skirt and spaghetti straps. It would do for the afternoon tea event. The bridal party would be dressed in full antebellum finery. Victoria had chosen a green-sprigged dress reminiscent of Scarlett O'Hara's gown in *Gone with the Wind.*

Downstairs, she stopped at Victoria's suite where all the girls were getting ready. When the door opened, she stood for a moment, amazed at the scene. Jenny wore a pale blue frock decorated with lace and ribbons. She twirled a matching parasol. Mindy's dress was peach-colored silk with flounces and decorative beading. The make-up crew was touching up her face. Victoria, already dressed, was holding Georgie's hands as Victoria's maid pulled the laces tight on her corset.

"This is too tight. I'm never going to be able to breathe," Georgie said.

"Just a little more. You need to fit into the dress." The maid yanked harder and secured the laces.

"Think about it," Jenny said. "Back in the 1850s, the girls had waists of eighteen inches. They were so tiny."

"No wonder, they probably couldn't eat when they were trussed up like a chicken," Georgie moaned.

The maid dropped a pink satin dress over Georgie's head and began to button up the back. The dress had tiers of ruffles and miniature pink silk roses along the deep neckline.

"You all look beautiful," Morgan said, and she meant it.

Downstairs they met Brad and the groomsmen, who also wore antebellum garb: dark cut-away coats, slim-fitting dove-grey trousers, colorful brocade vests and matching cravats. They were a dashing group.

Morgan laughed when Carter came over, bowing deeply and swishing his top hat. "Madame, how may I be of service?"

"If you could be so kind as to direct these ladies to their waiting carriage, I would be most grateful."

Jill and Rex photographed from every angle as the group made its way to the waiting golf carts. Once over the bridge, they would take the Magnolia van over to the Eden Gardens.

***

The Eden Gardens were closed to the public for the afternoon. Security guards manned the gates and surrounded the property. The kitchen helpers and Kendal, the pastry chef from the resort, had laid out a beautiful table of cakes, cookies, scones, clotted cream, jam, tea and champagne. Floppy pink peonies stood in a low vase in the middle of the round table, atop a lace tablecloth. Before sitting down, the wedding party planned to take pictures under the 600-year-old live oak known as the wedding tree, as well as photos in the Camellia Garden.

But first the group made their way across the lawn to the white mansion that evoked a Southern plantation. Jill and Rex shouted orders to the wedding party as they posed together on the wrap-around porch, the girls gracefully poised in large floppy hats, the guys leaning against the white pillars twirling walking sticks. Every detail evoked gracious Southern society of the 1850s.

The house photos finished, a video recorded their graceful promenade across the grass as they strolled over to the Camellia Garden. To Morgan, they moved differently from twenty-first century people, as if they'd taken on their roles. Probably that had to do with the wide skirts, tight corsets and uncomfortable shoes. After Jill and Rex had taken many more pictures and videos, the group walked over to the tea table under the massive live oak. Morgan kept well out of camera range, parking herself in a rocking chair on the porch. From her view, it didn't look like the girls ate much of the delectable food prepared by Kendal and his crew. *What a waste,* she thought. *All that culinary effort, just for show.*

She pulled out her phone and sped through her text messages. Itzel was handling the set-up for the barbeque and the wedding rehearsal down at the beach. They texted back and forth about final details. Then a message from Grady popped up: *We're about to take*

51

off. Plan to take some time off in two weeks. We'll go to Fairhope and I'll fulfill your every desire! Love always, Grady. The message was followed by a red heart and a smiley face. Somehow this missive annoyed her. *Love always, right!*

She was still staring at her phone when Carter sat down next to her. His chair squeaked as he rocked back and forth. "Bad news?"

She answered without thinking. "None of your business."

"Whoa." He held up his hands. "Just trying to be friendly."

She forced a smile. "I apologize." Things must really be getting to her, or she'd never have barked at a guest like that.

"Is it the boyfriend?"

She tried to make a joke of it. "I could say that's none of your damn business, but I'm too polite."

"Fair enough." They rocked back and forth. Across the lawn, they could see the bridal party seated around the table. Jill and Rex were filming. Victoria was absent.

Finally, Morgan said, "Yes, he left on a fishing trip with some buddies. We had to cancel some plans we'd made."

Carter shook his head. "I don't know how he could possibly choose his buddies over an hour with you...a minute with you...a second with you."

He was coming on a little strong. Morgan smiled, keeping it friendly but neutral. "Shouldn't you be over having tea and crumpets with the gang?"

"I'm not a tea and crumpets kind of guy. And I am really hot and really uncomfortable in this get-up." He stood up and pulled off his coat, then loosened his shirt collar. Morgan glanced up at him. He was a handsome guy; the red beard and dark red hair made her think of a Viking warrior.

Just as he was about to sit back down, a scream echoed across the grass. Startled, Morgan looked over. Georgie was jumping up and down. Draped over her head and shoulders was something that looked like a grey feather boa. Victoria was laughing hysterically.

"Oh my god, what an idiot. That's Spanish moss." Carter took off across the lawn. He ran over to Georgie and pulled the grey fluff away from her hair and shoulders.

52

Victoria had stopped laughing. "What's the big deal? It's only Spanish moss."

Carter spoke angrily enough for Morgan to hear him from across the grass. "Which is inhabited by chiggers and spiders, to name a few critters. What were you thinking?"

Georgie had burst into tears. Brad stared at Victoria. Morgan wished she could see his expression clearly. Something in it must have upset Victoria, because she turned away from Carter and Georgie and shouted at the film crew, "Cut that scene. I don't want it out there."

Chapter 13
Friday Evening

Before leaving the Eden Gardens, Morgan asked the staff to pack up the leftover tea cakes and deliver them to the park employees. She couldn't stand to see all that food go to waste. The group was subdued on the way back. Georgie had some welts on her smooth white shoulders. When they got back to the resort, Morgan hurried her to the nurse who maintained an office in the Magnolia Spa. The rest of the party headed to their rooms. They had a couple of hours before the wedding rehearsal on the beach and the Texas barbeque.

Morgan went up to her apartment and took a quick shower, then dressed for the evening's events. The wedding party would wear square dance outfits with a western flair. Resort employees would be dressed in jeans and Magnolia t-shirts. Morgan pulled on a pair of indigo jeans and a royal-blue tee. As she applied make-up, she studied herself in the mirror. As a girl, she'd been a tomboy and run wild with her brothers. She'd been uninterested in dolls, clothes or her looks. Now, with her job, it had become important to maintain a carefully disciplined beauty regimen. It was all part of the Magnolia mystique.

The subtle shades of her blush and eye shadow enhanced her smooth oval face and clear blue eyes without being obvious. She nodded at her reflection with a sense of satisfaction, then took a moment before going downstairs to open her computer and look at the weather again. The forecast predicted a perfect evening, seventy-four degrees with a light breeze. Before she closed the screen, she checked on the storm swirling its way up the coast of Mexico. Now rain was predicted for Sunday at five AM. By then the tent and wedding banquet would be cleared away, so no problem.

Downstairs, the lobby was bustling with the arrival of wedding guests. Lionel and Marco were at the desk checking people in. Porters wheeled luggage carts toward the elevator and a noisy group of kids chased each other around the potted plants. Morgan poked her head into the Orchid Lounge. A group of people dressed in cowboy gear were standing at the bar having a drink. Everything looked on track for the evening.

Morgan continued down the hall to the security office, where she found the head of security checking out multiple TV screens. In the one to the left, she could see the beach and the chairs set up for the wedding rehearsal. A couple of security guards patrolled the area. Other screens showed the Japanese bridge, the causeway entrance, and the lobby as well as the tent where the barbeque would take place.

"Is everything okay?" Morgan asked.

The security chief nodded. "Yes, we're on top of it. There's no way anybody could sneak in here tonight."

"Great, just making sure. Thanks, Roberts."

***

Morgan went back through the lobby and out the main entrance. The air was still warm, the sun low in the sky. This was her favorite time of day. She made her way down a path along a bubbling man-made spring. At the end, the path opened up to the Mimosa Garden where the tent was set up for the barbeque. White and red roses in blue vases decorated the tables that were covered with red-and-white checked tablecloths. Bouquets of roses cascaded down pillars crowned with Texas flags. The band was setting up at one end beside the dance floor. For the occasion, Victoria had booked top country entertainers: The Zac Blue Band, Tanya Swain, Terry Overwood and Bart Crooks.

Itzel stood in the middle of the tent directing the set-up crew. It looked as though she had things well in hand. The rehearsal dinner was for one hundred guests who would soon begin to arrive.

The buffet was a magnificent spread. Along with beef brisket, there were slabs of ribs and platters of barbequed chicken. Another table held bowls of pinto beans, coleslaw, potato salad, Texas toast, cornbread and green Jell-O. Morgan could just imagine what Chef Pierre thought of that typically American dish. For dessert, there would be banana pudding, pecan pie and fruit cobbler with vanilla ice cream. Morgan wondered if Victoria would eat any of it, and if she would allow Georgie to eat a bite or two.

A murmur of voices and hearty laughter heralded the wedding party, coming up from the beach. As Victoria and Brad entered the Mimosa Garden, the crowd applauded. Behind the young couple were Victoria's parents and they received a round of applause as well. Then the Zac Blue Band started playing "The Eyes of Texas."

Morgan had met Victoria's father several times, but Mrs. Palmer had remained a mystery. Either she was uninterested in her daughter's wedding or, more likely, Victoria didn't want her mother involved. After the parents were seated at their table, Morgan made her way over to say hello. Victoria's mother was a buxom woman, with a dour pancake face, wispy grey hair and small grey eyes. She looked absolutely nothing like Victoria. It was difficult to think these two women were related. Victoria's father, on the other hand, was maybe six foot six, with thinning blond hair and a considerable paunch. His blue eyes, like his daughter's, demanded respect. Victoria had also inherited his strong jaw and straight nose, along with his brusque and impatient manner. In his youth, he must have been incredibly handsome. Like the wedding party, Mr. and Mrs. Palmer wore matching cowboy and cowgirl outfits with fringed leather vests, jeans, boots and cowboy hats.

"Mr. Palmer, how nice to see you," Morgan said.

Big Bob, as he was called, gave her a broad grin. "Ah, Miss Morgan. I don't believe you've met my little wife. Norma Lee, this is Morgan Lytton. She's the wedding planner and responsible for this lovely event."

Norma Lee looked critically up at Morgan. "I'm sure this is all Victoria's doing and you're just one more yes-man, or in this case a yes-woman. Victoria has never wanted to be dictated to." She picked up a martini glass and took a sip, effectively dismissing Morgan.

Big Bob chided his wife. "Now, honey. You're not giving Morgan her due. She's a clever gal."

Just then a crowd of tall, burly people showed up at the table. While Big Bob introduced Morgan to his extended family, Norma

Lee remained placid in her seat and didn't look up. The relatives seemed to take her incivility in stride.

After a few pleasantries, Morgan slipped away and circled through the tent, chatting with people and sending wait-staff to clear plates from tables or fill water glasses. On the whole the Magnolia staff was well-trained and did their jobs seamlessly. Itzel was behind the stage dealing with the various entertainers and their needs, freeing Morgan to keep an overall eye on things.

Surveying the crowd, she spotted Victoria and Brad circulating among their guests, Rex and Jill in tow. Victoria stood out in a white peasant blouse with red flowered embroidery. Under her knee-length red skirt, several petticoats swirled. On her feet were neat little black booties, and she'd tucked a red rose in her jet-black hair. As always, her beauty and charisma drew stares. Brad wore a red shirt with black jeans, and studded black cowboy boots. Always the gentleman, he smiled and listened intently to the doting matrons. Later, Morgan saw him laughing with the oil barons that made up Big Bob's social circle. *Quite a successful pair*, she thought.

When the desserts arrived, the dancing began. Soon the dance floor was a pulsating mass. Morgan stood back in the shadows and sipped a glass of Perrier and lime. She usually didn't allow herself to drink anything at these events. The band had started to play their rendition of Sheeran's "Perfect." She watched as Jenny and Lars danced together, their bodies pressed close. From behind, an arm encircled her waist. She turned to find Carter staring down at her in the semi-darkness.

"Come dance with me," he said.

"I don't know. I'm the hired help."

"One dance. Come on." He took her hand and led her to the floor.

She moved effortlessly into his arms. He rested his cheek on top of her head and they began to move as one, not talking but listening to the words of the song. At one point he looked down at her and said, "You are perfect, you know."

Morgan pulled back and looked up at him. "I'll bet you say that to all the girls."

They both laughed, and he pulled her back into his arms. She felt almost like she belonged there. Then she thought, *what am I doing? Carter will be gone in two days and I'll never see him again.* As she eased away, she heard screams from across the tent.

At first Morgan couldn't see what was happening. She left Carter and ran across the dance floor, pushing people aside, dimly aware of him close behind. At the edge of the pavilion stood a near-naked man, wearing nothing but a tiny speedo. Tattoos covered his body. Morgan noticed a red and blue dragon tattooed up his leg. His chest bore the word *Victoria* wreathed in roses. He was dripping wet and laughing hysterically. "Hey, Victoria. I'm here. I know you want me." As he gyrated his hips and made lewd gestures with his hands, the security officers reached him and smashed him to the ground.

Chapter 14
Saturday Morning

Morgan didn't sleep well. That crazy tattooed guy kept popping up in her dreams. Apparently, he'd swum across the lake and made his way to the rehearsal dinner through several private gardens. According to Roberts, he'd been stalking Victoria for a year. Victoria seemed almost pleased by the incident. Rex had filmed the entire thing, and it had likely gone viral by now. More followers for Victoria.

Morgan lay in bed, reliving the evening. On the whole, her planning had been a big success. The dinner, the decorations, the music and the dancing had gone off without a hitch. Even the bridal party had seemed to enjoy each other. She'd seen Jenny dancing with Lars and Georgie with Josh. The two of them had great moves.

Her mind turned to that dance with Carter. It had felt good to be in his arms, like she belonged there. But how could she feel this way? She loved Grady, didn't she? They were almost engaged. Were they? Her mind went back to the dance, the feel of Carter's hand at the small of her back and his broad chest beneath her cheek. Then she remembered the crazy stalker. He'd brought their dance to a halt. It seemed as though every time she and Carter connected, a disaster occurred.

***

This morning the wedding party was having breakfast in their suites. *Thank goodness*, Morgan thought. Per tradition, the bride and groom would not meet until the actual wedding at five o'clock. The bridal party would spend a good part of the day in the spa doing hair, nails and make-up. The groomsmen were free until later when they would have their hair trimmed and an application of light make-up as well.

After a cup of coffee and a bowl of oatmeal, Morgan felt ready to face her work day. She got dressed in a pink shift and designer sandals, combed her hair into a pony tail, and put on silver earrings and a matching necklace. Theoretically, she would not deal with the wedding party until later, but she never knew when she might be needed. It was important to look professional.

As usual before leaving her apartment, she logged on to the Weather Channel. What she discovered worried her. The storm that was supposed to be hanging out on the west coast of the Gulf had turned and was coming right toward the Florida Panhandle. Not only that, but it had gained strength and momentum. According to the radar screen, it would make landfall right on the Emerald Coast. From what she deduced, the storm would arrive about three AM Sunday. Without bothering to log off, Morgan started for the door. During the planning stages of the wedding, they had made alternate plans for inclement weather. She had to convince Victoria to move the wedding inside to the ballroom, and they had to do it right then.

Morgan raced down two flights of stairs and ran down the hallway to Victoria's suite. She banged several times on the door. Across the hall, Mindy stuck her head out. "What's going on?"

"I have to talk to Victoria. We've got to move the wedding inside."

"How come?" Mindy came out of her room and crossed the hall. She had on a green sleeping shirt and her feet were bare.

At last, Victoria opened her door. She was wearing a sheer pink night gown and black sleeping mask pushed up on her forehead. Even with tousled hair and sleepy eyes, she looked exquisite.

"Victoria, we've got to change the wedding venue," Morgan said. "It looks like a big storm is coming this evening. We'll have to move it indoors."

Victoria yawned. "What time is this storm making landfall?"

"I don't know exactly, but it looks like maybe three AM."

"We'll have finished by then. I don't see the problem." She stepped back as if to shut the door.

"The rain and wind will start before then," Morgan said. "It could be a disaster.

Even Victoria's little-girl frown looked pretty. "I can't change the plans. It will ruin everything. The wedding has to be special. I owe it to my fans."

Morgan kept her voice smooth and calm. "I know you're disappointed. But we need to make this decision now, so my staff can set up in the ballroom."

Victoria stamped her foot. "No, I won't do it. We'll go ahead with the tent. If necessary, we can close down the reception early instead of going into the early morning hours."

Morgan raised her eyebrows and shook her head in frustration. "You're making a mistake."

"Morgan, this is my wedding and we will do it *my way*." Her tone held an acerbic edge. "You've already been paid plenty of money, so back off." The door thunked shut in Morgan's face.

Speechless, Morgan threw up her hands in defeat and turned to walk down the hall. She almost ran over Mindy, who was standing right behind her. The girl looked smug. Morgan grimaced and said, "I tried. You heard me."

***

Downstairs, Morgan went into her office to make some calls and check her email. Itzel was at her desk, a harried expression on her face. Morgan figured she probably looked equally distraught. This was how things went the day of a big wedding. "Itzel, I've got some terrible news."

Itzel looked up from her computer, where she was printing some last-minute instructions. "What happened? Did Victoria Palmer call off the wedding?"

"No. I almost wish she had."

Itzel laughed nervously. "So, what's up?"

"A big storm is heading our way. I suggested we move the wedding inside. It's an enormous job to move all the tables, chairs, flowers and everything into the ballroom, but I'm worried the tent will blow away and everyone will get drenched or worse. Victoria refused."

Itzel grimaced. "Well, she's the boss. It's her wedding."

Morgan sighed in frustration. "I just don't feel good about this."

She and Itzel went through the intricate plans for the wedding and reception. Normally she enjoyed this, but today it only added to her tension. They divided up the myriad tasks and went their separate ways. Morgan headed down to the kitchen to talk to Chef Pierre and go through the menu again. The crawfish hadn't arrived for the *vol-au-vent* appetizer and he was in a snit. She calmed him down somewhat, then met with the wait-staff and detailed the activities for the cocktail reception and the dinner. Using a printed map of the Magnolia Park, she clarified everyone's station.

Those tasks finished, Morgan checked her watch. Before going out to the tent, she went down the hall to talk to Roberts in the security office. His face red with embarrassment, he again apologized profusely about the breach the night before. "Listen, Morgan. We had no clue this nutcase would swim across the lake. I had guys posted at key points, but he snuck past them."

"I understand, but this *must not* happen tonight."

He nodded, picking up on the vehemence in her tone. "Sheriff Simmons will have his men around the perimeter of the lake. We'll have floodlights sweeping the water. The beach is being patrolled by our men and also the Coast Guard offshore."

"All that sounds good. But the paparazzi are swarming along 30A. They all want to post that first shot of Victoria Palmer getting married. I imagine there'll be some helicopter action."

"No, I think Big Bob Palmer paid big bucks to keep the air traffic away." Roberts shook his head in frustration. "Man, this wedding is crazy. I'll be glad when it's over."

Morgan could feel the tension creep up her spine. "You and me both."

Chapter 15
Late Saturday Morning

Morgan went down to check out the tent where the reception would take place. Magnolia Park was a beautiful setting for the wedding. The Sweet Silver stream gurgled down one side of the garden. Live oaks shaded the green lawn and a path meandered through the garden amid a profusion of flowers. Several days earlier, resort staff had erected a specialty tent with a trellis of pink roses at one end. At the other end was a gazebo constructed for the band. Diaphanous silk curtains hung from poles and were tied back with pink silk ribbons.

As Morgan walked into the tent, an army of Magnolia staff and florist assistants were hard at work putting on the finishing touches. They'd attached bouquets of roses to the pink ribbon bows. White tablecloths with swags of pink covered the numerous round tables. In the center of each table was a bowl filled with pink, lavender and white roses, atop a round mirror that reflected the muted colors. An intricate array of ribbons crisscrossed the ceiling and fairy lights glimmered. In the garden, artificial topiaries were festooned with flowers and artificial birds. Several gazebos had been constructed for guests to sit amid the gardens. The entire set-up was super girly-girly, Morgan thought. She'd been surprised that Victoria chose the pink and white theme. Morgan had suggested a more exotic motif with purple orchids or blue lotus blossoms. But Victoria said her fans would swoon at a pink and white wedding. It was every little girl's dream.

An air-conditioning system was set up inside the tent for the day. Plastic walls and flaps also helped to keep out the heat. Morgan wondered how they would withstand winds of a hundred miles an hour. The thought of it made her shudder.

Ralph, the technician in charge of the sound system, was having problems with the wiring. He was yelling at his assistants using some very colorful language. All the action and noise inside the tent made her think of a busy beehive. She gazed around the space again, filled with a premonition that things could go very wrong that evening.

***

With the bridal party safe in the spa for several hours, Morgan decided to take an hour off and try to relax. She needed to get away from the resort and find some momentary peace. After, checking with Katarina on the number of wedding guests who'd arrived thus far, she ran upstairs and grabbed her purse and her iPad. She would go to Rosemary Beach and chill.

Driving down the causeway, she looked up at the perfectly blue sky dotted with little puffy clouds. To her left, the Gulf was calm, and seagulls danced on the waves. Mother Nature was keeping her secrets. No way could anyone imagine She would turn this paradise into a roiling fury.

After driving along, the shore of the lake, Morgan arrived at a checkpoint manned by three sheriffs. The gate swung open and she drove through. When she hit 30A, she was bombarded by lightbulb flashes and a milling crowd. Along with Victoria's adoring fans, a heavy media presence had shown up. Morgan knew several big Hollywood stars, TV personalities, and music idols would be attending the wedding. Many of them were not staying at the resort and would arrive in the late afternoon. All this churning humanity was waiting to spot the celebrities.

Morgan drove east down 30A, past The Hub, where a spillover crowd was drinking and eating. The locale's enormous Jumbotron would undoubtedly feature the wedding that evening. Beyond it, the white buildings near Alys Beach looked pristine in the sunshine. Even here there seemed to be an increased number of people. George's was doing a rip-roaring business. Why was it that all these people wanted to be in the vicinity of this social-media extravaganza? They certainly weren't all invited to the wedding.

Five minutes later, Morgan pulled into a parking place in front of The Hidden Lantern bookstore. She turned off the engine and reached for her purse. As she was about to exit the car, she looked up and saw Josh and Brad standing several feet away. They were arguing, but she couldn't hear what they were saying. Josh was gesticulating, as if pleading with Brad. Brad held his arms straight at his sides, his hands balled into fists. It looked as though he was about to lunge at Josh.

Morgan didn't want them to see her. Luckily, she wore big sunglasses and the driver's-side sun visor was down. Even if they spotted her, they'd think she was a tourist or just some local. As she watched, Carter came out of the bookstore with Lars. They were deep in conversation and didn't look up at first. Immediately, Josh and Brad stepped back. Their expressions became bland. Clearly, they didn't want Lars and Carter to know they'd been quarreling. What was going on here? Morgan reminded herself it was none of her business. After today, all of these people would be out of her hair and out of her life.

She sat still and waited for the four of them to walk away past Wild Olives, towards Rosemary Beach City Hall. Then she left her car and headed toward Amavida.

Chapter 16
Saturday Afternoon

Morgan sipped her latte and turned a page of her book. She'd successfully lost herself in the plot and forgotten the wedding. She sighed with contentment. Then a shadow fell across her table. She glanced up. Carter was looking down at her, a sardonic smile on his lips. "Ah-ha, you've escaped the Magnolia prison and the Black Queen's wedding. Pretty irresponsible." He chuckled.

"You've caught me in the act. I'm shirking my responsibilities. For shame!" Morgan gestured to the chair across from her. "Please, sit down."

Carter sat and removed his sunglasses, placing them on the table along with a cup of coffee. "What are you reading?"

"*The Nightingale*." She held up the book, so he could read the title.

"Who's the author?"

"Kristin Hannah. I've read some of her other books. This is about two French sisters during World War II and how they cope with the German occupation. One of them is in the resistance and the other has to deal with a German billeted in her house. It's a great read."

"Hmm, I haven't read much fiction for a long time. I've always got medical journals to read. Then I need to keep up with the latest research in my field." He tapped his cup with his finger. "So, what happened to that poor slob with the speedo and the tattoos last night?"

"They arrested him and took him off the premises."

"Poor guy!"

"Poor guy?" Morgan looked at him quizzically.

"Yeah, another man who lost his mind over Victoria Palmer. She's been driving men nuts forever."

"Why did you agree to come to this wedding if you think so little of the bride?"

"Because Brad begged me to come and I actually thought it would be good to see everyone again, but I was pretty stupid. I *in*conveniently forgot what it was like to be in Tory's orbit."

He fell silent. Morgan sipped her coffee, thinking about the scene she'd witnessed earlier in front of the bookstore. "So where are the other guys? I thought you might be playing golf this morning."

"We had some breakfast down the way, at the Summer Kitchen Café. I had the best French toast ever. Then the three of them drove back to the resort. I just needed a little more coffee."

"Do you guys see each other often?"

"No, not really. I hadn't talked to any of them for a while. Sometimes, Josh sends me political cartoons or sports updates." He took a sip of his coffee. "Everyone's so busy and I think we've all moved on. You know what I mean? College was over almost ten years ago."

"What about the other guys? Do Josh and Brad get together? Don't they both live in Texas?"

Carter laughed. "Right, but Texas is a pretty big place and I can't imagine their paths would cross...a big-shot lawyer and a high school coach."

"Yes, I see what you mean." Morgan looked down at her phone. Her free hour was up. She had to get back to the Magnolia. "I better get going. Can I give you a ride?"

"If you wouldn't mind. That would be great."

Once they were settled in the car, Morgan told him about the storm on the horizon. "I tried to get Victoria to move the wedding and reception inside, but she won't hear of it. I'm just hoping everyone doesn't get drenched and the tent doesn't blow away."

"Whatever Victoria wants, Victoria gets. You should know that by now. And I'm sure the storm will obey her command," Carter said wryly.

Morgan suddenly thought of Grady, out in the middle of the Gulf with his fishing buddies. Certainly, he would know to get out of the storm's way. She wondered where he was. He hadn't texted or called her. Inadvertently, her hand went to her cheek.

Carter glanced over at her. "What's up? You look upset."

"I do?" She lowered her hand to her lap. "It's nothing."

Carter reached over and clasped her hand. "I'm sorry our dance was cut short last night…" he said quietly.

Morgan blushed, pulled her hand away and set it firmly on the steering wheel. "I was thinking about my boyfriend. He's out in a fishing boat in the Gulf…what with the storm…" She trailed off.

Carter didn't respond. She was fully aware of his hands spread on his thighs.

As they neared the resort, the crowds along 30A increased. Cops were patrolling the road, making sure the throng didn't spill onto the roadway. Tension charged the air.

Morgan clutched the steering wheel. "Look at these people, all here to get a glimpse of someone famous. It's crazy." She turned onto the service road and they went through the roadblock.

"I can't wait until this damn wedding is over and I can get the hell out of here," Carter said with vehemence.

Morgan swallowed and continued to look straight ahead.

***

Back at the resort, Carter thanked Morgan for the ride without looking at her. Then he disappeared towards the beach. She sighed. She hadn't meant to hurt Carter, but she needed to put a stop to whatever he was going to say about the two of them and last evening.

The lobby was bustling. There were people in the restaurants and she could see kids tossing a beachball in the pool. Morgan went through the passageway that led to the spa, to check on the bridal party. Natasha was at the desk when she walked in. "How's it going?" she asked. A tall redhead, Natasha had a muscular body and Morgan knew she gave a killer massage.

Natasha smiled. "We're very busy, with the bride and her maids but also with other guests in the hotel. I've got all my girls working today."

"That's good for the resort. Where is the bridal party?"

The smile vanished. "In the blue salon. I think they're doing hair and make-up now. But Ms. Palmer has her own stylists. She wanted none of ours." Natasha sniffed, definitely displeased.

Morgan gave her a sympathetic look, then entered the spa through the ladies' changing area. She was about to make her way around a screen when Georgie's high-pitched voice made her stop and listen. "I'm really thinking on pulling out. After the wedding, I'm going to find another job. I know I could get a job as a model. Everyone knows me, because of Victoria."

"For sure. You're almost as famous as she is," Jenny said.

Morgan peered diagonally past the screen at the mirror that reflected the three bridesmaids. They wore white cotton robes with the Magnolia symbol on the pocket. Three beauticians were working their magic, creating intricate curls on top of the bridesmaids' heads. Across the room, Victoria lay nude on her stomach, while her Thai maid rubbed some heavily perfumed cream onto her smooth, curved back. She made Morgan think of an Impressionist odalisque. With earbuds in both ears, she probably couldn't hear the other girls.

"She's really used me. I mean, she's paid me and all, but I have no freedom. It's like I belong to her, like a puppy dog or something," Georgie said.

Mindy leaned in. "I'm planning on pulling out, too. I'm fed up and I know I can get a job somewhere else in the hi-tech film world. I've been her slave for long enough."

"I don't know why Lars and I came down here. After everything that's happened, we almost left the other night," Jenny said.

Georgie slid a glance her way. "Why did she ask you to be in the wedding?"

Jenny giggled. "No clue?"

"You know why, it's because you photograph well," Mindy said. "You and Lars make a very cute couple. Let's face it, Victoria is all about her social media feed. She wanted beautiful people in her wedding." Then she added, "Of course, that might make you wonder what I'm doing here."

The other two girls looked at her as if for the first time, "Gosh, Mindy, you actually look pretty good yourself," Georgie said in unabashed amazement.

Mindy turned away, clearly annoyed, "No, I don't. I'm a plain-Jane."

Morgan agreed with the other girls. She studied Mindy's reflection in the mirror. She was a knock-out.

Chapter 17
Saturday - Late Afternoon

Morgan took a golf cart and drove back out to Magnolia Park. She wanted to check on the set-up again. Happily, everything was in place. In a few hours the reception would begin and five hours later the wedding would be over. All she would have left to worry about was the morning brunch. It would be a simple affair, with pastries, fruit, cheeses, omelets and coffee. Chef Pierre would have that well in hand if he made it through the banquet tonight.

While she was checking out the topiary, she got a text from Sheriff Dax Simmons, her friend Claire's fiancé. Morgan called him back. "Hey, Dax."

"Just wanted to confirm that we're in place. I've got extra men stationed around Lake Nawatchi. The problem will be to get the wedding guests through the front gates, so they don't get mauled. Man, we've never had a crowd like this, even during the music festival in January."

"Thanks, Dax. The resort is grateful for the crowd control and the extra security."

"I'll be on the island, so I'll see you later."

"Excellent." Morgan felt relieved. She'd been worried about security after last night's shocker.

Back at the resort, Morgan dressed for the wedding. She chose a short peach-colored cocktail dress, with a smooth fitting bodice of duchess satin. The skirt was several layers of diaphanous organza with a thin peachy-pink ribbon at the waist. It was one of her favorite dresses to wear at weddings, chic and elegant. She rolled her hair into a smooth bun at the nape of her neck and applied make-up. *Just a few more hours, and then things will get back to normal.*

***

The ceremony was a huge success. Three hundred people, in white chairs set up on the beach, witnessed the wedding vows. The ceremony took place under a silk and ribbon canopy. Potted orchids and ferns delineated the aisle, which was strewn with rose petals. Victoria looked exquisite in a peau de soie silk mermaid dress. It fit her curves beautifully and swirled out below the knee. Delicate seed pearls in an intricate pattern enhanced the lines of the gown. Her hair was swept up in a mass of curls at the back of her head and soft tendrils framed her face. Morgan had to admit she was a stunningly lovely bride. Brad and the groomsmen wore white tuxes and the bridesmaids were dressed in delicate pink gowns of full-length floating chiffon.

A well-known TV evangelist, Ron Bates, officiated at the wedding. Big Bob had insisted on the man and Victoria had agreed, enthusing to Morgan that he had an enormous following *and* was young and flat-out gorgeous. Bates had a sonorous voice and a brilliant smile. He was famous across America and had been invited several times to the White House. Morgan found him a little pompous, but this wasn't her wedding.

From where she stood at the very back, Morgan let her gaze rest on Carter's wide shoulders. In the late afternoon sunlight, gold highlights glinted in his dark red hair. Watching him, she felt guilty again. She should have been kinder that afternoon. He was a really nice guy.

After the ceremony, while the photographers took the traditional wedding photos, the guests were guided to Magnolia Park. Some people chose to walk, others rode over in beribboned golf carts. Itzel stuck around to supervise the dismantling of the wedding set-up. She and Morgan had agreed that with the storm coming, they couldn't take a chance and leave the chairs and canopy out. Morgan hurried over to the reception.

As she approached Magnolia Park, she saw clouds moving in, covering the low afternoon sun. A breeze ruffled the trees. She shook off a sense of foreboding and plunged into the crowd. Guests were spread out across the lawn, some sitting in the pink and white gazebos, others under the live oaks. A flute, guitar and bass trio played background music. Waiters circulated with trays of hors-d'oeuvres: mini crab cakes, caviar and crème fraîche tartlets, lobster toasts with avocado and many more. Along with glasses of champagne, there were flutes of Kir Royale, Victoria's favorite aperitif. Morgan circulated among the guests, making sure they had what they needed.

At seven-thirty the Red Roof Band began to play "Here Comes the Bride". At that moment floodlights illuminated a golden gondola gliding down the Sweet Silver stream. Victoria and Brad sat in the gondola on pink satin cushions and waved to their friends and acquaintances. Victoria was indeed the queen. Behind them two more gondolas arrived with the rest of the wedding party. At an artificial gold-painted dock, they exited the gondolas with the aid of a boatman dressed as a Venetian gondolier, including a pink-ribboned straw hat. The crowd cheered, and Victoria curtsied while Brad bowed.

Morgan looked at Brad as he walked beside Victoria smiling and shaking hands. She felt as though she didn't really know him. During the last year, he had only accompanied Victoria to the resort twice. Both times he was incredibly polite but somehow distant. It had been obvious he was leaving the wedding in Victoria's hands.

After Victoria and Brad took their seats on a pink satin-bedecked dais, dinner was served. There were toasts and laughter. As best man, Carter talked about their college days. "Although we all knew each other back then, it wasn't until recently that Brad saw the light." He raised his glass to Victoria. "He found a real live princess." To Morgan's surprise, Victoria actually blushed. "We're all wondering if Brad is going to give up his job at Triple S and become a media socialite. I know Tory's fans would love it." As Carter said this, Morgan saw a cloud come over Brad's face. The groom forced a laugh.

Carter's toast wound down, and after a couple of glasses of wine, Georgie stood up. She talked about her friendship with Victoria and told some stories about their travels together. "I love you, Tory. I hope you'll be happy now." Then she burst into tears. Recalling her extraordinary outburst on Thursday morning, her claim that she'd always loved Brad, and her gossipy declaration this afternoon that she was done with Victoria Palmer, Morgan figured the tears owed as much to the champagne as to genuine emotion. Victoria smiled coolly, patting her face with a napkin. Perspiration beaded her forehead.

Big Bob got up next and talked about his beautiful little girl and how she had made a name for herself. Morgan glanced at Norma Lee. Victoria's mother wore her usual dour expression. Even now she didn't smile fondly at her daughter.

"I am happy my darling girl found someone who makes her happy." Big Bob turned to Brad. "Take good care of my little girl. She has a mind of her own, but sometimes she needs a little prodding. You know, a hand of steel in a glove of velvet." Everyone laughed. Victoria smiled vaguely, still blotting her face with a napkin. Big Bob turned to Norma Lee. "Thank you, honey, for raisin' my little darlin'. You did the best you could."

Norma nodded but didn't smile. Morgan didn't get it. It was almost as though she resented her daughter.

The toasts finished, Morgan circulated among the guests, making sure they had everything they needed. Later she reminded Victoria it was time to cut the cake. It was a ten-tier extravaganza. After the bride and groom made the first cut and fed each other, the pastry crew began cutting pieces to be boxed up for the guests. After that, they brought in the ice sculptures. A myriad of pastries, mousses, profiteroles and ices were displayed on little shelves among the sculpted flowers and birds. Guests helped themselves to dessert and then the dancing began. Victoria and Brad started it off dancing to "All of Me". Then they split up. Victoria danced with her dad, but it looked as though Norma Lee refused Brad's invitation. Soon everyone was on the floor. Morgan saw Carter dancing with Mindy, then Georgie and some cute girl she didn't know. Unexpectedly, she felt a pang of jealousy.

The photographers circulated and took pictures of the guests. At some point, someone yelled, "Let's have a Talbot picture." The alumni all went up onto the dais and crowded around Victoria and Brad. When they were almost in place, Victoria shouted to Rex and

Jill, who were filming but not part of the official wedding photographers. "Hey, you guys, come up here. You're Talbot Tigers, too."

Rex and Jill climbed up on the dais. The wedding photographers took several shots while the Tigers clowned around, making faces and gestures. Several times they switched places laughing uproariously. Suddenly, Victoria's face twisted into a rictus of pain. She fell forward, crashing to the floor in front of the dais.

Several people screamed—Morgan couldn't tell who. Victoria's security detail rushed forward, then halted in apparent confusion as Carter and Brad jumped down and fell to their knees beside her. The band stopped playing. As the crowd hushed, dancers looked over wondering what had happened.

Carter felt Victoria's neck for a pulse. Then he leaned down and listened to her heart. His face turned ashen.

"She's dead."

As a murmur raced through the crowd, there was a crack of thunder and a loud rush of wind. Morgan ran forward and crouched beside Carter. "Are you sure she's dead? She was laughing a minute ago." The whole situation felt unreal, like a waking nightmare. It didn't seem possible that Victoria Palmer was alive and clowning around one moment, dead on the floor the next.

"I'm sure." He looked over at Brad, who was white with shock. Carter stood and put his arm around his friend. "I'm sorry, Brad."

Victoria's father lumbered towards them, tears streaming down his face. "What happened to my baby? Is she all right? Is she—"

"Sir, your daughter is dead," Carter said gently. "My best guess is, she had a sudden heart attack."

"No." Big Bob shook his head. He knelt and gently smoothed Victoria's cheek, crooning softly to her. "Baby wake up. Wake up now, sweetheart."

Another clap of thunder echoed, and the wind picked up with terrific force. It blew down the rose trellis and whipped up the silk curtains. The entire tent seemed ready to take off. Wedding guests screamed and stampeded toward the paths leading back to the resort, tripping and pushing each other in their haste. The band grabbed their instruments and headed down the pathway toward the bridge and the safety of their truck.

Morgan crouched beside Carter and Brad and poor Victoria's corpse, trying to think what to do. The wind increased to gale force and sent the topiary flying along with the flimsy wooden gazebos. Inside the tent, tablecloths flew off the tables, bringing with them mirrors, flowers, dishes, silverware, and champagne flutes. The sound of splintering wood and shattering glass and china added to the mayhem. Georgie and Jenny were crying. Lars had his arms around both of them.

"Anything I can do? Josh yelled over the din. His eyes were moist.

Morgan yelled back, "Find Sheriff Simmons. You can get one of the Magnolia security guards to locate him." Josh left, running. Some of the others followed him.

Rex and Jill had remained behind and were still on the dais, busily videoing Victoria's lifeless body. "What in the hell are you doing?" Carter yelled up at them. "She's dead. Leave her in peace."

"She'd want us to film it, man," Rex said, with a near-smile on his lips.

Morgan felt appalled. Was he enjoying all this? *How many people would take pleasure in viewing Victoria's death?* It was a sobering thought.

Along with the vicious wind came the sound of torrential rain, pouring off the tent like a waterfall. Rivulets streamed onto the tent flooring. "What should we do? We shouldn't move the body. But she'll be drenched down here," Carter yelled over the howling of the storm. He watched as a stream of dirty, brown water inched its way toward Victoria's pristine white dress. Beside him, Brad stared at Victoria's lifeless body, his eyes vacant. Big Bob was sobbing, caressing Victoria's cheek with one chubby finger.

Lightning flashed, and thunder cracked violently, joined by the sound of a terrible crash as the other end of the tent came smashing down, flattened by an enormous branch from a live oak. Frantic, Morgan stared upward. It seemed as though the rest of the tent would come down on them at any minute.

76

"Mr. Palmer, we better get out of here." Carter helped Big Bob to his feet. Then he gently scooped Victoria up in his arms and started off towards the resort. Brad took Big Bob's arm and followed along with Rex, Jill and the security guys.

Morgan trailed along behind, her dress plastered to her body. She seethed with anger and frustration as she watched Rex filming their macabre procession. Did he have no respect for the dead?

Chapter 18
Sunday

The storm lasted for only two hours, but it was disastrous for the resort. A mini tornado had swept across Lake Nawatchi and whirled its way into the beautiful Japanese bridge, spinning the wooden structure into the air like a stack of toothpicks. The causeway had suffered damage and was down to one lane. For several hours, the island had no electricity, but by noon it had been reconnected.

Except for the resort, the Emerald Coast didn't sustain much damage. It was as though God had sent the tempest right at the Magnolia.

Some wedding guests made it off the island before the tornado hit, but many were trapped. They'd camped out in the lobby and the ballroom, where staff tried to make them comfortable.

Initially, Victoria's body was laid out in a small meeting room. The local ME had arrived at five AM. After he left, Victoria's body was taken to the morgue for an autopsy. Thus far, no one knew the cause of death, despite Carter's suggestion of a heart attack.

None of the wedding party left the Magnolia. Morgan reminded Katarina and Lionel that Victoria had paid for everyone's rooms through the following Friday. At one point, she saw Georgie and Mindy wandering through the lobby, but she was too busy to talk to them.

In the afternoon, a crew arrived to help with the clean-up at Magnolia Park. The detritus of the wedding decorations, the tent and the tree branches filled several dumpsters. Morgan figured that by nightfall, the park would be returned to its pristine condition.

The kitchen staff prepared a simple breakfast for the crowd of stranded guests. By noon, most of them were transported off the property and things began to quiet down. Morgan filled in here and there to give employees a break. She checked her phone several times to see if Grady had contacted her. No texts, no calls. *Well, no news is good news*, she said to herself. But she was worried.

At seven o'clock after nearly thirty-six hours on her feet, she looked into the Orchid Lounge where the wedding party was gathered. She decided to see how they were doing. She went to the bar, got a glass of wine, and brought it over to the table. "Hello, everyone."

Brad and Carter both stood up. "Join us, Morgan," Brad said. He looked terrible, with dark circles under his eyes and a grey tinge to his skin. He pulled over a chair. Then he and Carter sat back down.

"Thanks, Brad. How are you doing? I'm so very sorry about Victoria. I can't imagine your pain."

Brad swallowed. "Thanks, I'll get through this somehow."

"How about the rest of you?" Morgan looked at the others around the table.

"We're still in shock," Georgie said. She twisted a lock of golden hair around her finger. Her long pink fingernails gleamed in the dim light.

"Yeah, I can't get my mind around the fact that Tory's gone." Lars shook his head. "She was a major figure in all of our lives."

"I remember I met Tory in the hallway when I moved in freshman year," Jenny said. "I remember thinking she was gorgeous." Tears filled her large brown eyes.

"Yes, she was," Georgie said.

They both nodded their heads.

"I saw her first at Rinaldo's," Lars said. "Remember that pizza joint near campus? It was late at night and my roommate and I were picking up a sausage pie. She was in this booth, yelling at this guy. We turned to look."

Rex lifted his beer. "She had the tongue of a viper when she was angry."

"Shut up, Rex." Josh glowered and started to stand. Carter gripped his elbow, and he sat back down.

All of them avoided looking at Brad. He was staring at his glass, turning it in his hands.

"Sorry, man," Rex said.

Georgie teared up. "Brad, I was just thinking you were only married for a few hours."

Interesting, Morgan thought, that Rex and Jill were part of the group tonight. Could it be that only Victoria had made them feel like they didn't belong?

"What I don't get is what she died of. It seemed like a heart attack. Did she have any problem that you know about?" Josh asked.

Brad looked over at Georgie, "Didn't she have a mitral valve issue?"

Carter frowned, "What do you mean, a mitral valve issue?"

"I don't really know." Georgie pushed a lock of hair behind her ear. She looked exhausted. They all did.

"Do you mean a mitral valve prolapse?" Carter insisted.

"I don't know." Brad drummed his fingers on the table "Carter, it doesn't matter now."

"I disagree. You should know the cause of death. What happened was not natural," Carter said.

"We'll know after the autopsy." Josh looked around the table, his eyes questioning.

Georgie shivered. "I hate to think about an autopsy, cutting Tory up like that."

"My god, Georgie, can you just *shut up*," Mindy snapped. The girl was pale and looked haggard.

They were all quiet for a minute. Everyone took a sip of their drink. Morgan noticed the sandwiches they had ordered sat uneaten on the plates.

"What I'm thinking about is my job," Rex said. "Let's face it, several of us were dependent on Victoria."

"Right, she was our meal ticket," Jill added.

Josh glanced at Brad. "Is this the time to talk about that?"

"It's a fact," Rex continued. "Jill and I will film the funeral and then we'll be out of a job."

Josh rolled his eyes. "Oh, my God, give it up."

Mindy shrugged. "Rex is right. Georgie and me, we'll be out of a job, too."

Brad pushed back his chair. "I'm going to bed. You guys can talk about your uncertain future without me." He turned on his heel and left the bar.

Josh glared at Mindy. "Look what you did."

"I just stated the obvious."

"I'm going to bed too." Josh got up and almost ran from the room. Now they were down to just seven Talbot grads.

Lars looked over at Morgan. "What's the status of access to the Magnolia now? Are they working on the causeway?"

The change of subject came as a relief. "Apparently, they've got a crew building a pontoon bridge to connect the resort to the parking lot for members and their guests. I understand it will be done by tomorrow."

Carter chuckled. "I'll bet some of your members with deep pockets want everything back to normal, pronto. They probably have the money to move heaven and earth."

Morgan nodded but said nothing. It was true the Magnolia Corporation wielded a lot of power.

"Well then, tomorrow we'll be able to leave," Jenny said.

Lars frowned. "I just hope our car wasn't damaged in the storm."

"Go to the front desk and give them the license number and type of car and they'll check on it for you. They're in contact with the security detail at the parking lot."

With that, Morgan got up and said good night to everyone. Dealing with the wedding party, let alone the bereaved groom, had exhausted her. Carter followed her out and joined her in the elevator. "Morgan," he said.

Their eyes met in the mirror on the back wall.

"So...about yesterday. I apologize if I offended you.'

"No problem." She smiled at him. "Apology accepted. I was feeling stressed."

The elevator reached the third floor. Carter put his hand out to keep the door open. "You must know, I think you're very special."

Morgan looked down at her feet.

"Good night," he said.

"Good night," she murmured.

Chapter 19
Monday Morning

Morgan woke up slowly. She rubbed her eyes and stretched. Little by little she cleared the cobwebs from her brain. What day was it? Ah yes, Monday morning. Soon her life would be back to normal. Since Grady was gone, she would have a few days to just relax and catch up on errands.

Grady! Wouldn't he have contacted her by now to say he was all right? Angst clutched at her heart. She looked over at her alarm clock. It was nine AM, so she'd slept nearly twelve hours. She reached for her phone. Dax Simmons had left her a voice mail and a text.

She called, and Dax picked up immediately. "Hello, Morgan. Thanks for calling me back."

"No problem. I just woke up. Yesterday, I was up for thirty-six hours straight."

"Know how you feel. We've been working round the clock. Listen, I'd like to talk to the wedding party. Are they all still there?"

"I think so. Let me contact the front desk and find out. Can you hold?"

"Sure."

Morgan called downstairs. Katarina picked up. "Hi, Katarina. Do you know if any of the Palmer wedding party have checked out?"

"Let me see." A minute later, Katarina was back. "No, everyone is still here. I think they're in the dining room. The Johanssons checked out and are leaving after breakfast." Her voice sounded different...tired or stressed.

"Please go into the dining room and tell them they need to stick around for a few hours. Sheriff Simmons would like to talk to them."

"Okay, will do."

Morgan ended the call and returned to Dax. "They're having breakfast together. When will you be here?"

"I'll be leaving the station in a few minutes. Is there a place I could meet with them?"

"Yes, I'll set up one of the smaller meeting rooms." Morgan stood up and went over to the window, still clutching the phone. "Dax, I'm worried about Grady. I haven't heard from him."

"What do you mean?"

"He's somewhere out in the Gulf and he usually texts or calls me. What with the storm…" Her voice trailed off.

"I'll get someone to check with the Coast Guard."

"Thanks."

"Oh, and could you sit in on my meeting with the wedding party? I need another pair of eyes."

"Sure."

After she hung up, Morgan realized she hadn't asked about Victoria. Would the sheriff's office know the cause of death by now? Probably that was why Dax wanted to talk to the wedding party.

Morgan slipped into a sleeveless pale grey dress and twisted a flowered scarf in muted colors around her neck. Before leaving the room, she walked over to the window, pulled back the sheer curtains and stepped out onto her balcony. It was a balmy, sunny day with just a light breeze. Below her the pool was crystal clear. Yesterday, it had been filled with sand and debris. The shore was pristine with Magnolia blue deck chairs lined up under round blue umbrellas. The water was smooth with barely a wave. Her eyes moved to the horizon, a sharp edge of turquoise cut across the deep, blue sky. Mother Nature was taking a moment of repose, before She lashed out again.

***

Downstairs, Morgan went into the dining room. Georgie beckoned her over. "Have breakfast with us, Morgan."

There was an extra chair beside her and Morgan sat down. Several members of the wedding party were dressed in the Vineyard Vine shorts and shirts from last Thursday morning. Thursday morning—it seemed like years ago.

Morgan ordered a spinach, mushroom and cheddar omelet with whole wheat toast. She realized she hadn't had much to eat the previous day and was starving. Unfortunately, she had only eaten half the omelet when she spied Dax at the entryway to the dining room.

"Sheriff Simmons is here. Are you all finished with breakfast?" Morgan asked. They all nodded, unnaturally subdued. Morgan folded her napkin, placed it on the table and stood up. "Follow me."

They trooped out of the dining room. On the way out, Morgan instructed one of the waiters to bring coffee to the Gardenia Room. The nine of them trailed her down the hall. Dax stood at the entrance to the meeting room. He gestured for them to come in and sit down.

The Gardenia Room walls were striped yellow and beige with walnut chair rails. An elegant walnut marquetry table stood in the middle of the room. Under it lay an oval Persian carpet that picked up the tones of the walls. The group sat down around the table. Dax sat at one end and Morgan at the other.

"Let me introduce myself, I'm Sheriff Simmons." He looked around the room. "First off, I would like to extend my condolences at the loss of your friend, Victoria Palmer."

Brad stood up. "It's not Victoria Palmer, it's Victoria Hughes." He said it loudly, almost shouting. He was perspiring, and his hands were shaking.

"Right, excuse me. You must be Bradley Hughes. This must be a terrible time for you. I'm sorry for my error."

Slowly, Brad sat back down. Georgie patted his arm.

Morgan looked at Dax. He was a handsome guy with a rugged face, straight nose and dark penetrating eyes. He could have fit right into Victoria's wedding party. He also radiated authority and strength. No one would mess with Dax, Morgan thought.

"We are not yet sure exactly how your friend, and your wife Victoria Hughes, died. The results from the autopsy should be in today. For now, I'd like to hear from you. Were there any signs she wasn't feeling well yesterday? Did anything happen before she collapsed? I'm interested in anything you can remember."

No one said anything. Dax looked around the room, waiting.

Then Morgan said, "I noticed at the reception that Victoria was perspiring a lot. Did anyone else notice that?"

Georgie leaned forward. "I did. Tory kept patting her face with her napkin. Normally, she would stop the film rolling and have Rosa fix her make-up. But I thought, this was her wedding reception and she couldn't stop the show." Georgie blushed and gave a half-smile.

"We didn't actually see Tory until she came down the aisle at the beach. I mean, the girls were at the spa most of the day and the guys stayed away." Josh spoke quickly, his rushed words tumbling out.

Mindy looked like she had that first night when Morgan met her in the lobby, with her big glasses back on and wearing shapeless grey pants and an over-sized grey hoodie. Her hair was in a messy pony tail. "I remember Tory complained about a stomachache or indigestion when we were in the spa." Her voice sounded rough, as though she were coming down with a cold.

"Yes, I remember that," Jenny said. She was sitting close to Lars, the two of them holding hands.

"Isn't that how you feel before a heart attack? "Jill said. "Like maybe it was coming on…" Her voice trailed off. She looked around the room. With her straight bangs and large grey eyes, Morgan thought she looked younger than her twenty-eight years.

Dax turned to Brad. "Did you notice anything? Did your wife mention that she didn't feel well?"

Brad slowly nodded. "I don't know…she seemed her usual self. She was having a wonderful time. This wedding was her dream come true. It's all she talked about for the last year." His low voice quivered with emotion.

Dax's phone vibrated against the table. They all stopped talking and stared at it. "Sorry, I've got to take this, I'll be right back." He scooped up the phone, went to the meeting room door and opened it just as a waiter arrived with a cart containing coffee, cream, sugar and a platter of Chef Pierre's fabulous mini-cinnamon rolls.

While Dax was out in the corridor, they helped themselves to coffee and rolls. Georgie looked over at Jill. "Now I can eat two or even three sweet rolls if I want." Then she blanched as she looked over at Brad. He didn't seem to be listening.

A few minutes later, Dax poked his head into the room. He beckoned to Morgan. She placed her mug on the table and went out into the hall. "What's up?"

Dax shut the door and slipped his phone into his pocket. "Morgan, Victoria was murdered."

Chapter 20
Monday Morning

Morgan didn't know how to respond. In her mind, she saw Victoria plunge to her death, the frightful rictus pulling at her beautiful face. Right now, Morgan's thoughts were going in a million different directions. Finally, she said, "How? What happened?"

"She was poisoned. From the contents of her stomach, they found she'd been poisoned with an arsenic compound earlier in the day. But that's not what killed her."

Morgan frowned, her eyes questioning.

"Just before she died, she was injected with a high dose of R27. A nerve agent. It killed her instantly."

Morgan leaned against the wall, shaking her head in disbelief. It wasn't as though she'd been terribly fond of Victoria, but the fact that the girl had been murdered was horrendous. Who could possibly have hated her so much? Murder? Here at the Magnolia?

"So she was killed minutes or even seconds before she fell off the dais?" Morgan asked.

Dax nodded.

"While they were taking all those pictures..." she said slowly. "That means it has to be one of her friends. Someone in the wedding party."

"Exactly. I'm going to need to see the wedding pictures."

Morgan shivered, "I was there watching the whole thing. "But I didn't see anything. At least, nothing that points to this."

"Morgan, I need your help. I'm going back in there to announce the cause of death. Could you please study everyone's faces? Watch how they react?"

"I'll do my best."

Dax opened the door and walked to his seat. The chatter stopped. All eyes were on him. Morgan slipped back into her chair.

Dax cleared his throat. "Ladies and gentlemen, I've received the autopsy report." He looked around the room, as did Morgan. Brad appeared a little pale. Georgie was frowning and twirling her hair.

"Dr. Robbins, the medical examiner, found a large dose of arsenic in Victoria's system. Apparently, someone tried to poison her."

"Oh my God!" Jenny turned to Lars and the two of them clutched at each other. Brad looked horrified, Carter speculative. Georgie burst into tears and Mindy shook her head as though she didn't believe it.

"The arsenic isn't what killed her, though." Dax's words seemed to vibrate in the still room.

Again, all eyes were fixed on him.

"What do you mean?" Rex asked. His lanky frame was slouched in his chair.

"We have learned that Victoria Hughes died from a lethal dose of R27, administered by means of a hypodermic needle to the back of her arm. Death occurred within seconds."

Morgan scanned the faces around the table. They all seemed equally shocked. She looked for some tell-tale sign of guilt but saw nothing obvious.

Carter said, "You're telling us someone tried to kill her with arsenic. Then they tried again with R27?"

"Maybe. Or there might have been more than one person, as well as more than one attempt."

Brad cradled his head in his hands. Morgan couldn't see his expression.

"Jesus Christ, I don't believe this." Josh's dark eyes were round with shock.

His arm around Jenny, Lars looked around the table. "It couldn't be one of us? It must be someone who snuck in, like at the barbecue. Some crazy person."

Jill nodded. "Yes, that must be what happened. I mean, there were so many people at the wedding. A murderer could have pretended he was a guest."

Carter narrowed his eyes. "If death was instantaneous, then the poison was administered while we were posing for the Talbot pictures. Right? Before Tory fell forward?"

"That is the most likely scenario," Dax said.

"Well, then it must be obvious in the photographs," Josh said. He was on the edge of his chair, his hands braced on the table.

Georgie gasped. "But we were the ones being photographed before Tory keeled over."

"That's right, baby-cakes. So one of us murdered Victoria," Rex said.

Georgie looked at Rex and Jill. "Did you guys take pictures of us up on the stage?"

Jill shook her head. "No, we were up on the stage, too. Remember? Tory asked us to get in the picture."

"Right, so those professional wedding photographers might have a picture of the murder." Rex turned to Dax. "You should talk to those guys. Maybe they've got a video or a picture of the person plugging her with the needle."

"God, can you stop talking that way, like Tory wasn't our friend and, and…" Georgie halted as if searching for a word, tears running down her face.

"Listen, I worked for Tory, I did a great job for her. I put up with all of her bullshit. But that doesn't mean I liked her." Rex stabbed his finger at Georgie. "You were her little puppet. She pulled the strings, you danced. But don't tell me you loved her. Stop acting like you're all broken up."

Mindy entered the fray. "How do we know it wasn't you? If you felt like this about Tory, maybe you killed her?"

"Me? Give me a break. Let's see." He looked around the table. "I'm thinking it could be Lars here. Tory was a bitch to him the other night. Hell, maybe he did it for Jenny." His laugh held a mean edge.

Lars turned white and pulled Jenny toward him. "That was unnecessary, Rex."

Jenny glared at the videographer. Morgan saw that Dax wasn't about to stop this argument. He was following it carefully.

Josh stood up and banged on the table. "Come on, you guys. Let's not play the blame game. We're all friends. The sheriff here will find out what happened."

For a minute, silence reigned.

After a moment, Jill asked, "What does R27 do?" She was hunched forward, her face pale.

"It's a nerve agent similar to Novichok, the drug the Russians used to kill former spies living in England. It prohibits the nerves from communicating with the muscles. It acts within several seconds because the heart stops pumping," Carter said.

Again, they went quiet.

Dax stood up. "Ladies and gentlemen, I will need to interview each of you individually to get a better picture of what happened yesterday. I'll ask Morgan to give me a list of your names. I'll go through the list alphabetically. Please remain on the premises."

"Oh, my God, we'll never get home," Lars grumbled.

Dax ignored him and continued. "If you know anything, saw anything, or heard anything, please come forward…even if the information seems trivial." His eyes traveled from face to face. Morgan noticed Josh was frowning and looking down at his hands.

As the group stood up to leave, the door flew open. Big Bob strode in, his face bright red, perspiration running down his flabby cheeks. "You killed her, didn't you?" He lurched across the room and started pummeling Brad with both fists. Brad held up his arms to ward off the blows. Morgan figured Brad could probably have beaten the man to a pulp; he was much stronger and in better shape as well as a lot younger. But he didn't defend himself. After all, this was his father-in-law.

Through tears, Big Bob blubbered, "You killed her. You killed her. You never loved my baby. All you wanted was her money."

Dax reached over and pulled the man off Brad. Big Bob made a strange guttural sound and crumpled in a heap. The floor vibrated with the weight of his fall.

Chapter 21
Late Monday Morning

After the paramedics left with Victoria's father on a stretcher, Morgan went down the hall to her office. She shut the outer door and leaned against it. Itzel was there working on her computer. She looked up, surprise on her face.

"What's up? You look upset."

"You obviously didn't hear the latest."

"No, what happened?"

"Mr. Palmer had a heart attack. The paramedics took him to Sacred Heart Hospital." Morgan sat down in one of the chairs facing Itzel's desk. She took a breath. "Victoria was murdered...poisoned." She blurted out.

"Oh, my God." Itzel blanched. Then she said, "Do you think Mr. Palmer was murdered too? Gosh, do you think we're safe?" She looked around her office as though an invisible attacker was hiding inside the file cabinets.

"I'm sure we are. Sheriff Simmons is going to be interviewing all the wedding party and also some of the staff. He'll probably want to interview you, to see what you remember from the wedding."

"So, how was she murdered?" Itzel asked.

"Someone poisoned her using a hypodermic syringe." Morgan decided not to go into further detail. "Did you see anything suspicious during the reception?"

"Listen, Morgan, I was running around like a chicken with my head cut off. I didn't really notice what the wedding guests were doing. I was too busy keeping the food coming and the plates picked up. I did see Victoria dancing with her new husband. They made a beautiful couple." Itzel stopped talking as she remembered the scene.

They sat together quietly for a few moments.

Itzel pulled out a Kleenex and dabbed at her eyes. "Over a year's time, we get to know these brides pretty well. We want them to have a beautiful wedding and then go off into the sunset and live happily ever after."

Morgan nodded.

Itzel took a deep breath and picked up a notepad where something was scribbled. "Here's another small problem that occurred after the reception." She stopped and blew her nose. "I got a call from Joe Middleton, the wedding photographer. He said one of his cameras was stolen."

"When? What happened?"

"He said when the storm broke, they stuck around for a few minutes and then they headed back to the resort. Remember how it was a zoo in the lobby? Well, Joe went to the desk to see if he could get a room for the night. Meanwhile, his partner needed to use the bathroom, so he left their bag of equipment in a corner, thinking no one would bother it. When they got back to their place the next day, a camera was gone. They figure someone stole the camera while their gear was unattended."

"We'll have to put a sign up asking if anyone has seen it," Morgan said.

"Joe said he really needed it because it had all the pictures taken at the reception. He sounded pretty panicked."

"Did he now?" Morgan frowned. "I'm going to give him a call. Oh, and Itzel, could you please type up a list of the wedding party? Sheriff Simmons needs it as well as a list of Magnolia employees who worked the wedding. The sheriff is down in the Gardenia Room. He'll be using it for a day or two, I imagine."

"Okay, Morgan." Itzel's eyes reflected concern. "This is supposed to be your day off. Why don't you get out of here and I'll take care of things?"

A day off. Suddenly, Morgan longed for it. "After I call Joe, I think I'll go to yoga. But I'll check in with you later. I can't really disappear with this investigation going on."

In her office, Morgan dialed Joe Middleton's number. He picked right up.

"Hey Joe, this is Morgan Lytton from the Magnolia Resort. I'm calling about the camera you lost here after the wedding."

"Yeah, we figure someone stole it right out of our bag during the circus in the lobby. We really need that particular camera."

"What pictures did it contain?"

"Pictures of the reception."

"The very end of the reception?"

"Well…yes…"

"Did you take pictures of Victoria Palmer's dead body?" In all the panic and mayhem when the storm hit, Morgan couldn't remember who was standing nearby while Carter checked Victoria's vitals.

"Well…maybe I did. What do you care?" Now he was on the defensive.

Suddenly she was furious. "I'm thinking you hoped to sell those pictures to the *Enquirer* or some other rag. Am I right?"

He sounded placating when he answered. "Morgan, you and I have a good relationship. Let's not ruin it. Just find my camera."

"If I find your camera, I'll give it to the police. It will be taken as evidence."

"What do you mean?"

"Bye, Joe." After she hung up, Morgan stared at her phone. Victoria might have been a royal pain in the ass, but it sickened her that someone wanted to profit from the girl's death.

***

Morgan went back to the Gardenia Room and told Dax about the stolen camera. "I'll want to interview Joe Middleton and his partner," he said. Then he added, "Morgan, I've got a forensics team going over to Magnolia Park."

Morgan frowned. "I don't know what they'll find. A crew worked there all day yesterday cleaning up after the storm. They threw everything in a dumpster that's been hauled off."

"Nonetheless, we need to comb the area and look for that hypodermic needle."

***

Morgan went up to her apartment to change clothes for yoga. The Magnolia fitness center was in a separate wing. As she walked through the weight room, she saw Carter and Lars on the machines. In another corner, Mindy was lifting weights.

The yoga studio was an attractive room in peach and beige tones. Rhea Bell, the instructor, had her own studio in Lemon Cove, but three times a week she gave classes at the resort. Several women were in the room laying out their mats. In one corner Morgan spotted Georgie. She was wearing red yoga pants and a red top. Only someone with a perfect body could get away with that, Morgan thought.

Rhea began the class and soon they were all at work. The good thing about Rhea's classes was that they fully occupied your mind and your body. Morgan always came out of the studio feeling mentally refreshed. That was what she needed today. What with the murder investigation and her continued worry about Grady, she needed to relax.

Rhea put them through their paces. It was a hard workout and Morgan felt as though she'd never used some of these muscles before. After a week off, it was as though her body had turned to jelly. After class, Rhea left in a hurry as did the other women. Morgan was rolling up her mat when Georgie came over.

"That was a great class," Georgie said.

"Rhea is excellent." Morgan smiled at Georgie. "How are you doing? After all, you spent more time with Victoria than anyone else." *And you're in love with her husband. If that wasn't all just histrionics...*

"Yeah, we traveled together six months of the year...all over the world for these crazy photo shoots. Bali, Hong Kong, Paris, Singapore, Moscow. Tory wanted to stage her videos in all these places...so her followers could travel with her vicariously." She sighed.

"What will you do now?"

"I really don't know...maybe model."

Morgan remembered Georgie had said that at the spa on the wedding day. Morgan pulled on a grey tunic. "Could you take over the website? Maybe all those followers would follow you."

Georgie gave a bitter laugh. "I could never do that. I'm not the narcissist Tory was. Maybe I don't love myself enough." She wiped her face and hung the towel around her neck. "Have you ever looked up the definition of narcissism?"

"No, I never have."

"Well, I have. Narcissists talk about themselves, need constant praise, have a sense of entitlement, take advantage of others, and they envy others. Basically, Tory was never really happy. Her beauty, her fame, her adoring fans... Nothing was ever enough. She was jealous of everyone. She wanted what she didn't have. That's the story with Brad."

"What do you mean?" Morgan was curious.

"In college, she hooked up with just about every guy. I mean, they were all crazy about her. But she wanted Brad and he didn't pay any attention to her back then. They didn't start dating until a year ago. I think they texted and then he showed up at the studio. I couldn't stand to see them together. I would leave when he arrived." Georgie sat down on a bench and slipped on her flip-flops.

Morgan sat next to her.

Georgie stared down at her feet. "Are you familiar with the opera *Carmen*?"

"I know some of the music," Morgan said.

"Carmen is this gorgeous, sexy femme fatale. All the men love her, but she wants Don José who takes no notice of her. There's this famous song called the Habanera; where she says exactly that: she loves what she can't have, then when she gets it, she doesn't want it anymore." Georgie sang some words of the song in French.

"L'amour est oiseau rebelle
Que nul ne peut apprivoiser,
Et c'est bien en vain qu'on l'appelle
S'il lui convient de refuser."

Morgan recognized the tune. As she listened to Georgie's sweet, clear voice, she thought about her original opinion of the girl. Georgie was not as flighty as Morgan had initially thought. Did she act like a ditz as a defensive mechanism?

"What happens next in the opera?" Morgan asked.

"Basically, Carmen dumps Don José. He can't get over it and at the end he kills her."

Chapter 22
Monday Afternoon

Upstairs, Morgan dressed in shorts and a polo shirt. This afternoon she would keep a low profile; after all, this was her day off. She gave Claire a call to invite her for lunch. They agreed to meet at 1:30 at George's in Alys Beach.

Morgan had a few minutes before she needed to leave and decided to go out to the patio above the pool. She found an empty table under an umbrella and ordered a glass of raspberry iced tea. Below her, giggling children jumped in and out of the pool. Beyond lay the beach and the gently rolling waters of the Gulf. There was a light breeze and for the first time in days, Morgan felt herself relax. From her purse, she pulled out her iPad and began to read.

A few minutes later, she became aware of someone standing at the railing looking out at the water. She glanced up and saw Jenny, who for once was by herself. Her shoulders were trembling, her arms wrapped around her torso as if she were cold.

"Hi, Jenny. Do you want to sit down?" Morgan said.

Jenny turned, and Morgan could see she'd been crying. "I don't know. Maybe. Yes. I guess." She came over and slumped in a chair, then turned her tear-stained face to Morgan. "Lars and I had a fight. We never fight. It's this wedding. This whole damn weekend." She banged her fist on the glass table. "I wish we'd never come. Victoria was evil when she was alive and she's still spreading her poison in death."   _sarcastic remarks_

Her vitriol startled Morgan. This girl really hated Victoria. "Why did you come to the wedding?"

"I guess we were flattered to be asked. And of course, it was a free vacation, including all the silly costumes. But even at Talbot, Lars and I weren't in the inner circle. I don't really know why she invited us."

The waiter came over and asked Jenny what she wanted. The girl looked perplexed, so Morgan suggested the raspberry iced tea. Jenny nodded distractedly. "I just wish we could go home now. There's too much tension here."

"Well, you should be able to leave soon," Morgan took a sip of her tea.

"Even at the reception, there was tension. Tory made fun of Lars because... never mind, it was cruel."

"I guess Victoria didn't mince words," Morgan said.

"And then I saw Victoria arguing with her mother. Did you see that?" Jenny's eyes glimmered with the pleasure of shared gossip.

"No, I didn't." Though Morgan remembered the barbed looks Norma Lee had shot at her daughter during the rehearsal dinner. They definitely hadn't gotten along.

"I heard her mother say something like, 'I wish you'd never come to live with us.' Then, Tory said, 'I know you hate me because Daddy always loved me more than you. Now you're old and ugly.' She had this mean look on her face and she said, 'He's probably fucking another mistress now.'"

"Wow." Morgan felt shocked at this revelation. She drank more iced tea as she thought about Victoria and her mother. They certainly didn't look alike. In fact, Victoria had many of her father's traits. Maybe she was Big Bob's love child. "Did you tell all this to the sheriff?"

"No. I didn't think about it when I was in there."

"He probably should know. Make sure you share that information."

The girl nodded but Morgan could tell she wasn't listening. The waiter came with Jenny's glass, set it down, and left. After he'd gone, Morgan asked, "Jenny, where's Lars now?"

"I don't know. He dumped me in the lobby and went off somewhere." Jenny stood, leaving her iced tea untouched. "I'm heading up to the room. I'm going to take a nap. See you later."

Troubled, Morgan watched her go. Then she shook off her unease, left money for both iced teas, and left the patio.

In the lobby, she ran into Carter. He was dressed in tennis gear. "Hey, have you seen Josh? We were going to meet and hit some balls," Carter said.

"No, I haven't."

"I had my interrogation with your friend, Sheriff Simmons. He told me we still need to stick around." Carter paused and looked away. "Is he another boyfriend of yours? You seemed pretty cozy."

"Cozy?" Caught between amusement and annoyance, Morgan laughed. "Dax Simmons is engaged to my friend Claire. I'm having lunch with her today."

Carter gave a sheepish smile. "Sorry, that was uncalled for."

"It was." Annoyance came to the fore, and she continued in a clipped tone. "Maybe Josh is waiting for you down at the tennis courts. Go look."

"We agreed to meet in the lobby a half hour ago. He said he wanted to check on something and then we'd play." Carter tapped his racquet against the palm of his hand. "Maybe you're right. I'll go down there." He strode off through the front entrance doors.

***

City authorities had installed a temporary signal near the causeway to control the one-way traffic. Morgan waited at the red light, then drove across. Once she arrived on 30A it was a quick trip to George's. Claire was already there at a table on the terrace.

"Let's have a glass of wine and a nice leisurely lunch," Claire said after Morgan sat down.

"Sounds good to me. I could use some down time. Things have been crazy at Magnolia."

Claire nodded. "Dax filled me in a little. I get the feeling I won't be seeing much of him for a couple of days."

"I think you're right. He's going to be questioning a lot of people."

When the waiter arrived, Morgan ordered the sesame crab and avocado salad and Claire ordered a California lobster roll. "And a carafe of your house chardonnay," Claire added. The wine arrived promptly, and the waiter poured two glasses. After he left, Claire said, "Tell me about the murder."

Morgan told her all about the last four days, the adventure at Eden Gardens, the rehearsal dinner and the wedding. Claire listened, wide-eyed. "Dax texted me that Victoria Palmer was murdered, but he didn't say how."

Morgan sipped her chardonnay. "He told us she'd been poisoned. Twice."

"Twice?" Claire set down her wine glass. "What do you mean?"

"She had arsenic in her system, probably administered through food early in the day. Then at the wedding, while they were taking pictures, someone injected her with R27. Dax said it's a nerve agent. That's what actually killed her."

"Oh, my God. This is like some crazy thriller on TV," Claire said.

"Yes. It's as though she died like she lived; you know, bigger than life."

"Arsenic sounds like the poison of choice for a little old lady in an Agatha Christie mystery. Where do you even get arsenic, I wonder?" Claire said, her eyes round.

"Or R27?" Morgan said.

"Maybe on the Dark Web."

Just then their lunch arrived. After the waiter left again, Claire said, "This story is going to go viral. Victoria Palmer could be one of the most famous people in the world right now. Thousands will mourn her passing."

They were silent for a few minutes as they began eating. Unwittingly, Morgan's mind switched to Grady. She still hadn't heard anything from him.

As if reading Morgan's thoughts, Claire reached over and took her hand. "Have you heard from Grady? Dax said you were worried."

"No, I haven't. He hasn't communicated with me since he left. With the force of that storm, I'm anxious about him out in the Gulf."

Claire squeezed her hand. "I'm sure the Coast Guard will find him."

Morgan smiled at her friend. "Let's talk about something else. Where are you looking for a wedding dress? I've got some great suggestions for you."

They spent the next hour talking about Claire's wedding. As it turned out, it was a short-lived happy moment

Chapter 23
Monday Afternoon

As Morgan drove back along 30A, she heard sirens heading in her direction. She pulled over as an ambulance and several police cars raced past. After they went by, she pulled back onto the road and followed them. To her surprise, they turned into the Magnolia access road. She followed them down the causeway and into the staff parking lot.

As Morgan exited her car, a paramedic jumped out of the ambulance and hurried towards her. "How do we get down to Magnolia Park?"

"What happened?" Morgan asked.

"We understand there's been an accident."

As calmly as she could manage, Morgan explained the route to Magnolia Park for vehicles and watched as the cavalcade of cars headed for the park. *What could have happened now?*

She entered the resort building through the back and hurried to the Gardenia Room, looking for Dax. The door was wide open, and no one was inside. Further down the hallway, three waiters were seated on chairs lined up along the wall outside the Iris Room. There too, the door was open and the room was empty.

"Are you waiting to be interviewed?" Morgan asked.

A rangy, blond waiter responded. "Yes, ma'am, but the policeman got up and ran outta there. We don't know if we should wait here till he gets back, or what."

"Why don't you go back to work? They'll call you in a little while."

The three men exchanged glances, then got up and went down the hall toward the lobby. Morgan followed them. A woman's voice, loud and angry, reached her ears. *Good Lord, what now?*

A crowd surrounded the front desk. There was a distinct feeling of uneasiness. An irate woman stood there, pounding on the counter and yelling at Katarina. The woman's face was bright red under a canvas sun hat, her rotund body stuffed into a tight flowered dress. "We came here to relax and enjoy our vacation," she shouted. "But can we relax? No! All these sirens, and the police are running all over the place, telling us where we can go and where we can't. We're checking out right now, and we want our money back!"

Katarina looked stressed, a frozen smile plastered on her face. The woman's husband, as skinny as his wife was plump, stared down at the floor. The hotel manager appeared, drawn by the commotion, and spoke gently to the furious woman. A baldheaded man with a mini moustache and a suave manner, Hans Bern had decades of experience soothing frantic guests. For once, it wouldn't be Morgan's job.

Morgan continued through the lobby. When she glanced into the Orchid Lounge, she saw most of the wedding party sitting at several tables at the back of the room. Carter looked up and saw her standing at the door. He beckoned to her. "Come join us."

She hesitated. *Why was she drawn to these people? She wasn't sure if she even liked them. And of course, one of them could very well be Victoria's murderer.*

She walked over to Carter's table. He stood up and pulled out a chair for her. "What can I get you? Wine? Beer? A cocktail?"

"How about some soda water and lemon," Morgan said.

Carter walked over to the bar. Mindy, seated nearby with Rex and Jill, gave Morgan an anxious look. "Do you know what happened?"

"No clue. I followed an ambulance and some police cars into the resort. Apparently, there's been an accident," Morgan said.

Rex cleared his throat. "The sheriff was interviewing me, when he gets a call on his walkie-talkie and he was up and out of there."

"Did you hear what happened?" Georgie asked him.

"No, I couldn't hear a thing."

"I'll bet it's Victoria's mother. She probably keeled over just like her husband," Jill said.

"Not that battle-axe. She'll never die. She's immortal like the Wicked Witch of the East." Brad slurred his words. He and Lars were sitting at a third table, Georgie and Jenny at a fourth. A tumbler

103

of brown liquid sat in front of him, probably scotch or bourbon. "She hated me, that woman, she hated Tory...but now Tory's gone...but I've got you guys." He reached over to hug Lars, who tried to extricate himself from Brad's grasp. "You love me, don't you, Lars? We're friends? Right?" Brad placed a slobbery kiss on Lars' cheek.

"Yes, we're great friends," Lars said as he pushed Brad away.

Carter returned and handed Morgan a tall glass. Then he sat down next to her and leaned in close. "Any word about your friend out in the boat?"

Morgan felt a wave of angst. "Nothing yet. Sheriff Simmons has got someone looking into it." She smiled at him briefly. "Thanks for asking."

Carter sat back and studied the rest of the wedding party. "We're sticking together, although we're fed up with each other." Then he leaned in close again. "Let's face it. I'm pretty sure one of us killed Tory."

Morgan raised her eyebrows. "That's a pretty incriminating charge."

"It is. But just about everyone here had moments when they wanted to kill her. Like a true narcissist, she was oblivious to others."

"Yes, that's what Georgie said." Georgie and Jenny were deep in conversation, Morgan noticed, and Jenny hadn't once looked toward Lars. They must still be on the outs. She wondered where Josh was. Sleeping in his room or walking on the beach, or somewhere else away from this bunch, if he had any sense.

Rex, Jill and Mindy had their heads together as well. "Why don't we form a company of our own? We've got the reputation. We could build off of Victoria's followers," Jill said.

Rex glanced toward Georgie and Jenny. "I think we've got to convince Georgie to work with us. Maybe she could bring in some other gorgeous chick with great boobs and a killer ass."

"Shut up, Rex. You're such a sleazebag. You make me sick," Mindy snapped.

Then Brad started to sing the Talbot school song.

"Oh, Talbot College, Oh, Talbot College.
To our school we will be true.
Oh, Talbot College, Oh Talbot College.
Unfurl the flag of red and blue."

No one else joined in. They all looked at him with pity.

From across the room, Morgan saw Dax approaching, a grim expression on his face. "Would all of you please follow me, back to the meeting room. We need to talk."

Everyone stood up like obedient children and filed out of the bar.

Chapter 24
Monday - Early Evening

Morgan was the last to enter the Gardenia Room. Again, they took seats around the polished oval table. This time Lars and Jenny sat across from each other. Their rift had not been healed. Morgan noticed Jenny was avoiding Lars's soft brown eyes. He seemed to be silently pleading with her. Jenny stayed close to Georgie, apparently her new best buddy. Mindy and Jill sat beside her. The guys were all lined up on the other side. *Boys against girls*, Morgan thought.

Dax stood with his hands on his hips. There was something threatening about his posture. "An hour ago, we found the body of Joshua Brown. He was killed earlier this afternoon, probably between twelve noon and two o'clock."

"Oh my God." Georgie burst into tears. So did Jenny. Both women hid their faces in their hands. Jill's mouth went slack, and her eyes looked wild. Rex swore under his breath. Lars looked stunned, like someone had hit him. Mindy paled, as if she were about to throw up. Brad merely looked dull and uncomprehending. In his inebriated state, Morgan wasn't sure if he'd taken in what Dax said.

Carter surveyed the group with narrowed eyes. His gaze met Morgan's and he nodded slightly.

"Where?" Mindy blurted out.

"In a small garden, near Magnolia Park where the reception took place. A member of the forensic team found him while searching the area for evidence from Victoria Hughes' murder."

"So, who killed him?" Rex's voice vibrated with anger. He had turned bright red. "You think it's one of us, don't you? We're all under suspicion."

"Shut the fuck up, Rex. Let the sheriff talk," Lars barked.

"You shut the fuck up." He gave Lars the middle finger. "You probably killed him. Back at Talbot, you were plenty racist. You led the white supremacist march down fraternity row."

"It was perfectly legal. Those blacks had taken spots from white kids who were better students. It was inverse discrimination." Lars glared at Rex. "But I didn't feel that way about Josh. He deserved to be there."

"You're goddamned right. He was a hell of a lot smarter than you," Rex snarled.

"Come on, you guys, give it a rest," Carter said. Morgan eyed Dax, who seemed willing to let this verbal skirmish go on.

Jenny leaned forward on her elbows. "Why would it be us? We all liked Josh. Remember, there was that creepy guy at the barbecue. Then Tory died and now Josh. I think it's some crazy fan that has it in for all of us."

"Oh my God, Jenny, that's totally lame. It's got to be one of us." Jill was sitting forward in her chair, like a cougar ready to pounce. Her blond bangs lay sleek on her forehead.

"How…did…he die?" Georgie asked between sniffles.

"He was shot at close range."

"Shot…with a gun," Jenny sputtered.

"Yes. Do any of you carry a handgun?" Dax asked.

They all looked at each other. Then Georgie raised her hand. "I do and so does Tory." She blanched. "I mean, she used to have one. We get threatening emails and stuff. Being famous on social media means a lot of crazies say nasty things about you."

"Where is your gun now?" Dax asked.

"I put it in the room safe when I got here. It should still be there," Georgie said.

"I'll need you to get it and bring it down, so we can have ballistics check it out."

Georgie nodded.

"We will be questioning all of you as to your whereabouts this afternoon," Dax said.

"Wait a minute. So, we're all suspects?" Jenny's eyes were huge, like a kewpie doll's.

107

Jill stared at her. "Of course, we are. Ninety percent of the time, a crime is perpetrated by a close friend or family member."

Georgie looked as though she was working it out in her head. "So, one of us killed Tory and then moved on to Josh."

"But why him?" Jenny asked. She dug a tissue from a pocket and dabbed at her face with it.

"Because he knew something he shouldn't have," Rex said. "He must have seen the killer murder Victoria."

"I saw Josh texting a few hours ago," Georgie said. "We kind of met in the lobby. I was waiting for the elevator and he was standing by that huge ficus tree. Maybe you should find his phone?"

"His phone was not on or near the body. Our murderer was careful about that." Dax pressed his lips together.

For the first time they all went quiet. Then Brad seemed to wake up from his stupor. A rivulet of drool ran down from the corner of his mouth. "What are you guys talking about?" His dead eyes surveyed the room. "Where's Josh? What did you say about Josh?"

"Josh is dead. Murdered," Rex said.

"No, Tory was murdered. You got it all wrong." Clearly, Brad was having trouble focusing.

Dax opened a notebook. "As I said, please remain here at the Magnolia until further notice. All of you."

"We can't go home?" Jenny whined. "Lars and I were going to leave this afternoon."

"Yeah, right. You don't even want to be in the same car with me," Lars said, his tone petulant.

Dax consulted his notebook. "In a few minutes, Officer Rodriguez will join me. We'll interview all of you again." He surveyed the group, his eyes resting briefly on each of them. "In the meantime, I want all of you to remain in the hotel building where we can find you. Also, we've obtained warrants and we'll be searching everyone's room."

There was a lot of grumbling as they got up to leave. Carter put an arm around Brad's chest and helped him up and out of the room. Dax placed a hand on Morgan's arm as she passed him, forestalling her departure. When everyone else was gone, he shut the door and turned to face her. "So, what are your thoughts? I see you're embedded with the enemy. Have you got some inside dope?"

"I watched everyone while you announced Josh's murder. No one looked particularly guilty; no shifty eyes or sly smile or anything like that. They all reacted true to character."

"Is there anyone you wonder about? Anything that happened today?"

She shook her head. "I had lunch with Claire, so I was gone this afternoon during the time when Josh was killed. I do know Carter Perry was looking for him when I left. He said they had a date to play tennis, but Josh had disappeared. Maybe you should talk to him."

"I will, in due time."

"Do you think Josh was killed because he knew who killed Victoria?"

"Yes...either that, or he killed Victoria, and someone saw him do it."

The unreality of it was getting to her. "Gosh, I can't see Josh killing anyone. He was this nice, warm person who was always putting out fires when the others were swiping at each other." She paused, fighting off a wave of sadness. "Can you tell me exactly where he was killed?"

"He was shot near the stream that runs along Magnolia Park and dragged behind a wall of bougainvillea."

"Dragged? He was a big guy." Morgan envisioned someone grabbing Josh by the shoulders and pulling him across the ground. "It would have to be someone strong. Probably a man."

Dax looked down at his notebook. "That means Bradley, Rex, Lars or Carter."

"Or a very strong woman," Morgan murmured.

Someone knocked at the door. "Come in," Dax said.

Detective Rodriguez entered the room. A short man with a powerful build, he had sharp hooded eyes and a military buzz cut. Dax introduced Morgan. She said hello and started to leave. As she pulled open the door, she heard Rodriguez say, "We've found a syringe somebody tossed into that man-made stream in Magnolia

Park. The needle was stuck in the bank. It's pretty muddy. I don't
know about fingerprints…"

Chapter 25
Monday Evening

Morgan desperately needed some downtime. With two murders in as many days, the police seemed to be everywhere, and helicopters hovered overhead. Someone had leaked the news of the latest murder to the media, and reporters were gathered at the entrances to the resort. She had no desire to rub elbows with the wedding party even though Dax had asked her to play spy. And there was still no word from Grady, or about him, which had her close to panic.

After locking up the office, she walked through the lobby towards the elevator. Hans spotted her and waved her over. Usually unflappable, right now he was visibly distraught.

"We've got a problem. All our guests for the week are checking out. They've heard about the murders and don't want to stay. They're cancelling reservations left and right. Soon this place will be empty. This is *not* good for business. Nor are those checkpoints the sheriff's department set up. I understand they need to control who comes and goes from the property, but…" He gripped the edge of the counter and seemed ready to hurdle himself over it.

Morgan looked around the lobby. In a low voice she said, "I know, Hans, but the police have to investigate these murders. It will take a few days."

"Can't you get them out of here? Couldn't they do their questioning over at the sheriff's department?"

"For the time being, they've set up shop here. They need to question everyone who worked or attended the wedding."

Hans frowned. "We never should have agreed to that wedding. That Victoria Palmer was trouble from the get-go."

Morgan didn't know how to respond. Hans shook his head and stormed off.

Katarina, manning the front desk, wore a strained expression and had deep circles under her eyes, probably due to all the angry people she had to deal with.

"When does Lionel take over? You look worn out," Morgan said.

"I am. He should be here any minute."

A distinguished-looking man somewhere in his fifties approached the desk. "We're cancelling the rest of our visit here. Please prepare the bill for Mr. DuPont, that's Michael DuPont. We came here for peace and quiet..."

Morgan turned away and headed for the elevator. In a corner, on one of the sofas, she saw Lars and Jenny. They weren't sitting close together, but they were talking. It looked as though Jenny had been crying. Whatever they'd been arguing about, they seemed to be patching it up. Good for them, Morgan thought absently as the elevator pinged its arrival.

Upstairs, she opened the door to her apartment and quickly stepped inside, then double-locked the door. She didn't normally do that, but with two murders in the last twenty-four hours, it seemed like a good idea. She took a deep breath and looked around the living room. Finally, she could relax.

She kicked off her shoes and padded into her kitchenette. Inside the fridge was an open bottle of chardonnay. She poured herself a glass and curled up on the sofa. Using the remote, she turned on the TV. Maybe she could distract herself and watch a movie. After flipping through the channels, she switched it off. No way could she concentrate on an inane family comedy or a gory crime show, not when a real-live murder investigation was going on right below her. She got up, pulled open the sliding glass door and went out onto the balcony. Gently rolling waves swooshed onto the beach. Their constancy was hypnotic. But as her gaze moved out to sea, her worry about Grady returned. Was he out there? Was he safe? The waters of the Gulf didn't respond. She would go nuts if she didn't think about something else. On a whim, she went back into the living room and opened her desk. She rummaged around in a drawer for a sharp pencil and found a legal notepad. Then she went back out to the patio and sat down on one of the turquoise and blue striped deck chairs.

Down the left margin, Morgan wrote the names of the wedding party, beginning with the girls. She left a couple of lines empty between each name, giving herself space to write down what she knew about each one. A momentary shiver came over her when she'd finished. One of these people had killed Victoria and probably Josh as well. That they were all downstairs, walking around free, was frightening.

Georgie…what did she know about Georgie? The girl was beautiful and jealous of Victoria. Morgan remembered her confession that she loved Brad and couldn't stand him marrying Victoria. She wrote down *jealous* and *loved Brad*. What else did she know about Georgie?

From inside, Morgan heard the soft chimes of her doorbell. Who could have come up here? The staff knew never to bother her when she was off duty. Would it be wise to open the door when she was alone? She stayed on the deck chair, notepad across her lap, frozen by indecision.

I won't be afraid. Not in my own home. She stood and strode to the door.

Chapter 26
Monday Evening

Through the peephole, she saw Carter grinning. In one hand he held a bottle of wine, in the other, a platter. Against her better judgement, she unlocked the door and opened it a slit. "Hi, what are you doing here?"

"I brought sustenance." He held out the platter. She recognized the Magnolia's classic cheese plate: perfectly aged Camembert, full-flavored Roquefort and a nice wedge of Comté, along with pâté, grapes and a neatly sliced baguette. "And I need to talk to someone."

Morgan was tempted. It looked delicious, yet caution held her back. "Can't you talk to one of your friends downstairs?"

"No. I need a third party. Someone who doesn't have emotional ties to Josh or Tory. Besides, you've been around us enough to have drawn some conclusions."

Morgan still wasn't convinced. "How do I know you're not the murderer?"

He grinned wider. "You don't. But I think you trust me."

She bit her lip, wavering.

"Come on. Let me in. This pewter platter is heavy," Carter groaned.

Morgan undid the chain and stepped back. Carter walked quickly over to the glass dining table and put down the cheese platter and the wine. He looked around. "Wow, this place is beautiful: pristine and yet comfortable." He surveyed the room, admiring the furnishings and the Impressionist paintings.

"Thank you. Very few people have ever been up here. With my job, I'm constantly dealing with people. At night, I need a hideaway where it's quiet and relaxed...where I won't be disturbed," she said pointedly.

Instead of responding, he looked at the legal pad in her hand. "What's that?"

Morgan blushed. "It's a list of the wedding party members. I was doing some investigative research."

"Ah-ha! Great minds think alike." He grinned again. "Come on, let's get to work."

Morgan fetched a wine glass, small plates and silverware from the kitchen. She set the table and went outside to retrieve her own glass of wine.

"No, you can't possibly drink white wine with cheese," Carter said at the sight of her chardonnay. "You've got to have some of this French Beaujolais."

"Okay, if you say so."

"I do say so. My mother was French, and I spent a fair amount of time in France as a kid."

"Not drinking wine, I hope?"

"I started with a quarter-inch mixed with water and graduated to a full glass at eighteen or so."

There wasn't much chardonnay left, so she drained her glass and waited for him to refill it. "So, an alcoholic since childhood...nice."

"Not an alcoholic...a wine connoisseur."

They sat down and served themselves cheese, bread and grapes.

"I'm sorry about your friend Josh," Morgan said. "He seemed like a really nice guy."

"He was a nice guy. That's why his death makes no sense unless he witnessed Victoria's murder." Carter held up his Beaujolais. "To Josh, that his killer be found and brought to justice."

"To Josh," Morgan said. They clinked glasses. She took a sip of the smooth wine Carter had brought. It was delicious.

"I think we should think about Victoria's murder first. Whatever happened to Josh was in reaction to, or as a result of, Tory's death," Carter said.

"I totally agree." Morgan cut a wedge of Camembert, spread it on bread and took a bite. Then she pulled the pad of paper closer. "Okay, tell me about Georgie."

Carter frowned as he took a sip of wine. "Back in college, I don't think she and Tory were BFFs. As a matter of fact, they were rivals. Georgie was the homecoming queen senior year and Tory was pretty bitter. But the queen and king were chosen for popularity as well as attractiveness. Georgie probably had a lot more friends." He paused. "Now that I think of it, Josh was the king." He stared at his glass, swirling the wine. "Back then it all seemed so important. But none of it matters now." He sighed.

"This morning, I talked to Georgie after yoga down in the spa. I was impressed by her knowledge. She comes across as a ditz mostly, but I honestly wonder if she's putting on an act," Morgan said.

Carter considered this. "As I remember, she was a pretty good student…particularly interested in the arts. Maybe ditz was the role Tory assigned to her and she's embraced it."

"That makes me wonder if all her tears this morning were real or were they an act too."

"Well, she'd been almost living with Tory for the last few years. She would certainly be upset," Carter said.

"If she and Victoria weren't great friends, why did Georgie work with her?"

"I think Tory wanted another gorgeous chick to complement her in all these YouTube videos." He popped a grape in his mouth.

Morgan drank more wine, debating how much to tell him. Then again, maybe he knew already. "That first day when Georgie wouldn't come down for breakfast, I went upstairs, and she was in a terrible state. She told me she loved Brad and that she would hate seeing Victoria marry him."

His eyebrows shot up. "Interesting. I didn't know that. But I haven't been around these guys for a long time. I suppose Georgie would have seen a lot of Brad this past year during the engagement."

"Did she date him back in college?"

"Probably. I dated Tory for a brief couple of weeks. I couldn't take her longer than that."

Morgan spread some Roquefort on a piece of bread. "Let's move on to Mindy. I talked with her at length when you guys were playing tennis."

"The day I stomped off like a jerk?" Carter asked.

"Why did you stomp off like a jerk?"

116

He gave a lopsided grin. "When we were kids, Brad always had to win. It was a juvenile reaction on my part." He shook his head, his eyes narrowing. "However, Brad has been acting weird since we got here and there was a mean edge to his game."

Morgan tapped her pencil on the yellow pad. "Anyway, Mindy told me she'd been Victoria's student slave and fixer since freshman year in college."

"Wow! That's a pretty vicious accusation. What did she mean by that?"

"Victoria sent her on errands...like getting her books from the library when she left them there or picking up her laundry. But then one time, Mindy set up an abortion for her in a nearby town. Apparently, Victoria paid her for her efforts."

Carter gave a low whistle. He finished his glass of wine and poured more for each of them. "Mindy would have needed the money. She was awarded some special scholarship, but she probably needed to work."

"And after college, Victoria was still paying her..."

Carter looked somber. "If Mindy got fed up, she could have snapped like a taught rubber band."

Morgan leaned back and crossed her arms. "Georgie, Mindy, Rex and Jill all worked for Victoria. It seems to me they'd want her to remain alive. She was their meal ticket. I know Georgie has a thing for Brad and was jealous of Victoria. Mindy was Victoria's handmaiden since freshman year. Rex and Jill followed Victoria around and filmed her every movement."

"And Tory would have treated them all like shit."

"Right, but they needed her. Why would they kill her? It makes no sense."

"Not to us, but the killer had his or her motive. And he or she wanted Tory dead," Carter said darkly.

Chapter 27
Monday Night

Morgan and Carter carried the dishes to the kitchen, where Morgan wrapped up the leftovers and put them in the fridge. Then they took their glasses of wine and went out on the deck. Morgan brought her legal pad and pencil with her. They sat down and continued their discussion.

"What about Jenny and Lars?" Morgan asked.

"They got married right after graduation. They met in that infamous biology class. They were lab partners along with me."

"Why do you say infamous?"

"Didn't I tell you about the lab experiments?"

Morgan frowned.

"We were working on this DNA experiment, doing research for Krishna and the professor. Remember I told you about Krishna?"

"Right," Morgan said.

"Well, the experiment was tampered with. Someone destroyed the DNA samples we were working on. Krishna went nuts. It put his research way behind schedule. We all got a grade based on classwork and tests, but the lab work could not be evaluated. No big deal now, but it was at the time."

Morgan sipped her wine. "What were Jenny and Lars like then?"

"Jenny was Miss Prim and Proper. She was a strict church-goer...no nonsense. Lars had a similar background, but he was testing the waters. He dated several girls, joined a fraternity, got drunk, smoked pot."

"And he dated Victoria."

"Yes, but not for long. You know, she made fun of him the other night at The Red Bar. She said he, well..." Carter paused and looked out at the expanse of water. "Well...that he couldn't perform sexually. Jenny had been talking about trying to get pregnant. I guess it isn't working."

"Okay, I can see them getting angry and being embarrassed, but would that be a reason to kill Victoria? It seems far-fetched to me." Morgan made notes beside Jenny and Lars' names. "Didn't Rex say this afternoon that Lars was a white supremacist? What do you think of that?"

"He did lead this march about white students' rights, but I never saw him go after any minorities. I think it was more about the principle of the thing."

Morgan pulled a footstool over and put up her bare feet. She looked out at the Gulf, where the moon had made a path of light across the water. It led right to them. "By the way, Jenny told me Victoria argued with her mother at the reception sometime before she died. I wonder what it was about?"

"Hey, how about we pay Mrs. Palmer a visit? Maybe we'd learn something," Carter said.

"I'm game. Let's go tomorrow." Morgan was enjoying this detective shtick.

Carter slipped off his leather sandals and put his feet up on the footstool beside hers. "Do you mind?"

Morgan gave a low laugh. "No problem." She took another sip of wine. She was enjoying Carter's company. He had nice legs, well-muscled with tawny hair. His feet were even nice-looking. She smiled to herself. She'd better get back to concentrating on the murders.

"What about Jill?" she said.

"Oddly enough, she was in the biology class too. So was Rex. But they really weren't part of our little gang. I do remember Jill had OCD. She wore gloves all the time because she didn't want to touch anything or anyone. On the whole, she had it under control, but I remember one time she kept having to repeat a step in the lab we were working on. Her partners got pretty ticked off."

"Who were her partners?"

"Let's see… I think it was Brad and Georgie. Yeah, it was Brad who lost patience with her." Carter stopped talking, a thoughtful

119

look on his face. "I remember what Tory did then. It was pretty mean," he said slowly.

Morgan stopped writing and looked up. "What happened?"

"Jill didn't like to be touched and she had a fear of rubbing up against other people's clothes. Tory was wearing a wool scarf, and she took it off and wrapped it around Jill's neck. Jill went nuts trying to get it off. I remember her eyes…frightened, like a wild animal."

Morgan let out a breath. "Victoria could be vicious. It seems like she enjoyed going after everyone."

"Yes, but people were also drawn to her. She had a hell of a lot of charisma."

They both fell silent, pondering everything they'd discussed. Then the doorbell rang. Morgan looked at Carter, frowning. "Who could that be?"

He raised his eyebrows. "No clue. Better answer the door."

Morgan got up and went through the living room. Carter came up behind her. She looked through the peephole and saw a man in uniform, his hat in his hands. *Coast Guard.* She started to tremble. "Who…who…is it?" Her voice shook. As if he sensed her fear and sorrow, Carter put his arm around her shoulders.

"I'm Commander Cummings with the Coast Guard," the man said.

Morgan pulled open the door. She knew what was coming.

"Ma'am, I have some bad news." Cummings looked down at the floor and then into her eyes. "We found the *Black Lion*. It was in bad shape, nearly destroyed by the storm. I'm sorry to tell you we found no one on board."

Morgan fainted into Carter's arms.

Chapter 28
Tuesday Morning

After Carter left, Morgan collapsed on the sofa in a ball. She felt empty, like a Raggedy Ann doll without the stuffing. She didn't cry. She didn't scream. She just remained curled up, her brain on hold. Much later she tried to conjure up an image of Grady, but he wouldn't appear. Finally, she pulled herself up and stumbled into the bedroom. Beside the bed was a picture of the two of them taken in New Zealand when they were on vacation. With a sense of relief, she clutched at the picture. She gently traced Grady's face with her finger, trying to print his image into her brain. It wasn't until much later that she fell into a fitful sleep.

***

At eight AM, Morgan's cellphone rang. She shot straight up in bed, looking frantically around the room. For a minute she didn't remember what had happened. Then it all came flooding back. The phone was insistent. She reached over and tapped the green button without looking at the caller.

It was her dad. "Morgan, what the hell is going on?"

It took her a minute to realize what he must be calling about. He wouldn't know or care about Grady. The two had met a few years earlier and it hadn't gone well. Her dad thought Grady had no substance even though he'd made a fortune with his app. Consequently, she'd avoided mentioning Grady's name these last two years. So her father couldn't be calling about the accident. It had to be about the murders.

"Good morning, Dad."

"I've talked to Hans. He told me people are fleeing the resort. This has to stop."

She sighed and took a breath. "Dad, there have been two murders on the premises. The police are investigating…"

He interrupted her. "You need to tell that sheriff to do his investigation elsewhere. He's spoiling the reputation of the Magnolia Resort. I won't have it."

"I can't control the police. When they've finished questioning everyone and done their forensic investigation, I'm sure they'll leave."

"How long will that take?" His tone was snide.

"I don't know."

"Hans says the sheriff is a personal friend of yours. Tell him under no uncertain terms that he must leave."

In spite of herself, Morgan started to laugh. "Give me a break, Dad. I can do no such thing."

"You never should have agreed to do this wedding. It was irresponsible of you."

"Irresponsible? That wedding brought in several million dollars. You love money, so you should love that." Now she was fully awake and in a fighting mood. "Listen, I'm busy right now. I'll have to talk to you later." She jabbed at the red button on the phone and tossed it across the bed. Almost immediately, it started to ring again, but she didn't answer it. The phone went silent. Then it rang again. Angrily, she reached over, grabbed the phone and looked at the screen. It was Claire.

With relief, she answered. "Hi, Claire."

Her friend's voice came over the line, warm and concerned. She must have heard about Grady. "How are you doing?"

"Not well right now. My dad just reamed me out. He said the Magnolia's reputation is ruined because of Victoria Palmer's wedding and the murders. He wants me to kick Dax out of here."

"Good luck, telling Dax what to do," Claire said. "Listen, I'm calling about Grady. What a terrible thing. How *are* you doing? How can I help?"

"I don't think I've really processed what's happened. I feel numb."

"Any chance he's on a life-raft somewhere in the Gulf?"

Her mouth felt dry. "Last night, the Coast Guard official said they would continue to search the area, but he didn't think there was much chance Grady or his buddies survived."

Claire choked back a sob. "This morning I was remembering all the good times we had together with you and Grady. I can't believe he's gone."

Morgan felt strange. She hadn't cried yet. It was as though she didn't believe it was true. She couldn't respond to Claire.

"Morgan, how about we get together tonight at The Bay? We can have dinner and toast Grady. I'll see if Olivia is free."

Why not, Morgan thought. She had nothing going on now. She'd been living the life of a nun when Grady was at sea and he'd been gone a lot. Now her monastic life stretched into the foreseeable future. "Yes, I'll meet you there. What time?"

"How about six-thirty?"

***

Morgan made coffee and carried her mug out to the deck. She looked out at her enemy, the Gulf of Mexico. It had swallowed up Grady. This morning the water was practically motionless, only a series of gentle swells. The Gulf was mocking her. She was a tiny, helpless human against the immensity of that ocean.

She got up and went back inside and slammed the glass door shut. She gulped down her coffee and headed for the shower. It was time for her to start her day. Wallowing in depression would do no good.

A half hour later, dressed in an indigo blue skirt and crisp white blouse, Morgan took the elevator down to the lobby. It was very quiet. Katarina was on the phone. The girl still looked out of sorts. Dealing with all the irate guests was taking its toll. Morgan gave her a nod and went down the hall to her office. Itzel looked up from her computer and seemed shocked to see her. She got up and came over to give Morgan a hug. "You don't need to be here. We've all heard about Grady. I'm so very sorry…"

Morgan extracted herself from Itzel's arms. "I prefer to be busy. Sitting alone upstairs wasn't doing me any good. I'm going to go online and look at some of the up and coming weddings. Maybe I'll make a few calls."

Itzel looked nervous. She twisted her fingers together. "We've had some cancellations. I didn't want to bother you about them."

"Cancellations?"

"Yes, The Crawford-Hanson wedding and the Beauregard-Chauncy wedding."

"Wait a minute, the Crawfords belong to Magnolia Club. They have a house on the property. That makes no sense."

"I think they're worried about what happened to Victoria Palmer," Itzel said tentatively.

"What does her murder have to do with their wedding plans? In six months, all this will be solved and forgotten." Morgan went into her office and slammed the door, feeling angry at the world.

Chapter 29
Tuesday - Late Morning

After several calls, promises and bribes, the Crawford-Hanson wedding was back on track. Both of the families were well known in Atlanta and Morgan didn't want to lose their business. The reputation of a fabulous wedding at the Magnolia Resort had to be protected.

She spent some time going through requests from various brides, and somehow managed to write friendly, encouraging responses. In addition, she emailed couples who were in the planning stages. It was important to keep an ongoing dialogue.

She ordered a curried chicken salad for lunch. A few minutes later, someone knocked softly at her office door.

"Come in," she shouted.

One of the waitstaff entered timidly. Itzel had probably told her Morgan was not in the best of moods. "Here is your salad, ma'am."

"Thank you, Lucia. Could you put it there on the table?"

"Yes, ma'am." She placed the tray on the conference table, then spent some time fussing with the napkin and silverware.

Morgan looked up. "That looks fine. Thank you."

Lucia held her gaze a moment, as if she wanted to say something, but then she rushed from the room.

Morgan smiled once Lucia had gone. Did she think Morgan was an ogre who would gobble her up? Granted, Morgan had been curt with Itzel that morning, but she usually treated the staff with kindness and consideration. Lucia had been working at the Magnolia for almost a year now. She should be feeling more comfortable, Morgan thought.

She sat down at the conference table and uncovered the plate. The salad was beautifully prepared: crisp lettuce, chunks of white-meat chicken, grapes and pecans, all in a delicious dressing. It was usually her favorite, but today she could only eat a few bites. The chicken stuck in her throat and the salad tasted unappetizing. She put the silver cover back on the plate and pushed it away. At her desk, she picked up the legal pad she and Carter had been working on. Then she got up and left the room.

In the outer office, Itzel was busy on the computer. She looked up, her expression tense.

"Sorry I slammed the door earlier. I won't do it again," Morgan said.

"Oh, you probably will," Itzel said with a smile. "Did you already finish that salad?"

"No, I can't eat it. Too riled up, I guess. I'm going to go down and talk with Sheriff Simmons."

"You need to eat."

She managed to grin. "Yes, Mother. I know. But not right now."

***

The lobby remained unnaturally quiet. Low murmurs came from the Orchid Lounge, probably what was left of the wedding party getting drunk. Morgan walked down the hall to the Gardenia Room. She knocked and a minute later Officer Rodriguez opened the door. Dax was seated at the table with a computer and several notepads. He looked up and then quickly got to his feet. "Morgan, how are you? What a shock this must be." His voice was filled with concern.

"I'm all right. I don't think I've fully internalized that…that…what's happened." Her voice was trembling. She realized she couldn't say Grady's name. Not saying his name made the shipwreck seem less real. A black wave of depression threatened to roll over her. She needed to think about something else. She tapped the legal pad she carried. "Do you have a minute?"

Dax looked taken aback at the sudden change in subject. Then he seemed to sense that she needed to come to grips with her feelings. "Sure, what's up?"

"Last night, Carter came up to my place and we did some detective work together. I thought you might like to hear what we discussed."

He frowned. "You mean about the murders?"

126

"Yes, we went through all the possible suspects. Would you like to hear what I learned?"

"Sure. Sit down. We're all ears."

Morgan sat down and proceeded to go through the information. Rodriguez and Dax took notes and questioned her from time to time.

"It sounds as though Victoria Palmer had a lot of enemies. She seems to have alienated all of her so-called friends." Dax tapped his pencil on the table in frustration. "Here's where we stand. Anyone could have plunged that syringe into Victoria's arm during the photo session. According to all the players, they switched positions several times. No one remembers who was where during the photo shoot before Victoria fell dead."

Morgan nodded. "Yes, they were clowning around."

"We need the photographers' camera, so we can isolate their movements," Dax said.

"Right, Joe Middleton said the camera was stolen from the lobby. I think Victoria's murderer hung around looking for an opportunity to grab it."

Dax nodded. "Agreed, and it's probably the same person who killed Joshua."

Morgan pushed back her hair. "It's hard for me to imagine any of those people in the wedding party would kill him. He was such a nice guy."

"He undoubtedly saw something or knew something. So he contacted the killer. It had to be someone he trusted enough to meet in seclusion."

"We've interviewed everyone in the wedding party. None of them have an alibi for the time of death, which would have been from twelve noon to two-thirty," Rodriguez said.

Dax caught his eye. "We need to establish a timeline for the afternoon. Then we can cross-reference everyone's location."

"I'll get on it, Chief." Rodriquez turned to his computer.

"Why don't you start with me," Morgan said. She told them about seeing Lars, Brad and Mindy in the weight room before the yoga class. "The class was from eleven to twelve noon. Then I talked with Georgie for fifteen minutes or so. I don't remember seeing anyone in the weight room when we left. Let's see, then I talked to Jenny out on the patio a little before one o'clock. She and Lars had had a fight."

Keys clicked softly as Rodriguez typed out her timeline. Morgan frowned, trying to recall what came next. "Okay, after the discussion with Jenny I went into the lobby. That's where I saw, Carter who was looking for Josh. It was about one fifteen. I left to have lunch with Claire—we'd agreed to meet at one-thirty—and Carter headed for the tennis courts."

"Right, and he claims Josh never showed," Dax said.

Rodriguez rubbed his chin with his stubby fingers. "Yeah, if we believe him. But he could have lured Josh over to Magnolia Park and killed him."

Morgan couldn't believe Carter would do such a thing. But maybe she was too gullible. The thought chilled her, considering she'd spent time alone with him last night. "I didn't see anyone else yesterday morning..." She looked down at her notepad. Her finger scrolled down the list of names and stopped at Brad. "Oh, I almost forgot. The morning of the wedding, I drove over to Rosemary Beach for coffee. I was sitting in my car and I saw Brad and Josh on the sidewalk in front of The Hidden Lantern bookstore. They were arguing. I don't know what it was about. I didn't get out of the car until they were gone."

"Interesting. I'll get Brad in here again and find out. He wasn't sober enough to make much sense yesterday."

As Morgan was about to leave, two police officers arrived, carrying a gun in a plastic bag. "Chief, Ms. Georgina Ralston gave us this gun out of her safe. It doesn't seem to have been used recently, or maybe ever. When the safecracker managed to open Victoria Palmer's safe, there was no gun inside."

"What about in the other rooms? Did you find anything of interest?"

"Well, I found some weed in two rooms. Other than that..."

"Let's not worry about that now. We've got two murders on our hands."

"Right, sir."

Chapter 30
Tuesday - Late Afternoon

Morgan walked back to the lobby. Georgie was exiting the elevator, dressed in black tights and a black long-sleeved turtleneck. The outfit made her face look even more washed-out and drawn. "Hi Morgan, you want to join us in the bar? We're all in there. Everyone is afraid to be alone. I mean…how do you know you're not next." She gave a forced laugh.

"That's a scary thought," Morgan said

Georgie looked at her closely. "You don't look so good yourself. Is something wrong? Something else, I mean?"

Morgan had no desire to share Grady's disappearance with this girl she barely knew. "Probably just tired. The last few days have been tense."

"You can say that again." Georgie started for the Orchid Lounge. The elevator doors slid open again and Carter walked out. When he saw Morgan, he looked concerned, "Hi, how are you doing?"

"All right, I guess. Listen, I'm sorry about last night."

"What do you mean?"

"Well, I fell apart and you were the only person there. I shouldn't have collapsed in your arms like that."

"I certainly didn't mind. I was glad to be there and be able to comfort you." He smiled wryly. "Do you need another hug?"

Morgan took a step back. "Not right now." To change the subject, she said, "I've just been talking to Sheriff Simmons. I shared our detective work from yesterday evening with him." She held up the legal notepad. "I think he was grateful for our insights."

Carter nodded. "Good. By the way, how about we go down and visit Victoria's mother tomorrow like we planned?"

Why not, she thought dully. "Okay, maybe tomorrow afternoon. Shall we call first?"

"No, I think a surprise visit would be better."

"See you then. I'm going upstairs." Morgan headed for the elevator, then changed her mind and took the stairs. On the second-floor landing, the security door flew open and Jill stepped into the stairwell. She was scowling.

"Oh, it's you. I'm ticked off. I didn't appreciate having those cops pawing through my things. What did they think they would find? Probably some pervert was happy to sniff my dirty underwear."

Taken aback by this outburst, Morgan said, "They were just doing their job. All rooms had to be searched. I wouldn't take it personally."

"Right, well, I don't like it and I'm ready to get out of here. Do you know when we'll get permission to leave?"

"No clue. Go down and talk to Sheriff Simmons." Sick to death of all of them, Morgan turned and started up the stairs.

"He's a pompous ass. I don't like that guy," Jill shouted after her.

Once inside her apartment, Morgan collapsed on the sofa. She felt incredibly tired and depressed. The last thing she wanted was to go out for dinner with Claire and Olivia. She picked up the phone and speed-dialed Claire. When her friend answered, Morgan blurted out, "Hi, can I take a raincheck? I'm just wiped out. How about dinner tomorrow night instead?"

"Are you sure you don't need some TLC tonight? I could come over there."

"No, I want to be alone tonight...go to bed early."

"If you say so, but I think it's a bad idea."

Morgan sighed. "See you tomorrow, Claire." Then she hung up.

Once off the phone, Morgan went to the fridge and took out the bottle of chardonnay. She poured herself a glass and went out on the patio. This evening, there were big waves and a strong breeze coming off the Gulf. Morgan sank onto a chaise and felt the tension pour out of her system. This had been a difficult day after a night with little sleep. She took a sip of wine and then sighed. From nowhere, tears slid down her cheeks. She just lay there and let them come. It felt good to give up and cry a little. Was she crying for herself or for Grady?

They'd had a lot of good times together. She remembered the trip to New York. They'd stayed at the Ritz-Carlton on Central Park. She remembered the fabulous meals at Carmine's and Bagatelle as well as the Broadway shows. They'd spent hours in the Met and taken long walks in the park. The trip was a once in a lifetime visit for her. Yet in spite of all the time they'd spent together, she felt she never really knew Grady. He'd kept a part of himself locked up, like a jewel in a box.

Would they ever have gotten married? If she was honest with herself, the answer was no. He was the archetypal bachelor. He wanted to be with her on his own terms and she'd gone along with it. Was she being unfair? No, she wasn't.

She remembered the time he was supposed to be at sea and she thought she'd seen him in Destin. He claimed she'd imagined it, but she'd sensed something evasive about his response. "Damn you, Grady," she cried out loud. More tears streamed down her face. She got up and went into the living room to get a Kleenex.

Much later, after more wine and more maudlin memories, she fell into bed.

***

At midnight, the doorbell chime and loud knocking woke her up. Half asleep, she grabbed her silk robe and went through to the front door. Through the peephole, she saw Carter. Should she open up? How much could she trust him? With misgivings, she opened the door a crack, leaving the chain on. "What's up, Carter?" she said, clutching the panels of her robe closed.

He looked frazzled. "Have you seen Brad?"

"Brad? I've been alone all evening. Why would you think he was here?"

"I'm covering all the angles. Brad's missing. We're worried," Carter said.

"Do you want me to come down?"

"Yes, if you wouldn't mind."

"All right. Give me a minute to dress."

Chapter 31
Wednesday - Early Morning

Morgan went into the bedroom and pulled on some shorts and a sweatshirt. Then she left her apartment and headed downstairs. Carter had gone down before her. The wedding party was huddled together at one end of the lobby, perched on a pair of sofas while Rex paced up and down in front of them. Mindy, Jenny and Georgie were in white Magnolia robes. The others still wore the clothes they'd been wearing that day. They all looked up as she approached.

"Tell me what's going on," Morgan asked.

Lars spoke first. "Jenny went to bed early. So, about an hour ago, I went looking for Brad to play pool in the game room. I couldn't find him anywhere. I texted him and I even went up and knocked on his door, but he didn't answer."

Rex spoke up next. "Yeah, so then Lars knocked on my door and the two of us searched the bar, the spa, the workout room. Everywhere we could think he might be."

"I ended up knocking on everyone's door, but no one had seen him," Lars continued.

"Do you think he's been killed?" Jenny's eyes were round with fear.

"Don't jump to conclusions, honey." Lars hugged her shoulders.

"We need to have security protecting us. The police should stand guard. It's not safe for anyone," Mindy said. Her face was blotchy, and she seemed highly agitated.

"Calm down, you guys. Brad could be out walking on the beach or somewhere on the property," Carter said.

"But Lars said he didn't answer his phone. Isn't that suspicious? I mean, he would have his phone if he was out walking," Georgie said.

Carter turned to Morgan. "Could you open the door to his suite? We could check if he's in there and just didn't hear us knocking."

Rex stopped his pacing, "Yeah, he could be passed out in there. Remember how drunk he was yesterday."

Morgan considered this request. "Okay. I'll get the pass-key and we can go up there and check on him." She gestured to Carter and Rex. "Why don't you two come with me and the rest of you can wait here."

Marco was manning the front desk. He must have overheard what was going on, because he held the pass-key out as Morgan reached him.

"Here, Morgan." A worry line appeared between his thick brows. "We're missing one key that's usually here in this drawer." He gestured at a spot under the desk.

"It's been crazy around here. I'm sure you'll find it." Morgan took the plastic keycard and they went up to the third floor. Carter knocked on Brad's door several times and both he and Rex called out, but they got no response.

Morgan slipped the pass-key into the slot and pushed open the door. It was dark inside, except for moonlight streaming in through the window and silhouetting the furniture. Carter reached around and flipped on the lights. The living room was empty.

"Hey Brad, are you here?" Rex called out.

Again, no answer.

Carter walked into the bedroom and turned on the lights. Morgan could hear him opening the closet doors and pushing drawers shut. "No one here. Let me check the bathroom."

Rex walked over to the patio door and checked outside. "There's no one out here, either." He came back inside, leaving the sliding glass door open, and flopped on the beige and turquoise sofa. A breeze off the Gulf rippled the curtains.

Carter came back into the living room. "His suitcase is there, and all his clothes are hanging in the closet. So he hasn't taken off."

"Maybe we should call the police," Rex said.

Morgan walked over to the writing desk. She noticed a brochure open on the mahogany surface, an advertisement for a casino up on Highway 98. "Does Brad gamble? Here's a brochure for the Nawatchi Casino. Maybe he Ubered it over there."

Rex looked at Carter, his eyebrows raised. "Do you know if he gambles?"

Carter shook his head. "I've no idea. I hadn't seen him for years until the wedding. I don't know what he does in his spare time." He rubbed his chin. "Let's go down and ask the others."

Downstairs, Jill and Mindy were still sitting with Georgie, who was chewing her nails. Jill sat with her shoulders hunched. Mindy's eyes darted around the lobby. Jenny and Lars sat on the other sofa, wrapped around each other.

"He's not in his room. But we found a brochure for the casino," Carter announced. "Do any of you know if he gambles? Maybe he broke Sheriff Simmons' order and left the property."

"How far away is this place?" Rex asked.

"Probably only twenty minutes from here." Morgan turned to Carter. "Do you want to go over there with me? We could see if he's there."

"Shouldn't we call the police?" Georgie said. She shivered. "I mean, he could be dead."

"Don't start imagining things. You're scaring all of us," Mindy yelled, her voice rising an octave.

"Calm down, you guys. Morgan and I will check out the casino. If he's not there, then we'll call the police," Carter said.

Georgie stood up abruptly. "I don't think any of us should be alone. Why don't you all come up to my suite and we'll hang out together until Carter and Morgan get back."

Morgan got what she *wasn't* saying…that one of them was a murderer and none of them were safe.

134

Chapter 32
Wednesday - Early Morning

"I'm sorry to have dragged you into this," Carter said as they drove down the causeway. "This is above and beyond your wedding planner responsibilities."

"No problem, I've got the car and I know where we're going."

"This could be a wild goose chase."

"I know. But I hope we find him."

They went quiet, each deep in thought. Then Morgan said tentatively, "Carter, who do you think killed Victoria and Josh, if you had to guess?"

In the dark, she felt his gaze on her. "So you've decided I'm not guilty."

She nodded. "For now, anyway."

He chuckled. "I've been racking my brain. I can't figure out a motive for any of us to actually have killed Tory. But I do think Josh was killed for what he knew or saw."

"I agree. But you do think someone in the wedding party killed Victoria?"

"For sure. The dose of R27 in that hypodermic needle would have caused almost immediate death. We know it had to be administered by someone behind Victoria while the wedding photographer was snapping those shots of all of us."

Morgan nodded. "I think that eliminates Rex and Jill. Remember, Victoria asked them to come up on the stage for the group photo. I remember thinking it was nice she included them. She asked them last minute, so they couldn't have planned to kill her."

"Right, but they could have had the syringe ready, waiting for the right moment."

"Come on...they've been traveling with her for a couple of years. Why kill her now?"

"She was going to fire them? I don't know…" Carter sounded frustrated.

"I've been thinking about the execution. I mean, how easy would it be to pull out a syringe without anyone noticing and then prime it?" Her brows knitted.

"They've got these syringes nowadays for diabetics that can be carried in a small case. It looks like a pen. It's primed and ready to go."

"For the guys, it would be easy. You had several pockets in your tuxedoes. I wonder if the bridesmaids' dresses had a pocket?"

The entrance to the Nawatchi Casino loomed up ahead. The building was shaped like a grandiose Taj Mahal and lit up like a Christmas tree on steroids. In spite of the hour, rows of cars filled the parking lot. The place was open twenty-four hours a day.

They parked the car and walked up the broad steps to the entryway. Lights flashed, and piped music filled the air. The gold and maroon interior was lit with gold sconces. An enormous round maroon carpet with a gold "N" in the middle covered most of the marble floor. Heavy brocade armchairs were grouped around the vast space. To the right was a large room filled with rows of slot machines, to the left the entrance to the game room. "Whoa," Carter breathed.

A tall Nawatchi native with strong chiseled features and black hooded eyes smiled broadly and welcomed them to the casino. When Carter explained they were looking for a friend, the man hunched his shoulders and held up his hands. "I don't know the names of people who enter our establishment. You will have to look on your own." He turned his back on them and approached another customer, who had followed them up the steps.

"Let's start with the slot machines," Carter suggested. They turned to the right and entered the softly lit room. Loud music echoed, accompanied by the jangle, ping and bang of people playing the machines. They went up and down the aisles, looking for Brad. Most of the gamblers were women. Some of them had little buckets of change, and all of them kept their eyes glued to the screen in front of them. After a few minutes, Morgan and Carter concluded that

136

Brad wasn't in there. "I don't think the slots are his thing. Let's try the gaming tables," Carter said.

They returned to the entryway and crossed the expanse to the game room. Heavy velvet curtains pulled back with gold cords marked the entrance. Crystal chandeliers overhead provided subdued lighting, and low-hanging lamps over green felt-covered tables created a sense of intimacy. Upbeat music played in the background. Even though it was well into the morning hours, there was plenty of action. Waitresses carried drinks to customers intent on games of blackjack or poker. Carter led the way through the tables, up and down the aisles. Morgan searched the faces of the people they passed. She recognized a bartender from the resort, as well as a man who owned a house on the island.

They'd just about searched every aisle when they came to a roulette table. Four people were seated around it. One of them was Brad. He sat hunched over, his eyes vacant. He looked wretched, Morgan thought. There were no chips in front of him, only an empty glass. He didn't seem to be following the action as the dealer spun the wheel.

Carter bent over him and spoke into his ear. Morgan couldn't hear what he said. Brad shook his head. Carter said something else and then he reached down and grabbed hold of Brad's arm. Reluctantly, Brad stood up. Carter led him toward the exit. Morgan followed behind. Outside, they walked to the car without saying anything. Morgan opened the passenger door and Carter nudged Brad into the front passenger seat. He got in the back. Morgan drove through the gigantic parking lot toward the highway.

Once on the road, Brad started to sob. Morgan glanced over at him. He was rubbing his eyes with his balled-up fists like a little kid. She reached into the console, pulled out a couple of Kleenex, and handed them to Brad. He mumbled thanks and blew his nose.

"It's over. I'm screwed," Brad said between sniffles.

"What do you mean?" Carter asked.

"I lost all the money and Victoria is gone and I have nothing to live for."

"Hey, man, don't say that. You have plenty to live for." Carter gripped Brad's shoulder. "Victoria's death is a terrible blow. We know that. But you do have a future. You'll get over this."

"Yeah…maybe…I don't know. Right now, I'm totally broke. I mean, I've really lost everything."

"You're talking about money?" Carter said.

Brad nodded. More tears streamed down his face.

"You've got your job. 3S is the biggest law firm in the country. You have to be making six figures."

"That's the thing." Brad's voice was low and tremulous. "I don't work there anymore. I was fired."

Morgan glanced in the rearview mirror. Carter looked at her, his eyes wide with surprise.

Brad sniffled some more. "I lost my job months ago. Victoria was supporting me until I found something."

"Ah, so you *really* lost everything," Carter said. He and Morgan exchanged another glance.

"See, she gave me twenty thousand on Wednesday when we got here."

"Dollars?" Morgan blurted without thinking.

Brad looked at her. "Yes, dollars. I came here tonight to see if I could double it. I've been doing pretty well lately. I was on a roll." Now he sounded excited. "I played some blackjack and then I went to the roulette table. I bet on Victoria's birthday, seven and eleven. Shit, I raked in all these chips. I kept playing, I kept winning. It was great. I felt like I was flying. I was invincible." He took a deep breath. "Then I put it all on the numbers of our wedding date. Victoria would have liked that. The croupier spun the wheel. It seemed to go around forever. And then it stopped. I lost *everything* in that one spin." His voice was full of wonder and pain. "I don't understand it. I was winning."

Morgan raised her eyebrows as she looked back at Carter. He was shaking his head in disbelief.

"Maybe you lost all that money, but your life isn't over," Carter said.

"Yes, it is. I don't have Victoria. I don't have a job. I've lost everything. And…and…I've got other problems…Josh knew. He was going to help me, but now he's gone too."

Morgan turned onto the back road that led to the causeway. The sheriff's deputies recognized her and flashed her through. It was dark under the canopy of trees. She glanced at Brad, who was slouched over in his seat. To her, he was diminished in more ways than one. She had truly misjudged him. It made her wonder how many other people she really didn't know.

Chapter 33
Wednesday - Late Morning

Morgan slept late. When she woke up, she felt groggy and out of sorts. After a couple of cups of coffee, she called the Coast Guard to see if they had news but was told they had nothing to report. The officer she talked to was empathetic, and yet she felt there was something off with the conversation, as though the man was being evasive. He probably thought she was wasting his time. After she hung up she gazed out at the Gulf. She felt a tightness in her chest and her eyes filled with tears. Poor Grady, he had suffered a terrible death.

After a shower, she put on a lavender sundress and sandals. Downstairs, she walked quickly through the lobby to her office. Luckily no one from the wedding party was in sight. She spent an hour working with Itzel on the small wedding that would occur the following Saturday. The couple was getting married in the gazebo down on Lake Nawatchi at ten in the morning, followed by an elegant champagne brunch under a tent. The wedding would be tasteful and low key... the opposite of Victoria's wedding.

At noon, she went back across the lobby and down to the Gardenia Room, hoping to talk to Dax. Rodriguez told her he'd gone to the station and wouldn't be back for a couple of hours. Morgan had an hour before she was to meet Carter. She slipped into the kitchen and a sous-chef made her a Salade Niçoise. She sat at one of the metal tables to eat it and chatted with the cooks as they worked.

***

The afternoon was hot and muggy. The air was motionless, and the trees dripped with moisture. Black flies buzzed around their heads as Morgan and Carter walked quickly down to the Palmer cottage.

"What should we say about why we're there?" Morgan asked.

"It's a condolence call. You can talk about Victoria and how sad you are that she died so suddenly. Then we can inquire about Mr. Palmer."

"Somehow we'll have to lead the conversation to what Norma Lee and Victoria were arguing about at the reception." Morgan brushed an annoying fly away from her face. "It might have been something totally irrelevant."

"Right, but we're on a fact-finding mission and anything we can glean from the conversation might be useful," Carter said.

The Palmer cottage was hidden from view by a high, trimmed hedge. They passed through the opening and followed a meandering path through a manicured lawn dotted with colorful flower beds. Large mature trees provided cool shade. Pots of red and white geraniums were placed on the steps leading up to the door. A screened-in porch stretched across the front of the two-story house. Flowered, chintz-covered sofas and white porch swings formed groupings at each side of the porch.

Carter tried opening the screen door, but it was locked. He pushed the buzzer. Almost immediately a short, dark-skinned man in a tropical shirt and white shorts came through the beveled glass front door. He beamed as he reached them. "Can I help you?" He spoke with a pronounced accent.

Morgan said, "We're here to see Mrs. Palmer. I'm Morgan Lytton, the wedding planner from the resort."

"Ah yes, important person. I go tell the missus. Be back." The man turned and went back into the house, shutting the door quietly behind him.

"Important person…nice to be appreciated," Morgan whispered.

Carter smiled. "*Very* important person."

A minute later the door opened again, and the manservant came out. "Mrs. Palmer said come in." He unlocked the screen door and they followed him into the house.

The two-story entryway was large and airy. A crystal chandelier hung over a rosewood marquetry table. Through an open door on the right, Morgan got a glimpse of a library with walls covered in bookshelves. To the left, a broad stairway led to an open landing above. Straight ahead was a wide doorway into a large, sunny room. She could see a sparkling pool beyond, surrounded by flowers and palm trees. The manservant led them through the hall and into the sun-drenched room.

Morgan glanced around. The space was decorated in white with green and blue accents. White sofas surrounded a circular sunken living area with a round glass-topped aquarium in the middle. To the right of the wall of windows was a baby grand piano, to the left a bar with a white marble counter. Behind the bar, open shelves displayed a myriad of glasses. In the back corner of the room she spotted a games table surrounded by eight leather-upholstered chairs.

She returned her attention to the sunken seating area. Norma Lee was sitting on the circular sofa, an enormous fluffy white cat on her lap. It made Morgan think of the green-eyed cat in the Fancy Feast ad on TV. In one hand, Norma Lee held a martini glass filled with a pink liquid. With her other hand she caressed the cat. Morgan could hear it purring.

"Ah, the wedding planner. I bet you're glad that one's over." The woman actually looked better than she had at the wedding. There was a bloom to her cheeks, probably from the alcohol. The yellow silk robe she wore showed an abundance of crepe-y cleavage and highlighted the flush in her face.

"Hello, Mrs. Palmer. We're here to express our condolences for the loss of your daughter." Morgan walked down the few steps to shake the woman's hand.

"Right. My daughter. I'm not sure I'll miss her." Norma Lee briefly clasped Morgan's hand, as if indifferent to it, and took a sip from her drink. Then she gestured to the sofa across from her. "Sit down. I can't stand people talking down to me." She looked at Carter and smiled. "Carter Perry, right? Vicky should have married you. You look like you've got a level head on your shoulders."

Morgan sat down on the edge of the sofa. Carter flopped back among the pillows smiling broadly.

Norma Lee held up her glass. "Would you like a strawberry daiquiri? There's a pitcher in the fridge." She pressed a pendant that hung between her breasts.

Immediately, the manservant appeared. "Yes, ma'am."

"Bayani, serve these two young people a drink."

He looked at them expectantly. "I'll just have some water," Morgan said.

"I'll have some of the daiquiri. It looks delicious." Carter smiled conspiratorially at Norma Lee.

Morgan groaned inwardly. Carter was unashamedly polishing up the woman. Bayani went to the bar and prepared the drinks.

"That's a big cat," Morgan said, nodding toward the beast in Norma Lee's lap.

"This is Angel. He's my baby. Over there is Lucifer. He wants nothing to do with me." She gestured to a fake climbing tree in the far corner, where a large black cat lay curled on a pillow halfway up. "Sometimes we take the top off the fish tank and let him catch a fish. He's actually pretty speedy."

Morgan looked down into the fish tank where blue and green fish zipped around among waving green aquatic plants. The thought of that black monster entrapping these little fish seemed alarming.

She brought herself back to their visit. "How is Mr. Palmer doing?"

"It was a heart attack of some sort. They put in some stents. I'm told he'll be fine. I haven't been to the hospital." Norma Lee took a long sip from her daiquiri. "I don't do hospitals."

"Have you made funeral arrangements for Victoria? Is there anything I can help you with?" Morgan asked.

"Big Bob will handle all that when he's better."

Silence fell. Morgan was trying to think what to say next when Bayani served her a tall glass of water with a lime slice. He served Carter and then poured more of the daiquiri mixture into Norma Lee's glass.

"You know, Victoria and I never got along," Norma Lee said as soon as the manservant moved away. "She was impossible from the day she got here. I tried to be a mother to her, but she was so headstrong. It was her way, or she would scream bloody murder. I finally gave up and handed her over to a full-time nanny…who didn't do much better than me." Her free hand rhythmically caressed the cat.

"This is a top-notch drink," Carter said.

Morgan smiled inwardly. *Top-notch, really*, she thought.

Norma Lee didn't seem to have heard him. "When she was little she had a bunch of American Girl dolls. Her daddy would buy her anything she wanted. He commissioned a dress designer to make matching wardrobes for the dolls and for Vicky. She would spend the day dressing herself and the dolls and parading in front of the mirror. The nanny would arrange her hair and she would admire herself. Even way back then, she was in love with herself and her image."

The black cat jumped down from its perch and padded silently over to the circular sofa. He jumped up behind Carter and stretched out along the sofa back. Morgan hoped Carter wasn't allergic to cats.

Norma Lee didn't notice. She took another sip of her daiquiri. "You see, Victoria was adopted. Her dad showed up one day when she was about six months old. He said someone out in the field had wanted to give her up and she needed a home. But I knew. She was his kid. Probably the child of some whore he knocked up."

Morgan considered Norma Lee's words. It was just as she'd thought. Victoria did look a lot like her dad but had nothing of this woman.

Norma Lee kept talking. "She was a narcissistic brat…a self-centered adult and she would have been a selfish wife. Mr. Bradley Hughes the Third got off lightly. I'll bet he's counting on all that money. Vicky must have left a nice fat bank account."

Morgan looked at Carter. Norma Lee apparently lived in her own little world. How drunk was she? Was it time for them to leave?

Catching Morgan's eye, Carter said, "I guess Tory was pretty difficult to get along with. It must have been hard." His voice reflected sympathy.

"You're damn right. She was a bitch right up until the end." Norma Lee's eyes narrowed. "Right there at the reception, she told

144

me she wished I wasn't there. That I always brought bad luck...bad karma. She was vicious. And I fought back, I told her I wished she'd never come to live with us. That she would come to a bad end..." Norma Lee smiled and swilled down the last of her drink. "And she did."

Chapter 34
Wednesday Afternoon

When Morgan and Carter got back to the resort, they headed to the Gardenia Room. Morgan knocked on the closed door. "Dax, it's Morgan.

"Come in," he called.

Carter opened the door and they went in. Dax and Detective Rodriguez were sitting at the table, studying a flow chart.

"Hey, Morgan, what's up?" Dax asked. At first, he didn't look up from the paper in front of him. When he saw Carter, a line appeared between his brows.

"We've been doing some unofficial snooping," Morgan said.

Dax shook his head. "You should be careful what you do and who you talk to. There is a killer in your midst and I think this individual is unhinged. I mean, it could be dangerous. You should leave things to us."

"I think you'll appreciate what we found out," Carter said.

Dax looked hard at him. "Maybe I will, but remember you're a suspect right now, like all the other members of the wedding party."

"Right, I understand that. For the moment, I can't prove my innocence. I can't prove to you I was nowhere near Tory when she was poisoned. And I can't prove I never met up with Josh yesterday afternoon."

Morgan interrupted him. "Dax, we've just been to see Mrs. Palmer. Did you know Victoria was adopted?"

Dax raised his eyebrows. "No, I didn't. When we spoke with Mr. and Mrs. Palmer, he did most of the talking."

"According to Norma Lee, Big Bob brought Victoria home, claiming her real parents didn't want her. But Mrs. Palmer is sure Victoria was her husband's love child, the product of one of his many affairs," Carter said.

"She looks just like her father," Morgan added.

"Apparently there was no love lost between Victoria and her mother. They despised each other and even argued at the reception," Carter said.

Dax looked from one of them to the other. "You're quite a tag team." He frowned. "Okay, Victoria was adopted but was actually Big Bob's natural daughter. I don't know where that information gets us. Did you think the mother poisoned her? How would she have managed that? Was she up on the dais for the picture? No, she wasn't." Dax seemed uncharacteristically irritated and on edge.

Morgan looked at Carter. They both shrugged. Suddenly, their visit to the Palmer home seemed meaningless.

Nonetheless, Morgan continued, "Dax, that's not all. Last night, Lars was looking for Brad and couldn't find him. He talked to the others and pretty soon everyone was searching the building. They were worried he'd been killed like Josh."

Now they had Dax's attention. "What happened? Did you find him?"

"Eventually. Carter and I drove out to the Nawatchi Casino. He was playing roulette and had lost all his money."

"I told everyone to stick around here." Dax shook his head in frustration.

"Brad's a compulsive gambler," Carter said. "He lost his job some months ago."

Morgan added, "Victoria has been giving him money. He lost $20,000 dollars yesterday."

"Wow." Dax sat back in his chair, tented his hands and squinted in thought. "So...he needed Victoria alive to keep him in cash..." he said slowly." Or he needed her dead, so he could inherit. I've got to say, killing her at the wedding reception seems pretty nervy."

"Did she have a will?" Morgan asked. "She's so young, maybe she didn't."

"Her lawyer is coming from L.A. tomorrow. We'll find out."

They all went silent, thinking about what the latest information could mean. Then Morgan gestured to the papers spread out on the table. "What's all this?"

"We've been working on yesterday's timeline." Dax pointed at Carter. "You worked out in the gym; then you were seen at about one-fifteen in the lobby. You went looking for Josh and you say you didn't find him. Then you went to your room where you worked and caught up on email. Right?"

"Yes, sir," Carter said.

"So, you have no alibi, right?"

"Right."

Dax ran a finger down the list of names. "Bradley was drunk all day. We couldn't get much information out of him. However, he did mumble something about seeing Josh walking down the hall with his phone to his ear."

He looked at Carter, who nodded. "Brad told me that, too. But I'm not sure we can believe him. He was smashed."

Rodriguez said, "Rex worked with Jill. Mindy joined them for lunch. Then Rex went up to his room and played Fortnite for the rest of the afternoon." He looked up at them. "Can you imagine all those hours playing a video game?"

Morgan certainly couldn't imagine Officer Rodriguez ever wasting his time that way. He had the bearing of a drill sergeant.

Dax continued. "Jill corroborated Rex's account of his whereabouts. After lunch she watched music videos in her room. No alibi."

Morgan bent over the table to study the timeline as Dax went on. "Lars worked out, fought with Jenny, then walked on the beach. It seems Jenny confronted him about his relationship with Victoria back in college. She was on the patio and talked to you, Morgan, at about twelve forty-five. Then she went up to their suite. Neither one has an alibi for the entire time frame when Josh was killed."

"I figured their big fight had something to do with Victoria," Morgan said.

"Mindy says she worked out," Dax continued. "At about twelve, she says she saw Josh in the lobby. He was running out the front door and she says she didn't talk to him. She had lunch with Jill and Rex and then hung out in her room. Again, no alibi."

148

"So we know Josh was alive and going to meet someone at twelve," Morgan said. "Who does that leave?"

"Georgie. She reported seeing Joshua texting near the elevators after our meeting. Then she was at yoga with you, followed by a bikini wax in the spa." He rolled his eyes. "Then she went up to her room for a nap. Another one with no alibi." Dax sighed. "That's everyone."

Morgan looked at some additional times listed in red. "What are these?"

"Those are the times we interviewed everyone about Victoria's murder," Rodriguez said.

"So no one has an alibi from about one to three," Carter said. "Everyone is still guilty until proven innocent."

Someone knocked at the door. At Rodriguez's invitation, a police officer entered, carrying a gun in a plastic bag. "Sir, we found this in some bushes along the path leading from the scene of the crime. It looks as though it's been wiped clean."

Chapter 35
Wednesday - Late Afternoon

Once out in the hall, Carter asked. "Have you got something to do right now?"

"I'm having dinner with some friends later. What did you have in mind?"

"I was thinking it might be worth driving to the hospital and talking to Big Bob. It could be another condolence call." He raised one dark red eyebrow and smiled conspiratorially. "What do you say?"

"Okay, I guess I have time. But we'll have to make it quick," Morgan said. "What do you want to learn specifically?"

"Anything that will give us a clue into Victoria's life since graduating from Talbot. Maybe she shared things with her dad that she never shared with her mom."

***

Robert Palmer's room was the last door on the right across from the emergency exit stairwell. When they entered the room, a nurse was pulling up the top sheet and smoothing it across Big Bob's massive chest. The man looked greatly diminished. His normally pink jovial face looked grey and sunken. He was hooked up to an intravenous line and several monitors. But his eyes were open and immediately registered their presence. He smiled wanly.

"It's Morgan and Carter." His voice was low and scratchy. "Are you here to see this decrepit old man take his last breath?"

Morgan smiled at him. "Hello, Mr. Palmer. We've been worried about you. We came to see how you were doing."

"I'm trying to think of a reason to keep on living. I haven't come up with one yet." His eyes filled with tears. "My girl's gone…"

"We wanted to tell you how terrible we feel about Victoria's death," Carter said. "No parent should live through such a nightmare."

"Thank you, Carter." Big Bob reached up and wiped his eyes with the edge of the sheet. Morgan found a tissue in the box by the bed and handed it to him. He dabbed at his eyes. "You know, when I met your gang down at Talbot, I thought Victoria should marry you. You seemed like the one with your two feet firmly placed on the ground. But Victoria wanted something else." He coughed up some phlegm and cleared his throat. Morgan handed him another tissue. He wiped his mouth. "At one time she had that movie star, Roy Holland. That guy spent all his time looking in the mirror. He was a total narcissist." Big Bob sighed and closed his eyes. "Like Victoria, I guess."

Morgan and Carter exchanged glances.

Big Bob continued, "Then there was an investment banker. I didn't like him. I always felt he wanted to get at her money. I got Jerry Ganz to make sure her wealth was protected."

"That was a good move," Carter said.

Big Bob kept talking. "I was always suspicious of Bradley. Initially, he came across as a solid citizen, but there was always something off about him." He coughed again and cleared his throat. "I don't actually think he killed Victoria. I blamed him at first, but since I've been lying here, I've changed my mind. I think he's too much of a wimp."

"He's pretty broken up about her death," Carter said. "I think he really loved her."

"That could be true, but he wasn't the right husband for her. She needed somebody stronger than herself." He moved his head back and forth on the pillow.

"Right." Carter raised his eyebrows at Morgan.

"Do you know of anything that occurred recently that might explain what happened to Victoria? Was there someone…" Morgan asked.

He eyed her suspiciously. "What do you mean?"

"We were just trying to figure out what could have happened." Morgan felt foolish. She should just shut up.

Big Bob squeezed the sheet between his big hands. A sheen of sweat broke out on his face. He seemed to be looking at something

151

in the distance and he was having trouble breathing. He kept repeating, "It just couldn't be… it just couldn't be…"

One of the monitors started beeping. Seconds later several nurses rushed into the room and shooed Morgan and Carter out into the hallway.

Frightened, Morgan looked up at Carter. "Oh my God, do you think I killed him?"

He put an arm around her. "No, but he sure got agitated about something he remembered."

They waited for several minutes and finally a nurse came out of the room. "Mr. Palmer is doing better now. He needs to rest."

Morgan let out a breath she hadn't known she was holding. "Thank God."

Chapter 36
Wednesday Evening

Morgan had agreed to meet Claire and Olivia at The Bay at six-thirty. On 30A she got stuck behind a giant construction truck that moved at a snail's pace. By the time she reached The Bay, it was six-fifty. She found Claire and Olivia in a corner of the restaurant, at a table overlooking the beach. A rock band was playing out by the sand pit and the place was lively for a Wednesday night.

Claire and Olivia had their heads together. As Morgan approached the table, Claire looked up and blanched. Olivia greeted her with one of those fake hundred-watt smiles. Something was going on. Her first thought was that the engagement had been called off and Claire was in a funk.

"Hi, sorry I'm late. I got behind a truck and couldn't get around it," Morgan said as she sat down.

"No problem. We ordered a bottle of chardonnay to share." Claire poured her a glass and smiled.

For a moment they were all silent. Something was going on. Morgan raised her chardonnay. "Here's to good friends." They clinked glasses.

"How are you doing? You've been through a lot lately," Olivia said.

"Let's just say I've been better. The Magnolia has been a zoo with these murders, the police and the paparazzi…and Grady…" She stopped as tears welled up in her eyes.

"Right," her friends said in unison, nodding vigorously.

Morgan narrowed her eyes and looked from Claire to Olivia. "All right, you guys. What's going on?"

They exchanged glances, and Morgan had the feeling they were consulting each other telepathically. Finally, Claire took a deep breath.

"Okay," she said. "Today, I went to my usual class at Sunshine Yoga. You know Rhea Bell, right?"

"Yes, I saw her yesterday as a matter of fact. She taught a class at the Magnolia spa."

"Well, there's this girl in the class. Her name is Sandy. She's been coming for about six months. She's a redhead. Petite, cute."

"Okay," Morgan said. Where in the heck was this going?

"Well, she was upset today." Claire looked at Olivia as if she needed support.

"So…" Morgan felt impatient, along with rising nervousness. What did she care about some strange girl being upset at yoga class?

"Well, Sandy was upset because…because her boyfriend…" Claire paused, then finished the sentence in a rush. "Her boyfriend Grady drowned during the storm Saturday night."

For a moment, Morgan couldn't process what she'd heard. "Her boyfriend *Grady*?"

"Yes. Sandy said she'd been in touch with the Coast Guard and they found the boat, the *Black Lion*, but no one was on board." Claire grabbed her glass of wine and took a gulp.

"This woman Sandy was Grady's girlfriend…?" Morgan repeated numbly. She sat back in her chair and closed her eyes.

Olivia got up, dipped a napkin in the ice water and pressed it gently against Morgan's forehead. "It's going to be all right, Morgan. I know it's a shock. You just need to get used to the idea."

"Drink some wine," Claire said.

Morgan opened her eyes and pushed away the wet napkin. "Thanks, Olivia." She grabbed her chardonnay and downed the entire glass in a couple of gulps.

Claire and Olivia stared at her, their eyes wide with concern. Then Morgan started to laugh, a little hysterically. She laughed and laughed, and pretty soon they joined in without really knowing why.

After a while, Morgan tried to catch her breath. Then she said, "Grady was a two-timing S.O.B."

That set them off again. As their laughter wound down, Claire said, "Yes, he was a cheating, lying, two-faced, double-crossing two-timing son of a bitch," and off they went again.

154

Olivia poured the rest of the wine into their glasses and they downed it. When the waiter came over, they ordered another bottle of wine and a couple of sushi plates to share.

Morgan sighed and smiled at her friends. "I guess I was pretty naïve. There were times when I thought he was at sea and he probably was on shore hanging out with Sandy. The truth is, I never really knew his schedule. It seemed to change all the time."

"Once I was in Destin and I thought I saw him with a girl. But you'd told me he was gone, so I forgot about it. That was a couple of months ago," Olivia said.

Morgan thought about this, "The night before he left this last time, he told me he wanted me to move in with him. But he never said he loved me or that he wanted to get married. I was angry with him when he dropped me off."

"Do you think he really meant it?" Olivia asked.

"I don't know. Right now, I wonder if anything he said was for real. I obviously didn't know him at all." Morgan's eyes filled with tears again. "We did have some great times together," she said.

Claire patted Morgan's hand. "Well, remember the good times."

Abruptly, Morgan started crying full out. "In spite of all this, I'm mourning him. When I think about how he must have died in the middle of that storm... drowning. It's horrible." She covered her face with her hands, her shoulders shaking.

Claire got up and wrapped her arms around her friend. "It's going to be all right," she crooned. Olivia looked on, her eyes moist. "I know it hurts, but we're with you, and you're going to be okay.

Chapter 37
Wednesday Night

Morgan arrived back at the Magnolia close to midnight. She, Olivia, and Claire had shared an Uber car since the three of them had polished off two bottles of wine. She'd have to pick up her own car from the lot at The Bay sometime tomorrow. For now, she wouldn't worry about it.

The car dropped Morgan off at the main gate. Media diehards still hovered near the entrance, and she noticed a contingent of mourning fans and paparazzi camped out along 30A. She wondered when they'd give up and go home. As she walked up the driveway, a car raced towards her, the headlights off. She jumped to the side as it whisked past. Some moron driving way too fast.

In the parking lot, she knocked on the door of the security shack to ask for a ride. One of the security guys, Renaldo, opened up. He was a heavy-set guy with a pudgy face and a small moustache. He'd obviously been fast asleep.

"Can you drive over to the resort?" Morgan asked.

"Sure, give me a sec."

A moment later he came out of the shack and they climbed into a golf cart. As they drove over the pontoon bridge, she noticed Lake Nawatchi was obscured by a thick layer of haze that drifted across the water. The air felt like a Finnish sauna.

"I hear things are bad in the hotel, Miss Morgan," Renaldo said.

"Bad? No. It's lovely. Herr Bern is furious and wants the police gone. Guests have been cancelling their reservations left and right. Last but not least, we have a murderer in our midst. Other than that, it's great." She must be drunk...she didn't usually run off at the mouth like this.

He shrugged. "I talked to some of the guys…they say the police have no leads. I'm thinking if they don't find Victoria Palmer's killer, the country will be up in arms."

She turned to look at him. "What do you mean?"

"On social media, there's all this talk. People are really angry and think the police are deliberately keeping secrets. They want to send in the FBI or the CIA or the army and storm the resort."

"Oh my God, people should get a life and forget Victoria Palmer." The cart rolled over a bump and she grabbed onto the hand rail to keep from being pitched overboard.

***

At the resort, Morgan thanked Renaldo for the ride. Slightly unsteady, she walked up the front steps and pushed open the glass door into the lobby. Hans was manning the front desk. He waved her over. When she got closer, he grimaced. "You look terrible. You look like a feisty raccoon with that smeared eye make-up."

Morgan felt like punching him. "How come you're working the desk tonight?"

"This afternoon, Katarina collapsed, and I sent her to her room. Lionel came in early, so I said he could go home at eleven." He looked out at the empty lobby. "Things are quiet around here. I'm going to close down the desk."

Morgan frowned. "What do you mean, Katarina collapsed?"

"Oh, it was a girl thing. She started to cry and said she couldn't stop. I figure she's exhausted or going to have her period, so I gave her the afternoon off."

Morgan didn't want to get into it with Hans, but she was seething inwardly. *A girl thing.* The man could be such a jerk. Maybe it came with being a Swiss-German stickler for detail. She bit back a sharp retort and said, "It was nice you gave her the afternoon off."

She left the front desk and took the elevator up to her apartment. Upstairs, the hallway was dim and quiet. Thank God there were no hotel guests on this floor. She frowned as she looked down the hall. Was that a bundle in front of her door? As she drew closer she saw it was a person curled up. Sudden fear jolted her. She felt like turning around and running for the stairwell. Instead, she took hold of

157

herself and kept walking. "Hello," she said as she approached the small shape. At the sound of her voice, the person uncurled and sat up. It was Lucia, the server who had brought her the salad yesterday. In the dim light, the girl looked like a ghost.

"Hello, Miss Morgan. I…I…I have to talk to you. I don't know who else to talk to."

Morgan reached down and helped her to stand. Lucia couldn't weigh more that ninety pounds. Her small hand felt moist. "Come on inside and we'll talk." She punched in the code and opened the door. Lucia followed her in. Morgan dropped her bag on the entryway table and turned on the lights. Lucia stood at the threshold, as if waiting to be invited into the living room. "Come in. Would you like something to drink? What can I get you?" She started towards the kitchenette.

"No, ma'am, I don't want anything." Lucia looked around the room in wonder. "It's beautiful here, so clean and white."

Morgan smiled. "Let's sit and you can tell me why you're here." She reached down and took off her shoes, feeling a little woozy. She'd had way too much to drink tonight.

The girl's gaze traveled the room, avoiding Morgan's eyes. Then she dared to make eye contact. "I…I…just need to tell someone…I feel terrible…I think I killed the famous Victoria."

Morgan stopped stock still. "You *what*?" Now she was wide awake, the foggy feeling gone.

Lucia's next words tumbled out. "I know I have to tell someone and I'm afraid of the policeman. I lied to him and maybe he'll want to have me deported."

Morgan led Lucia to the sofa and they sat. "Are you here illegally? Do you have a green card?"

"Yes, ma'am. I'm legal." Lucia's back was ramrod straight.

"Well, then you have nothing to worry about." Morgan leaned back against the cushions.

Lucia looked momentarily relieved. Then the dark cloud returned. "I have to tell you what happened and then you can tell me what to do."

Morgan raised her eyebrows. "Why don't you start from the beginning?"

Lucia took a deep breath as though she was going to dive into a pool. "You know the green smoothie Miss Victoria liked?"

"Yes."

"Since the first day all those wedding people were here, I was supposed to take the drink up to Ms. Palmer's room. The chef made it from a special recipe."

"Uh-huh."

"Every day, I went through the lobby and took the back elevator." She paused, and Morgan nodded.

"Upstairs, I would knock on the door and Miss Victoria would tell me to bring it in and I would place it on the little table."

"Uh-huh."

"Well, a couple of weeks ago, we got a new doorman. His name is Roberto."

Morgan nodded again. She'd seen the new guy. Though she couldn't see where this story was going.

"Roberto and I like to talk and stuff." Lucia's cheeks reddened. She looked down at her hands. "On the wedding day, when I went through the lobby, he smiled at me and, well, Katarina, you know Katarina at the desk?" Lucia squeezed her hands together. "Well, she said she would take the smoothie upstairs."

"Uh-huh."

"So, I didn't do my job and I'm worried Katarina poisoned Ms. Victoria."

Morgan sat up, fully alert. "Why do you think she did that?"

"Because she hated Ms. Victoria. I should never have let her take up the smoothie."

"How do you know she hated Victoria?"

"By her eyes, whenever Victoria came by the front desk. I could see it. By the way she talked about her."

Morgan narrowed her eyes. "That's quite an accusation. Are you sure about this?"

Lucia nodded. "When I worked in the lobby, serving cold drinks to the wedding guests, I would see Katarina's eyes. They were filled with hatred for Ms. Victoria. I don't know why."

Morgan thought, *one more person who hated Victoria Palmer.*

"That's not all." Lucia looked in agony now. "Katarina saw me with Roberto in the storage room. She said if I told anyone she took up the smoothie, she would tell Herr Bern about Roberto and me and I would be 'out on my ass.'" Her eyes brimmed with tears.

Morgan wished she'd gone easier on the chardonnay. "Let me get this straight. You and Roberto have been fooling around. Katarina knows about it. She hates Victoria and might have poisoned the smoothie she delivered. Then she threatened to get you fired if you told anyone about the switch. Is that right?"

Lucia's lips trembled, and a sob escaped. "Yes...ma'am."

Morgan got up and fetched a handful of tissues. She handed them to the shaking girl. "I think we should talk to Katarina about this before we go to the police, don't you think? Wouldn't that be fair to her?"

Lucia blew her nose and dabbed at her eyes. "If you think so."

Chapter 38
Thursday - Early Morning

Although it was already early morning, Morgan decided to drag Lucia over to Katarina's room right then. Most of the staff did not live on the premises, but Katarina and Lionel had apartments over the maintenance garage. As they took the elevator and walked through the silent hotel building, Morgan considered what she'd learned. Why would Katarina want to poison Victoria? Did she really think she would get away with it? It seemed pretty dumb. Morgan thought back over the last couple of days. Katarina had definitely looked stressed. Was it just from dealing nonstop with irate, frightened guests, or had she actually attempted murder?

They ascended the wooden staircase attached to the exterior of the garages and opened a door that led into a short hallway. Morgan had been up here a couple of years back when she'd been friends with a desk clerk who had since gotten married and moved away. The apartments were cozy, meaning small, but when you worked long shifts, it was nice to be able to "go home" nearby.

Katarina's apartment was the first door on the left. Morgan knocked. They waited. Then she knocked again. No response, or sound of anyone approaching. Could Katarina have flown the coop? If so, they would have to tell Dax and he'd go after her. Morgan knocked again and put her ear to the door. This time she thought she could hear rustling inside. "Katarina, it's Morgan. Could you please open the door? We need to talk."

A moment later, they heard a chain lock being pulled back and the click of a bolt. Then the door opened a crack. Katarina looked out at Morgan, her eyes bloodshot, her face pale. When she pulled the door open further and saw Lucia, her eyes widened in fear. "What do you want?" she said, her tone hostile.

"I think you know why we're here. Let's sit down and talk."

"Are the police here?" Katarina stepped out and looked up and down the hallway. She looked terrible, in a black thong and a dirty white tee-shirt with the red Talbot logo on the front.

"No, it's just us."

"Why should I talk to you?" She sounded belligerent now. "Do you believe *her*? She's a little liar and a slut."

Her harsh words startled Morgan. Katarina had always been so quiet and polite. She obviously didn't know this girl at all. "We really need to talk." Morgan took a step inside, pulling Lucia behind her.

The studio apartment was a mess. Clothes, dirty dishes, glasses and wine bottles covered every available surface. An acrid odor of dirty laundry and old pizza lingered. The room was dimly lit by one small lamp. Katarina stepped back from the entryway and stood in the middle of the room, her legs apart and her arms crossed, her face hard in defiance. Morgan wondered if it was all an act. The girl she knew at the front desk had always been friendly, if shy and hesitant. This current version of Katarina wanted to be in their faces. Maybe it was alcohol, evidenced by all the empty wine bottles around the room.

Morgan shut the door. There wasn't a clear space to sit down. She walked over to a small loveseat, picked up some clothes and tossed them on the bed. Then she sat, pulling Lucia down beside her. Lucia was trembling, her head down. Morgan cleared her throat. "I brought Lucia over here because I thought it was best if we discussed together what happened on the morning of Victoria Palmer's wedding…"

"Do you know it's the middle of the night?" Katarina snarled.

"Lucia made some accusations and I thought we should talk before we got the police involved."

"I don't care about the police. They can lock me up and throw away the key." Katarina was still trying to look defiant in her tee-shirt, underwear and bare feet.

"Why did you offer to deliver the green smoothie to Victoria on the morning of her wedding?"

"How do you know I did? Lucia's lying."

Morgan switched gears. "Did you go to Talbot College?"

Katarina looked surprised, then glanced down at her shirt. "Maybe I did."

"When did you graduate?"

"I didn't. I left." She kicked at a sweatshirt that lay crumpled on the floor.

"Why?"

Katarina stood her ground, tapping her foot.

"Were you in the same class as Victoria and the rest of the wedding party?"

"No, I was a year behind. But I hate all of them. Not so much the guys, but the girls. They're cruel, selfish bitches," she blurted.

"Why do you say that?"

"Because..." Katarina suddenly sat down cross-legged on the floor.

"Because?" Morgan repeated.

Katarina rubbed her legs. "They made fun of me because I was fat and I didn't get their jokes. They played tricks on me. They stole my bras and hung them out the window. It was Victoria who did it. She was the worst." She rubbed her legs harder.

Morgan remembered the story Victoria had told during the bridesmaids' shopping expedition, while they ate lunch in Seaside, of some poor girl the sorority sisters had made fun of in college. *Kati with an "i"*, she'd said. Jenny hadn't thought it was funny, Morgan recalled. "Did you take the job at the Magnolia because you knew Victoria's wedding was going to take place here?"

"Yes. I wanted to get back at her, to make her suffer." Abruptly, Katarina jumped to her feet. She paced back and forth across the room, stomping on the clothes littered across the floor. "Okay, I did take that smoothie up to Victoria on her big wedding day. And I did put arsenic in it. Now call the police and tell them I killed her." She rummaged through her bag on the floor beside the bed. For a split second, Morgan thought she would pull out a gun and shoot them. Instead, she pulled out her phone and tossed it at Morgan. "Okay, call." Her eyes were wild, and she hopped from one foot to the other like a crazed kid.

163

"Where did you get the arsenic?" Morgan asked.

She forced a laugh. "Online. You can order just about anything off the internet."

"Sit down, Katarina," Morgan said quietly. "Calm down. Listen to me. You didn't kill Victoria. You just made her sick."

Katarina's eyes looked ready to pop out of her head. "What do you mean?"

"Either you didn't put enough arsenic in the smoothie, or she didn't drink it. Either way, someone else killed her with a much more powerful drug. They injected her with it at the wedding."

Katarina slid to the floor like a deflated balloon. "I didn't kill her? Oh, my God." The girl flopped back and lay on the floor, inert. She'd fainted dead away.

***

Twenty minutes after Morgan called, Dax and two officers arrived. The three men seemed to fill the small apartment. Morgan had encouraged Katarina to get dressed before they showed up. The girl had put on some jeans and pulled her hair into a pony tail, but she still looked a mess.

As the men looked around at the chaos, Morgan explained what she'd learned from Lucia and Katarina. Dax sighed, looking from one girl to the other. "You could have saved us a lot of time and effort if you'd come forward earlier. Both of you were interviewed and both of you lied, or you intentionally withheld information. I'm arresting you Katarina Petrov, for the attempted murder of Victoria Palmer." He repeated the Miranda warning. Katarina stared straight ahead, unresponsive.

Lucia had turned chalky white. "Am I going to prison?"

Dax shook his head. "No, but I want you down at the station tomorrow morning at eight o'clock sharp to give your statement."

Lucia nodded and whispered, "Yes, sir."

The two officers took Katarina by the arms and led her out of the room. Dax followed. At the door he stopped and said, "Thanks, Morgan. Sorry you had to handle all this. But maybe we're a step closer to our actual killer now."

"Don't be too hard on her. Victoria was cruel and merciless. Katarina has been nurturing her pain for a long time."

Chapter 39
Thursday Morning

Morgan managed to sleep a few hours. During the early morning, a steady rain fell and deadened the sound of the waves. Now it was drizzling, and the world was enveloped in a cottony, gray mist. She made coffee and curled up on the sofa, looking out at the opaque world. A white seagull was perched on the patio railing. She could see nothing beyond its silhouette. This misty world was like her current life. She'd been blind to who Grady really was. She'd pulled the wool over her own eyes and believed what she'd wanted. His lack of sincerity and the series of lies he'd told her made her feel foolish as well as hurt. Yes, she'd been blind.

Similarly, the murder investigation seemed to be wrapped in mist. All the actors were insubstantial phantoms. She reached for the yellow legal pad and looked down at the list of names. Who were they really? Was Georgie a ditz or a calculating psychopath? Were Jenny and Lars as innocent as they seemed, or had Lars killed Victoria because of a slam on his manhood? Had Josh witnessed the crime, so Lars killed him? What did she know about Rex, except he seemed to go from zero to a hundred on the psycho-meter in a matter of seconds. And Jill was truly a mystery. Morgan remembered that first night in the lounge. Jill had been drunk and seething with hatred towards the in-crowd…which included all the wedding party. Then there was Mindy, with a years-long backlog of denigration and servitude. Killing Victoria would have provided payback and emancipation.

Of course, number one on the suspect list was Brad. He would probably inherit a pot of gold. He'd mentioned a prenup agreement in case of divorce, but he would undoubtedly inherit with Victoria dead. On the other hand, would someone Victoria's age even have a will? Morgan was nearly the same age and she'd never thought of preparing one.

Morgan realized her coffee was cold. She got up, warmed the cup in the microwave for a few seconds, sat back down and sipped the scalding brew. Who had she missed? Ah, Carter. She didn't want it to be Carter, and yet...that first day at the tennis match he'd displayed unrestrained anger. He was also a biochemist and would have access to drugs and poisons...even a hypodermic needle. Maybe he'd cozied up to her and played the detective game as a ruse, so he could get closer to Dax and the investigation. She took another sip of coffee and closed her eyes. But why would Carter want to kill Victoria? If he did, it must date back to their time at Talbot. That thought made her sit up with a jolt. Maybe that was it. Whoever killed Victoria and then Josh had been nurturing their bitterness since college, just like Katarina. She jumped up, nearly spilling her coffee, and went over to her desk. She pulled up the chair, sat down and opened her laptop.

First, she googled the university and the years the wedding party attended Talbot. She found some information about an alumni group but nothing else. Then she googled "Talbot scandals" thinking she would spot a familiar name. A few articles reported a rape that occurred in the last few months. Five years ago, a cheating scandal made national news. There was reportage about a basketball coach who had taken bribes and been fired. She found an article about Lars Johansson and the march for white students' rights. There was even a picture of Lars holding a sign stating: "No to Affirmative Action." He looked pretty much like he did now.

Going back ten years, Morgan came upon an article about a lab break-in. The name Madhavadity Balakrishnan caught her attention. Wasn't that the name of the research assistant Carter had referenced when they'd talked on the beach? She remembered Carter said they called the man Krishna. He'd been their lab instructor. Carter had also mentioned the entire wedding party had met in that class.

Morgan read through the article. Apparently, the students had participated in an important genetic study. Through an inventive procedure, Krishna and a professor named John Bender had discovered a simple and fail-safe genetic test. This was way before 23andMe. The research was ground-breaking, but a break-in at the

167

Talbot laboratory set the project back several months. The research samples had been destroyed and there was a police investigation. She needed to discuss this further with Carter, or maybe she should call Professor Bender.

Morgan sat back in her chair and looked out at the Gulf. The sun was peeping through the clouds and a cool breeze ruffled the curtains. It would be a bright, sunny day after all.

Chapter 40
Thursday - Late Morning

After a shower, Morgan pulled on some black leggings and a green and blue patterned tunic. She debated on a bowl of cereal in her apartment or an omelet downstairs. The omelet won out.

Hans was at the front desk, looking disgruntled. "I hear you had Katarina arrested. When will she be back?"

Morgan bit back her anger. "I don't know when or if she'll be back…and Hans, I did not *have* her arrested. The police did that."

"In any case, I've got several interviews lined up this afternoon. We need another desk clerk."

"Good."

"What about the wedding party? Ms. Palmer paid up-front for their rooms through tonight. They should be out the door tomorrow. Then we'll be back to normal." Hans rubbed his hands together.

Back to normal? "Right. I haven't spoken to any of them this morning."

"They're in the Jasmine Bistro." He sniffed. "It's kind of weird, how they're always together."

***

Before going in for breakfast, Morgan went to her office. She'd brought down her laptop and the yellow legal pad. She put the note pad in the bottom drawer of her desk. She'd continue her research later. She left her office and hurried into the Bistro. Talking about the lab break-in with the entire group might be revealing. Here was her opportunity.

Carter spotted her when she came in and hailed her over. It looked as though the group had finished breakfast and were lingering over coffee. Morgan claimed an empty seat next to Georgie and was greeted by a chorus of hellos. They all seemed eager for a new face.

The waiter came over, and she ordered her favorite goat cheese, spinach and bacon omelet. She glanced at the large glass in front of Georgie. There was a ring of muddy green goo at the top and a similarly colored sludge at the bottom.

Georgie noticed and giggled nervously, "I feel like Tory is watching me. I haven't been sticking to the mandatory diet. Now I'm back on track."

"If it's what makes you feel good, then go for it," Morgan said.

"Did you hear what happened last night?" Jenny asked, looking around the table.

Jill rolled her eyes. "Just tell us, don't make us beg."

"The maid who brought us coffee in our room this morning…she said the skinny blond girl at the front desk got arrested."

"You mean Katarina? She's so sweet. Why would they arrest her?" Georgie said.

Rex raised his coffee cup. "Duh-uh, maybe because she killed Tory?"

"That girl? I can't believe it."

Mindy, Carter and Brad looked perplexed, but said nothing.

Morgan's omelet arrived. The group kept silent until the waiter retreated across the room. Then Brad asked, "Did the maid tell you what she was arrested for?"

"No, but it had to do with someone else on the waitstaff in the hotel…that shy little one, I think her name's Lucia. She had to go give a statement to the police today." Jenny seemed to relish all the attention. She obviously felt important as the bearer of the latest news. Jenny looked over at Morgan. "Do you know what happened?"

Morgan considered lying, but undoubtedly the story would run rampant in the hotel. Lucia would tell Roberto and he would pass on the juicy gossip. She also had to admit to herself that she wanted this group to understand the cruelty Victoria had inflicted on Katarina. She knew some of them had participated in shunning the girl. Morgan took a breath, then told them what happened the previous evening and why Katarina had been arrested.

When she'd finished, Georgie said, "She tried to kill Victoria with arsenic? That sounds like an Agatha Christie novel."

Rex leaned forward. "Man, this is flat out crazy. Two people wanting Victoria dead. It *is* like some mystery novel."

"Could she have poisoned Tory at the wedding?" Jill asked. "Was she there?"

Carter drummed his fingers on the tablecloth. "If she did, she would have been on the dais with us for the wedding pictures. I'm pretty sure she wasn't among us."

"So she's the girl we called Kati with an 'i'. We were talking about her last week." Jenny's hand flew to her neck in a nervous gesture.

"Remember she was way overweight? Gosh, she's so skinny now," Georgie said.

Brad looked upset. Morgan wondered if he had ever really come to grips with how Victoria treated people. It would have made her hard to love. But maybe he didn't see how she acted. Love was blind, they said. Morgan had certainly been blind where Grady was concerned, but she wasn't sure she really loved him.

As the group discussed Katarina, Morgan finished her breakfast. She patted her mouth with a napkin and took a sip of coffee. During a lull in the conversation, she said, "What do you guys remember about the break-in at the biology lab when you were in college?"

Everyone looked at her quizzically.

"Why do you ask?" Georgie said, twisting her hair around her finger.

"It came up when I was researching articles about Talbot."

Morgan watched the group. Carter looked at her and frowned.

"What are you, a wannabe detective?" Rex asked. His tone was snide.

"I remember we didn't get a lab grade since all the tests we were working on were destroyed," Lars said.

"But that was the point of it," Jill said. "I always thought someone didn't want those results revealed."

Mindy's eyes narrowed. "What do you mean?"

171

"Once our DNA was public knowledge, people could find out about us. Like if we had a criminal record," Jill said.

Morgan could feel tension rising around the table. Jenny's normally rosy cheeks had lost their color.

"Ah-ha," Rex said. He looked at Morgan with new respect. "You think whoever destroyed the DNA is the same person who killed Tory."

"That's nuts! All that happened years ago." Lars pushed back his chair and stood up. Jenny did likewise. She followed him, stumbling slightly as they headed for the lobby. The rest of them fell silent, thinking private thoughts.

Chapter 41
Thursday - Late Morning

Morgan left the dining room with Carter right on her heels. He grabbed her arm. "Listen, you shouldn't be asking all those questions. Some totally deranged person killed two people and won't stop at another murder."

Morgan spun around. "Let go of my arm." She pulled it free and glared at him.

Carter released her. "I'm sorry." He pushed back his hair in a nervous gesture. Then his true-blue eyes nailed hers. "I'm worried about you. I just think you should forget about our sick little group and go on about your business. We'll all be gone soon..."

Morgan didn't want to stop this investigation. She felt like she was on to something. "Don't you think all this dates back to your college days? Doesn't it have to do with the group dynamics back then? Look at Katarina...her hurt and anger have been moldering all these years."

"You're right. It isn't about something that happened here at the Magnolia, but we have no clue what the motive was for killing Tory, let alone Josh. I'm just thinking that if you ask too many questions, our killer will want to shut you up." His voice turned hard. "Leave it to the police. Leave it to your friend Dax."

Morgan glanced down the hallway. Dax was there with a short, dapper man in a tailored grey suit and shiny black wing-tips. Dax beckoned them over.

Carter held her back. Again, he grabbed her arm. "Let's talk later. Okay?"

She nodded, and they moved down the hall. As they approached, Dax said, "Morgan, Carter, this is Victoria Palmer's lawyer Jerry Ganz. He arrived this morning from California." Mr. Ganz had a tanned, bald head and bright, inquisitive eyes behind black-rimmed glasses.

They all shook hands.

"Morgan, would you mind getting everyone down here?" Dax asked. "Mr. Ganz is going to read Victoria's last will and testament. Then I'd like to talk to everyone."

"Sure, we'll round them up." Morgan and Carter went back to the lobby. It took a few minutes but soon the wedding party was settled in the Gardenia Room. Morgan had ordered coffee and mini-pecan rolls. Everyone helped themselves and made small talk waiting for Dax and Ganz to appear. When the two men entered the room, they took seats at the head of the table.

Dax cleared his throat. "Good morning, ladies and gentlemen. This is Mr. Jerry Ganz, Victoria's lawyer. He has agreed to share portions of the contents of her will with you."

The little man jumped to his feet, holding his glasses in one hand. He made Morgan think of a wiry and wise gnome. "Good morning. I know the past few days have not been good. He looked at Brad. "Mr. Hughes, please accept my condolences. The death of your wife after only a few hours of marriage is most tragic. I know she loved you dearly and hoped for a long and happy life together."

Tears welled up in Brad's eyes. He nodded but he couldn't speak. Morgan noticed his hands were shaking.

Jerry Ganz looked around the group. "All of you were Victoria's close friends. I'm sure you are mourning her loss. I offer you my condolences as well."

Georgie and Jenny dabbed at their eyes. Everyone else remained stoic.

Ganz continued. "Several of you were included in Victoria's will. Since you're all here together, I thought this would be an opportune time to read it."

Morgan noticed a change in the atmosphere of the room. Suddenly, the wedding party were all very attentive. Carter caught her eye and winked. He'd never worked for Victoria, Morgan recalled. Neither of them would be mentioned, so they could enjoy the drama.

"Initially, Victoria, didn't want to bother with a will at this point in her life. However, because of the depth and breadth of her estate,

I suggested strongly that we prepare the document before her marriage." Ganz put on his glasses.

Everyone looked over at Brad. He was patting his face with a handkerchief. Rather than slumping in his chair, he sat straight and alert. She thought back to their drive from the casino the other night. He was probably hoping for a nice chunk of change, so he could head back to the roulette tables.

"I won't read the list of small amounts destined for Victoria's maids, make-up artists etc. Let's see…" The lawyer ran his finger down a page, then flipped it over and studied the next page. He cleared his throat. "To Jill Dixon and Regis Conrad, twenty thousand dollars each."

Jill and Rex high-fived. "Holy shit, that's the bomb," Rex said. Jill giggled.

"To Georgina Ralston, fifty thousand dollars." Ganz looked up and smiled at Georgie. He must have met her before.

Georgie had turned pale and looked shocked. "Wow, wow…"

Morgan noticed Jill was frowning now.

"To Minerva Fairbanks…" the lawyer continued.

"Minerva? Who's that?" Lars looked puzzled.

Visibly irritated at the interruption, Ganz said, "Let me repeat. To Minerva Fairbanks, two hundred thousand dollars."

Carter looked over at Mindy. "That's you, isn't it?"

Mindy nodded. She looked stunned. Morgan thought about everything Mindy had done for Victoria through the years. This was payback in a good way.

Rex started to laugh. "Minerva! What the fuck. I never even thought about what your real name could be. Minerva. Isn't that some Greek or Roman goddess?"

Everyone was laughing now, except Mindy. She sat hunched over, her hands clasped to her chest. Clearly, the bequest came as a major surprise.

Morgan noticed that Georgie looked offended. She was probably wondering why she didn't get the same amount as Mindy. What had Mindy done that warranted the more generous sum of money? Morgan figured Georgie wasn't privy to Mindy's servitude.

175

"Are you sure that's right?" Jill asked. "I mean, what did Mindy do that was so important? I don't get it."

"Yeah, I don't get it," Georgie repeated.

Ganz responded in a cool voice. "I read what is written here, and what Victoria wanted."

Rex laughed. "Listen, Jill. Ten minutes ago, you didn't have twenty thousand big ones. Let it go."

Ganz cleared his throat and took a sip of water. "The remainder of my fortune is to be divided equally. Half will be used to build and maintain a museum in my name: The Victoria Palmer Museum of Beauty. I bequeath the other half to my husband, Bradley Hughes III." The lawyer looked up. "However, Mr. Hughes's inheritance is conditional upon the following." He looked over at Brad with a stern expression on his elfin features. "The monies for my husband will be placed in a trust and will only be available when Bradley has given up his drug and gambling addictions. In addition, he needs to be gainfully employed. My executor Jerry Ganz will determine when my husband is fully recovered from his addictions, at which time he will initiate the disbursement of the trust."

Surprise crossed the others' faces. They avoided looking at Brad. Morgan wondered how many of them knew about his problems. She hadn't realized he was into drugs as well as gambling. It probably explained his conversation with Josh in Rosemary Beach that day, when Morgan had seen them arguing on the street. Josh must have been trying to reason with him. Another thought popped into her head. What was Brad's drug of choice? Heroin or cocaine? Did he use a syringe?

Brad's usually limpid eyes had narrowed and turned slate blue. "This is god-damned unfair. You want to control me, you bastard." He shot to his feet and shook a fist at Ganz. "You're the one who got her to write those terms. You've been my enemy from the start."

The tension escalated like a rocket taking off. Then the door burst open. Officer Rodriguez stood on the threshold. He looked upset. "Sheriff? I need a minute. In private."

Chapter 42
Noon Thursday

Dax left the room for several minutes. Brad paced, clenching and unclenching his fists. Jerry Ganz studied his papers. Jenny and Lars held hands and looked frightened. Rex and Jill had their heads together, whispering. Georgie fidgeted like a little kid, twisting her hair into a knot on top of her head and tapping her foot against the table leg. Mindy seemed to be in her own world as she chewed on a hangnail. Morgan looked over at Carter. He was leaning back and observing the others. It looked like he was enjoying himself.

Moments later Dax pushed open the door and returned to the head of the table. He sighed, and his shoulders slumped. For once, he didn't look in complete control. "Robert Palmer, Victoria's father, died in the early morning hours at the hospital…under suspicious circumstances."

"Oh my God," Jenny burst out. "When is this nightmare going to be over?"

"Not soon enough," Carter murmured.

"I have to go to the hospital now. I'll be back in a couple of hours. I ask that you remain here at the Magnolia. I'll need to talk to everyone again." Dax looked around the table. "It is difficult to imagine that this latest murder is not somehow connected to the murders of Victoria Palmer and Josh Owens."

"How did he die? Poisoned? Strangulation? Gunshot?" Rex asked.

Brad glared at him. "Shut up, Rex. You're being a total asshole."

"Look who's calling the kettle black. I'll bet you killed your main squeeze because you wanted that money." Rex chuckled. "Now you're going to have to wait."

Brad lunged at Rex, grabbing him in a bear hug. The two of them grappled together, growling like animals. Brad tore at Rex's ponytail. Rex leaned back and slugged Brad in the face.

Dax and Rodriguez rushed over and pulled the two men apart. "Cut it out, you two," Dax snapped, holding Rex's arms from behind. "Everyone is tense. You've got to keep your cool."

Rex stared at Brad. Hatred shone in his eyes. Brad stared back. Blood dribbled down his face from a small cut below his eye. Then he wrenched his arms away from Rodriguez's grasp. "I don't need your vicious insults." He looked around at his fellow alumni. "You all make me sick." Then he stomped out of the room.

Rex snickered. "Woo-ee, I think I hit a nerve."

"I'm going up to my room. You guys are crazy," Georgie said, and took off.

Dax left with Jerry Ganz and the rest of them hurried out of the room. Morgan dallied behind, hoping to speak to Carter.

He came up to her. "Hey, Inspector Morgan, how about we sneak out of here and I'll take you for lunch wherever you want? We need to talk."

Morgan felt drained after all the emotion in that room, but she was dying to discuss the latest. She hushed the small inner voice that reminded her he was still a murder suspect. Although she didn't really believe it. "Okay, let's go out the back way and I'll take you to The Perfect Pig for a brisket sandwich. How does that sound?"

"Sounds perfect." He smiled at her. Then without warning he bent down and kissed her. His lips were soft and full.

Without thinking, Morgan kissed him back. Then she pulled away. "Hey, what are we doing? We've got work to do." She smiled up at him. Then she reached up, curved her hands around the nape of his neck, pulled him close and kissed him again…longer this time. His arms went around her. She leaned in, feeling unbelievably at home.

***

As they drove down 30A, they discussed Big Bob's death. "I wonder what Dax meant by suspicious circumstances?" Morgan said.

"If it's our killer, it's probably the same drug, R27. A gun wouldn't rate as 'suspicious circumstances.' They'd know for sure it was murder." Carter laid his arm across the back of Morgan's seat.

178

She glanced at Carter, and he met her gaze. Quickly, she turned away, her mouth curved in a smile. Then she sobered.

"I can't get my head around this. I think Josh was killed because of what he saw or what he knew. But who would want to kill Victoria *and* her father? And why?"

"That's the crux of the matter."

"What about Norma Lee?"

Carter chuckled. "I don't think she could stop drinking long enough to carry out the dirty deed."

"Well, at this point she's the one with the most to gain. Maybe she hired somebody to do her dirty work?"

"I don't think so. Unfortunately, it's got to be one of us." His tone was grim.

When they reached The Perfect Pig, they decided to eat outside. They ordered beers and brisket sandwiches. When the food arrived, they dug in.

"You were right, this is delicious." Carter wiped his mouth with one of several paper napkins.

"I am so glad to be away from the Magnolia right now. I mean, that's my home, but it's been toxic lately." Morgan looked at Carter, her eyebrows knit in worry.

"Victoria brought all the drama…even in death." He took a long drink of beer. "Tell me again about Katarina and the maid, Lucia."

Morgan recounted the evening in more detail. "Victoria and her posse hounded Katarina out of school. The girl is a basket case. What happened to her was horrendous. I hope she'll be treated fairly. I don't think she's really a killer."

"Well, if she'd succeeded, she would have been. It sounds as though she'd been scheming Tory's demise for a long time…just like the real killer."

Morgan took a bite of her sandwich and chewed thoughtfully. "Do you think Brad killed Victoria for the money? You and I both know he's desperate for funds."

"No, I don't. And I don't think he killed Josh, either."

"Brad's turned out to be very different than the person I thought he was. When he came with Victoria to the resort for all the planning

179

sessions, he seemed like this intelligent, even-minded lawyer with a brilliant career and the manners of an English gentleman."

Carter nodded. "I've known Brad most of my life. Things came easily to him. He was good-looking, won all the awards, was the hot-shot quarterback, class president, et cetera. And he was a really nice guy on top of all that." Carter finished his beer and stared into the distance, as if deep in thought. "Then times got rough. Both of his parents were killed in an automobile accident. He was messed up for a while and seeing a shrink. I think he took some anti-depressants. Later, he got pretty banged up in football and used to take painkillers. Maybe he got into drugs through an opioid addiction? Which would mean he needed money. I'm guessing he was reasonably successful at the blackjack tables, and that led to his gambling obsession. Then he lost his job. I don't know. This is just conjecture. He doesn't seem to want to talk about it." Carter looked over at her, his eyes questioning hers.

"It seems as though Victoria knew all this and yet she went forward with the wedding. She must have really loved him," Morgan said. She picked up her sandwich and took another bite.

Carter nearly choked. He sipped water. "That's hard for me to believe. I never thought she could love anyone but herself. I think it's more likely she wanted to control him. Now she can continue to control him in death."

"That's pretty sick." Morgan put down her sandwich. Somehow, she was no longer hungry. She sat back. "What did you think about the will?"

"I think the lawyer convinced Tory to include bequests for all of her various minions. He must have had substantial power over her. I can't believe she would have been that generous on her own."

Morgan laughed, "Wow, you certainly have a low view of Victoria."

"I guess I should shut up or you're going to suspect me."

"No, Carter, I don't. But I'm a terrible judge of character." Suddenly, she realized what she'd said. Her face fell and she fumbled with her glass, nearly knocking it over.

180

Carter reached over and covered her hand with his. His blue eyes looked into hers with concern. "What's the matter?"

She closed her eyes and took a breath, then told him about Grady and his other girlfriend. "I had no clue what sort of person he was. I feel like a total idiot." She picked up her napkin and dabbed at her eyes. Then she folded it carefully before placing it by her plate.

"Morgan, look at me." When she did, his eyes searched hers. "You can trust me one hundred percent." He leaned over and kissed her ever so gently.

Chapter 43
Thursday Afternoon

When they got back to the Magnolia, the crowd had thinned out considerably along the highway outside the resort. Morgan surmised that the media had gone to the hospital in search of the latest news sensation. No one was in the lobby. Carter went upstairs, and Morgan went down to her office.

Itzel wasn't there. Thursday was her day off. Morgan went into her private office and spent some time on email. Every day, there were ten or twenty requests for information about a Magnolia wedding. She read through them, but her mind kept wandering. She couldn't stop thinking about the murders and the six likely suspects. Eventually she gave up and sifted through the actions and comments of each member of the wedding party.

Whoever killed Josh would have had to be strong enough to pull him into the bushes. That pointed toward Rex, Brad or Lars. What about the girls? From the yoga class, she knew Georgie was well-muscled. She'd seen Jill carrying heavy equipment around. Mindy had been lifting weights in the workout room. Only Jenny didn't seem that strong. Was that everyone?

Morgan reached down and opened the bottom left-hand drawer where she'd placed the yellow legal tablet with notes on each suspect. She felt around for it, then looked down. With a little screech, she pulled her hand back as if bitten by a snake. The tablet was gone. In its place was one single sheet with a single sentence scrawled across it: *Stop playing detective bitch if you value your life.*

Trembling, Morgan looked around the office as if someone might be hiding behind the furniture, ready to stick her with a syringe. Of course, there was nowhere to hide. She was alone. She pushed back her chair, got up and ran to the door. She slammed it shut and locked it. Then she stood in the middle of the room, shaking, her arms wrapped around her torso. Someone had been in here and left that poison pen letter. Someone did not like her questions about the past at Talbot. She was sure her not-so-innocent question about the lab break-in at breakfast had sent the killer into her office. She went back to her desk and looked around to see if anything had been taken and saw fragments of yellow paper in the trash basket. Her notes had been viciously torn into tiny pieces.

She pulled out her phone and texted Dax that he needed to contact her pronto. Her next thought was that she shouldn't touch anything. Maybe the forensic crew could find fingerprints or some DNA from her intruder. She picked up her laptop, left the room and locked the door behind her.

Lionel was at the front desk. Morgan asked him if he'd seen anyone go into her office.

He shook his head. "To tell you the truth, I haven't been here long. Hans was here, but he's doing interviews now. Those people are waiting. They've been here for a while. You could ask them." Lionel gestured towards a heavy-set woman in a purple shapeless dress and a young guy in a cheap brown suit. The woman had blond curly hair and the young man's black hair was sleeked back. Both of them were intent on their phones. They didn't look up when Morgan approached.

"Hello," she said. No reaction. The kid's thumbs flew over the tiny screen. He was probably playing a video game. From the woman's phone came the sound of voices.

Morgan raised her voice. "Hel...lo!"

That got a reaction. Both of them looked up, their faces blank.

"How long have you been waiting here?" Morgan asked.

The young man said, "I just got here. Sorry. I'm kind of late for my interview."

The woman looked over at him. "Don't worry, kid. The manager is way behind with the interviews. I've been here an hour."

"I'm sorry you've had to wait. I'm sure Herr Bern will talk to you soon," Morgan said.

The woman shrugged. "It's not so bad. I'm watching this show I like. No problem."

"In the hour you've been waiting, did you see anyone go down that hallway?" Morgan pointed in the direction of her office.

"Nope, I don't think so. You mean anyone in particular? What does this person look like?" The woman scrunched up her face like a Cabbage Patch doll.

"Probably young, about my age," Morgan said off-handedly. She didn't want to awaken this woman's curiosity.

"I don't think so. Like I said, I've been watching my show. I'd like to get back to it." The woman turned her attention back to the fascinating tiny screen.

Morgan was pretty sure neither of these people would be offered a job at the front desk of the Magnolia.

She stepped away, feeling restless. She needed to talk to someone. Carter had gone up to his suite. She didn't know his cell phone number. She stepped over to the desk, asked Lionel for Carter's room number and called him on the house phone. He picked up right away. "Carter Perry."

"Carter, it's Morgan. Could you come downstairs? I need to talk to someone."

"Sure, I was just getting on my swim trunks. I'm going to swim some laps in the pool."

She heard her voice wobble. "I'm in the lobby. Come soon."

Morgan paced the large room, hugging her laptop. Tension and fear kept her moving. Who had left that message in her desk? Was she in danger? She turned and started back towards the front desk, then felt a hand on her arm. She spun around, ready to knock off the hand that had grasped her.

"Miss Morgan..." It was Marina, the woman in charge of housekeeping. She let go of Morgan's arm and took two steps back. She looked startled, even frightened.

Morgan lowered her raised hand and got ahold of herself. "Oh, Marina, it's you. I'm so sorry. I thought it was someone else."

Marina took another step back. "I...I just found this in the ground floor laundry closet. It was behind a stack of tablecloths. I was looking for the peach-colored ones for Sunday's wedding brunch." She held up a camera. "Didn't someone lose a camera?"

"Yes…yes. One of the photographers said it was stolen after the Victoria Palmer wedding." Morgan managed an uncertain smile. "Thank you, Marina. I'm so sorry I acted like that. I'm a little off-kilter today. You know, a little nervous."

Still apprehensive, Marina continued to back away. "I better get back to work."

"Thanks, Marina," Morgan called after her as the woman rushed off.

Chapter 44
Thursday Afternoon

Carter came up behind her. "What's the matter? You sounded freaked out when you called."

She spun around, still holding the camera. He eyed it but made no comment. "I *am* freaked out," she said. "I need to tell you what happened."

"Let's go somewhere and talk. How about your office?" He started down the hall.

Morgan reached out and held him back. "No, we can't go into my office." She was trembling again. "Let's go upstairs to my apartment. If we lock the door, I'll feel safe."

Carter's eyes widened with concern.

As they started towards the elevator, she held up the camera. "Look what Marina found."

"Who's Marina?" Carter pushed the up button.

"Marina is in charge of housekeeping. I think this is the camera that was stolen from the wedding photographer. We'll have to turn it over to Dax, but maybe you and I could check out the pictures first."

When the elevator door slid open, Rex and Georgie stepped out. They had towels over their shoulders. Unobtrusively, Morgan hid the camera behind her back.

"There they are, the lovebirds," Rex said.

Georgie frowned. "Leave them alone, Rex."

Without missing a beat, Carter said, "You guys going down to the pool? I'll probably be down in a little while."

Rex laughed and looked from Carter to Morgan. "Maybe you will and maybe you won't."

Morgan's jaw clenched. *What a jerk.* She and Carter stepped into the waiting elevator and the doors closed.

"Sorry about that," Carter said. He squeezed her hand.

She rolled her eyes. "No problem. I know Rex pretty well by now."

***

Upstairs, Morgan tapped in the code and they entered her apartment. She placed the camera and laptop on the hall table. Then she double locked the door and pulled the chain across. As she turned around, she started to shiver again. Carter stepped over and took her into his arms. She clung to him for several minutes. He said nothing and just held her close. When she felt her heart rate slow down, she pulled away.

"Something terrible happened while we were out for lunch." She explained about the note and the torn sheets of paper.

"'Stop playing detective, bitch, if you value your life,'" Carter repeated slowly. "And this person saw the notes we'd made about every member of the wedding party."

"Yes. And tore them into a million pieces."

"I wonder if there was anything on that list that indicated we were on to someone? I mean, right now we have no idea who the killer is, right? But maybe he or she thinks we do."

Morgan felt cold. She hugged herself. "I see what you mean."

"Did you contact Sheriff Simmons?"

"I texted him, but he hasn't gotten back to me. I rushed out of the office and locked it. I figured the police might want to look for fingerprints or DNA."

"Good move."

Then she was back in his arms, clinging to him. He kissed the top of her head, then cupped her chin and raised her face to his. Their lips met. Their bodies were molded together. They kissed for a long time, soft gentle kisses and then they grew more urgent. Again, Morgan pulled away. She placed a finger on his lips. He kissed it.

"We're wasting time," she said, smiling.

"Wasting time? No way! Kissing you is a valuable use of time." He reached for her, but she stepped back.

"When Dax gets here, we're going to have to give him the camera. Let's look through the pictures right now, while we can."

Carter sighed. "You're right."

187

Morgan retrieved the camera from the hall table. She snapped out the memory card and slid it into her laptop. In the living room, she carried the laptop to the dining table. Carter pulled over a chair, so they could look at the pictures together. She downloaded the images on to her computer. "Oh my God, there are hundreds of pictures."

"What we really want is the last ones." Carter snaked an arm around her shoulders.

"Yes, maybe we can zip through some of these." She began to scroll through the images. Now and then she stopped if she spotted a member of the wedding party. "Look, here's Rex and Georgie dancing pretty close. Do they have a thing going? I thought she loved Brad."

Carter shrugged. "How would I know?"

"Well, we just saw them together." Morgan continued to scroll through the pictures. "I haven't seen very many of you dancing."

"I wasn't dancing much. I wanted to dance with you, but you were giving me the cold shoulder." Carter squeezed her shoulder as he said the word.

Morgan turned to smile at him. "Sorry." She kissed him quickly and turned back to the computer. "Here's Josh having a conversation with Mindy. Oh, here's Brad asking his new mother-in-law to dance."

"Norma Lee looks like she'd bite his head off."

Finally, they got down to the last pictures of the Talbot gang up on the dais. Morgan enlarged the first image. Brad had his arm around Victoria's waist. To her right were Jenny and Lars. Mindy and Jill stood to Brad's left. Lined up behind them were Josh, Rex, Carter and Georgie. In the next picture, they had all changed places, but Victoria and Brad were still front and center. After that everyone was joking around, making faces and holding rabbit ears over heads. They kept changing places, and at one point, Victoria wasn't visible, just her billowing white dress behind the guys. Then all the girls were clowning around in front. In the second to last picture, Victoria was back in place with Brad. In the last one, the rictus on her face left no doubt she was in pain. After that there were several pictures of Victoria lying on the ground with Carter and Brad at her side.

Morgan used the pointer, moving across the faces. "All these happy pictures make me feel incredibly sad. Here's Victoria looking...well, victorious. She has her man and the wedding she dreamed of."

"Yeah, I feel that way looking at Josh. Who in the world killed him? He was such a great guy."

They went back and looked at the images several times. Morgan tried to locate each person and when they were behind or to the side of Victoria. "How long before R27 takes effect? A few minutes? Thirty seconds?"

"I believe within thirty to sixty seconds," Carter said.

"So we should concentrate on these last six pictures, perhaps. What do you see?"

"I see a bunch of drunk people acting like idiots...and I'm one of them." He pointed to the third from last picture. "I'm smiling like a Frankenstein look-alike."

"Not one of your best headshots." Morgan giggled and sat back. Carter kept going through the images.

"I feel like it could be almost anyone at one time or another...except Jenny...she's never near Victoria...beside or behind." Carter frowned, peering closer. "Let's see...and Jill seems to be just standing there on the edge. She doesn't move much. She really doesn't smile, either."

Morgan leaned forward to get a better look. "That's weird, because she takes pictures and videos all the time, so you'd think she would be aware of how someone looks on camera."

Morgan's phone rang. She pulled it out of her pocket. It was Dax. "Hi, sorry I couldn't get back to you," he said. "I've had a lot going on here at the hospital. What's up? You sounded upset."

Morgan explained about the note and the yellow tablet.

"Don't touch anything. I'll send a forensics team over there. I doubt we'll find anything, but you never know."

"I've got some other news. We have the lost camera. One of our cleaning staff found it in the ground floor linen closet behind a bunch of tablecloths."

"Great! This might be the breakthrough we've been waiting for." Dax sounded ebullient.

Morgan didn't tell him he might be disappointed. She and Carter hadn't seen anything that pointed with certainty to any one person.

"I wonder why they left the camera in that closet where it could be discovered?" Dax said.

"That closet is usually locked. We've got silver vases in there and a bunch of other stuff. He or she probably couldn't get back in to retrieve the camera."

"Who's handled it?"

"Oh, gosh, I didn't think about fingerprints. Marina, the woman who found it, me and the thief. I guess."

"Maybe we'll be able to pick up some prints."

"Dax, what about Mr. Palmer?"

"He was poisoned, probably R27 just like Victoria."

Morgan drew a jagged breath. She thought of Big Bob lying in the hospital bed just yesterday. Now he had joined his daughter.

Dax was still speaking. "Morgan, I'm worried about you. You need some security. This maniac will stop at nothing. Are you alone now?"

"No, I'm with Carter."

"Okay, don't go anywhere alone."

"Right," she managed to respond. She felt a sense of elation. Dax didn't consider Carter a suspect anymore.

"Oh, and don't let anyone know you've got the camera. It's important evidence."

Morgan rang off, and then told Carter what she'd learned.

"Someone wanted Victoria, Josh and Big Bob dead. Why? We need to find out," Carter said.

"What did Big Bob say yesterday that set him off?" Morgan frowned, trying to remember.

"You mean, 'It just couldn't be…it just couldn't be'?"

"What do you suppose he meant? *It just couldn't be…* that Victoria died, or…?"

"Or it just couldn't be someone he knew that killed her."

If that was the case, then he had an idea who the killer was, Morgan thought.

Chapter 45
Thursday - Late Afternoon

Morgan and Carter took the elevator down. They met Dax as he came down the hallway from Morgan's office. "I've got a forensics team in there. They're checking for prints." He held up a plastic evidence bag. The poison pen note was inside. "This is going to the lab right, now."

Together they went down to the Gardenia Room. Once inside, Morgan handed him the Nikon D850. "I might as well tell you we looked at the pictures already." She blushed slightly.

Dax shook his head in frustration. "Morgan, you should leave this investigation to us. You've been very helpful, but I'm worried about your safety. So did you figure out who the perp was?"

Morgan glanced at Carter, who also looked uncomfortable. "We couldn't decide on one person for sure. But we did rule out Jenny and Jill. They weren't anywhere near Victoria during the series of pictures."

"I'm sending the camera to the lab. Hopefully, they'll see something you didn't." Dax slipped the camera into another evidence bag and handed it to the waiting police officer along with the bagged note. The man left the room.

"Dax, I didn't tell you Carter and I went to see Mr. Palmer yesterday afternoon."

"Man-oh-man, you two can't just leave well enough alone." He raised his hands in frustration. "Okay, what did you learn?"

"We made our condolences and talked for a while. At one point I asked him if he had any idea what could have happened lately to have gotten Victoria killed. He became very agitated and repeated, *it just couldn't be.* That set off his monitors and they asked us to leave."

"'It just couldn't be...'" Dax repeated the phrase. "You couldn't ask him what he meant?"

"No, they told us he needed to rest so we came back to the Magnolia."

Dax sat down and gestured to the chairs around the table. "Sit down. I might as well tell you what we know."

Morgan and Carter sat.

"From what we could learn, last night someone entered the hospital, probably through the emergency room. They made their way up the stairs right outside Mr. Palmer's room. They entered his room and injected him with R27. He'd been given a sleeping aid earlier in the evening and was probably too drowsy to fight back."

"What about the monitors and IV? Wouldn't the nursing staff have been alerted?" Morgan asked.

"Late yesterday, they removed the monitors because he was doing well. He ate dinner and he was supposed to go home this morning."

"The hospital staff didn't see anyone suspicious?"

"Apparently it was a busy night for the nurses. They had two code blues and were probably occupied when Mr. Palmer was murdered. One nurse said she thought she saw someone enter the stairwell, sometime around one AM. But she wasn't sure. Couldn't give us much of a description, either."

"What took them so long to contact the police if he died in the early hours of the morning?"

"Initially, they thought it was a heart attack. Only later, an observant resident noticed the puncture wound from a syringe at the back of his arm. Then they did tests."

Carter drummed his fingers on the table. "This killer got away with it again..."

Morgan interrupted him, "What about at the Magnolia? If someone left here and drove to the hospital, the security cameras must have recorded them leaving and returning."

"Detective Rodriguez is checking that out right now. He's down the hall working with your guy Roberts. They're studying the camera footage to see who left the resort and what time they returned."

"What about Norma Lee, I mean, Mrs. Palmer? Has she been notified of her husband's death?"

"I tried calling earlier but her household help told me she couldn't be disturbed, even when I said it was the police. I'm going over there now."

"I'll go with you if you want. She knows me," Morgan said.

"That might be a good idea. You could soften the blow."

Eventually, Dax decided Carter could tag along. Norma Lee had seemed especially charmed by him the day before. The three of them got into a golf cart and Morgan drove. In the late afternoon light, the Magnolia gardens were exquisite. Morgan could smell the heavy perfume of the gardenias as they whisked past the flowering bushes.

As they made their way, Dax got a call from Detective Rodriguez. He listened and then disconnected with a sigh of frustration.

"Nothing. They have nothing from last night. Apparently, the security cameras at the parking lot and the bridge were destroyed by the storm. The crew who worked last night have no recollection of a car leaving or returning by the front gate. They also checked the staff entrance. They have footage of my arrival to pick up Katarina Petrov and my departure. There were no other cars recorded either coming or going."

"Wait a minute, that's not right," Morgan said. "When I got home at midnight, a car came speeding down the driveway from the parking lot. It almost hit me. Whoever was driving had their headlights off."

"What did the car look like?" Dax asked.

"I don't know. It was dark, and the moonlight was filtered by the trees."

From the rear seat, Carter laid his hand on her shoulder. "Was the car you saw dark or light colored?"

She thought for a minute. "It must have been black or dark blue. But honestly, I didn't see who was driving or anything. It zipped by so fast."

Dax hit his forehead with his palm. "Each time we get a clue, we're stymied by incomplete information. We just can't get a handle on this killer."

"Sorry," Morgan said.

"Oh, it's not you. I just feel like this guy keeps outsmarting us."

"Or gal," Morgan said.

They came around a pergola covered with climbing roses and approached the Palmer cottage. Morgan drove up the meandering pathway to the house. She was struck again by its simple grandeur. In the shadows, it wasn't possible to see into the large porch. They got out of the cart and Dax went up the steps and rang the doorbell. As before, Bayani, the manservant, opened the door.

Dax spoke with authority. "Hello, I'm Sheriff Simmons. I must talk to Mrs. Palmer now."

"I will tell the missus." Bayani scurried back into the house, shutting the door behind him.

Quietly, Dax fumed. "This is like getting an audience with the queen."

Carter and Morgan exchanged smiles. Dax definitely did not like to wait.

A few minutes later, Bayani was back. He opened the door and then bowed. "Please to follow me."

They entered the huge front room with its circular sunken living area, the white sofas, the grand piano and the view of the pool. This time around, Norma Lee sat facing the pool. She didn't bother to get up or even turn around. The white cat was draped over her shoulders. As they got closer, Morgan could see she had a martini glass in one hand and a cigarillo in the other. She wore a fuchsia silk robe, and rabbit fur mules on her feet.

Dax went down the short steps and introduced himself. Norma Lee interrupted him. "I already know he's dead. You didn't need to come over here. Someone called me."

"Who called you?" Dax asked.

"They didn't identify themselves. I guess from the hospital." Her voice was slurred. Morgan looked closely at the woman. She had aged since yesterday in spite of a thick coat of make-up that covered her wrinkled face. Norma Lee's eyes were focused on the pool outside. Morgan turned to follow her gaze. Outside, lolling by the pool, was a gorgeous hunk dressed in a white speedo. He was leaning back on a deck chair, one leg stretched out and one bent at the knee. With long blond curls and his body slick with oil, he looked like one of those chick magnets on the cover of a romance novel.

Norma Lee looked up at Morgan. "He's gorgeous, isn't he."

Morgan nodded. Dax and Carter frowned.

"His name is Adonis. And he truly is an Adonis. He came over to help me feel better. I love looking at him." Norma Lee slurped her drink and held out the glass to Bayani. "I'm not going to offer you a drink today. I really don't want you to stick around. What do you have to tell me that I don't already know. Bob is dead. Victoria is dead. Now I'm alone to do what I want." She gestured towards the window with her cigarillo.

Dax sat down across from her, as did Carter. Morgan sat facing the pool. Adonis was changing positions. He lay on his side now, one leg bent. He flexed his muscles and smiled. He was putting on quite a show.

Bayani brought Norma Lee another drink. At that moment Lucifer, the black cat, jumped down from his perch and hopped up on the aquarium. He sat there twitching his tail and looking down at the darting fish.

Dax started again. "I'm sorry you had to learn of your husband's death from a stranger. The reason I'm here is to tell you that Mr. Palmer was murdered by lethal injection, like his daughter."

Norma Lee frowned in confusion. "Killed? Big Bob? Why?" She took a long drink, slopping some liquid on her silk robe. The dark stain spread across the silky folds.

"We don't know why. We wondered if you knew. Do you have any idea who would want to kill your husband?"

Morgan doubted Norma Lee was in any state to do any deep thinking. Nonetheless, the woman seemed to be searching her fuzzy brain for an answer.

"Bob was no angel," she said after several seconds. "He didn't get rich doing kind deeds. I'm sure he had enemies." She bent and flicked ashes into a purple ashtray.

"Mrs. Palmer, we feel his murder has something to do with Victoria's murder. Can you see a possible connection?"

Norma Lee looked at Carter. "Like I told you the other day. Victoria and her dad had secrets. I was the outsider. From the beginning, Victoria was number one in his heart." Tears formed in her eyes and ran down the crevasses of her cheeks.

Dax kept pushing. "Did something occur recently? Was there conflict about the wedding? Someone who called or texted?"

The woman took a long drag on her cigarillo letting the smoke filter out through her nostrils. "All I can tell you is that sometimes, very rarely, Bob got calls from someone. He would go into another room to talk. When he came back, he was always subdued." She sipped her drink. "He got a call like that the day before the wedding. He seemed upset."

Morgan looked out at the pool. Adonis stood on the diving board. The slanted rays of the afternoon sun illuminated his sleek body. Then he did a perfect dive into the turquoise water.

Chapter 46
Thursday - Early Evening

On the way back to the resort, they discussed their visit with Norma Lee. "Wow, that was weird," Carter said.

Morgan giggled. "And you weren't even watching Adonis perform."

"What do you think, Dax? She was pretty drunk. Do you think she was telling the truth about those phone calls? Or was she just setting us up?" Carter asked.

"Why wouldn't she be telling the truth?" Morgan said.

Dax eyed them both. "I think there really were secret phone calls, but they don't necessarily have anything to do with Victoria's or Mr. Palmer's murders."

But maybe they do, Morgan thought.

***

Back at the resort, Carter asked Dax if he had a minute to talk. They went down the hall to the Gardenia Room.

Georgie was on the house phone in the lobby. She beckoned Morgan over. Mindy stood beside her. Georgie wore a light blue off-the-shoulder dress and had piled her blond hair atop her head. Golden tendrils framed her perfect oval face. Mindy had on her usual baggy jeans and a grey hoodie.

"Hey, Morgan, we think Jill is boarded up in her room," Georgie said.

"What do you mean?"

"She won't answer the phone and we're sure she's in there," Mindy said. "Could you come upstairs with your pass key?"

Georgie slammed the phone down. "She won't answer. I'm worried she hasn't taken her meds and she's probably obsessing up there. We need to help her."

"Sure, I can help you out."

Morgan got the pass key from Lionel, and they went up in the elevator and down the hall. Georgie rapped on Jill's door and they waited. After a few seconds of silence, Georgie said, "Hey, Jill. It's me. Mindy is here, too. Can you open up?"

They waited. Georgie knocked again.

Mindy put her ear to the door. "I think I hear running water."

"We better go in," Georgie said.

Morgan inserted the keycard and the door clicked open. Georgie stuck her head in. "Hello...Jill?" Then she pushed the door open and they walked in. Jill's room was much smaller than the suites the bridal party had been given. From the door, Morgan could see into the bathroom. Jill's back was visible. The girl was in her underwear, wiping the mirror with a washcloth.

Georgie rushed over to her. "Are you alright?"

Jill looked at her blankly. "Yes, but I have to clean the mirror." She dipped the washcloth into the sink and scrubbed at the mirror. The basin was flooding over and there was water on the tiled floor.

"Honey, the mirror is clean." Georgie turned off the faucet and gently grasped Jill's hand. "You don't need to wash it."

"But I do. I can still see the writing. It's there. I can see it." She struggled to remove her arm from Georgie's grasp. She began to rub the mirror with her free hand.

"Jill, did you take your meds today?" Georgie asked.

"I don't know. I can't remember," she said vaguely.

Mindy went over to the open shelf where several pill bottles were lined up. While Georgie tried to reason with Jill, Mindy read the directions on the bottles and showed them to Morgan. "She's supposed to take one of these and one of these, morning and night. We don't know if she took one this morning but it's almost night now. Don't you think she should take one of each? I mean, it would be safe."

"What are they for?" Morgan asked.

"For her OCD, I guess. I mean, she's freaking out, right?"

"I don't know," Morgan said. "Georgie, you travel with Jill. Do you know about the pills?"

"Yes, I know she has to take them every day. Get a glass of water, Mindy."

Georgie had managed to bring Jill into the bedroom and helped her into a white terry robe. The girl looked young and fragile. Her blond bangs were plastered to her forehead. Georgie made her sit on the edge of the bed. Mindy brought over two capsules and a glass of water. Jill swallowed the meds like a little kid.

Morgan went into the bathroom and used the bath towels to wipe up the floor. Georgie was speaking soothingly to Jill and the girl seemed to grow less agitated. When Morgan came back into the bedroom, they were laughing quietly. Morgan felt relieved. Then, with sudden violence, Jill pushed Georgie away and struggled to her feet.

"I've got to wash off those words on the mirror," she said.

The others looked at each other in confusion. "What words?" Morgan asked.

"It says...*I know you killed Tory*." Jill rushed into the bathroom, picked up the washcloth, and resumed scrubbing hard at the mirror.

Mindy whispered, "Do you think she did it? I mean, she's always been a little screwy."

Georgie turned to Mindy, her face dark with anger. "That was mean. Jill has her problems, but she's not a killer."

"I'm sorry, I guess I don't trust anyone." Mindy got up and left the room, slamming the door shut behind her.

Morgan stayed on, until Jill had calmed down and they were able to reason with her. "You just imagined those words. It's like a nightmare," Georgie said.

Jill nodded. "You're probably right. Although..." She trailed off, looking vague.

Gently, Georgie shook her shoulder. "Come on, get dressed. We'll go down and have a glass of wine before dinner."

Chapter 47
Thursday - Early Evening

The wedding party agreed to have one last dinner together. They were fed up with each other, but no one wanted to be alone. They decided to escape from the resort and have dinner in Rosemary Beach. Georgie begged Morgan to come along. They used the Magnolia van, as they had the first night when they'd gone out for dinner at The Red Bar. That was only a week ago, but to Morgan it felt as though months had passed.

She sat next to Carter. He didn't say much during the short drive. He seemed to be deep in thought. The van dropped them off in front of Wild Olives in Rosemary Beach. They found a table outside. It was dark now and the stars were out. Lanterns provided a soft light. At the server's suggestion, they ordered a couple of bottles of red wine and a couple of white. The guys all wanted hamburgers and the girls agreed to share a rustic Provençal flat bread as well as several small plates including fried green tomatoes, goat cheese, crab cakes and seared scallops.

"I've had enough fancy food this week. I'm ready for a burger and fries," Rex said. He was sitting next to Georgie, their shoulders touching. Morgan thought about Georgie's tears only a week ago, when she was bemoaning her loss of Brad. Apparently, she'd gotten over it.

Brad had been pale and subdued all afternoon. He and Carter were deep in conversation. Carter patted him on the back and Brad nodded. Then he raised his glass. "Let's drink to Tory and Josh. I wish they were here with us."

Everyone raised their glasses. "To Tory and Josh."

Morgan could feel the tension around the table. Someone here was glad Victoria and Josh were no longer alive. But tonight, there seemed to be a tacit agreement to overlook the murderer among them.

"I saw you and Carter going off with the sheriff," Georgie said. "What's the latest? Was there something fishy about Mr. Palmer's death?"

Morgan looked over at Carter. He shrugged. She decided there was no big secret. "Mr. Palmer died from a lethal injection."

"Oh, my God," Jill said. Georgie slid a comforting arm around her shoulders.

Jenny's eyes widened. "Just like Victoria."

Rex leaned forward. "Did they see who did it at the hospital?"

Morgan shook her head. "No, the nurses were busy, and no one saw anything."

Lars sipped wine. "I can't believe that. Hospitals have video cameras all over the place."

"Well, big Chief Simmons hasn't been by to arrest anyone. So, Morgan must be telling the truth," Rex said. "Where were you guys going in the golf cart this afternoon?"

"We went with Sheriff Simmons to talk to Mrs. Palmer. They hadn't been able to reach her before."

"Oh, my goodness. She must be all broken up," Jill said.

Morgan decided to lie. She didn't know how to describe the weird scene they'd witnessed with Norma Lee. "Yes, she's quite upset."

"What does this mean for us? Can we still go home tomorrow?" Mindy asked.

"Yes, the police have nothing on us. And the Magnolia is kicking us out," Rex said.

"Please, let's talk about something else." Jenny gulped down some white wine.

Georgie cleared her throat and looked around the table. "So, what's everyone doing next week?" She looked particularly beautiful tonight, Morgan thought, like a Viking princess.

There was a moment of silence.

"Well, we're going home, first thing tomorrow morning," Lars said. "I filled up the car with gas this afternoon. We're planning on driving straight through."

"Yeah, I can't wait to get home and have everything turn back to normal." Jenny smiled up at Lars. The brown and white patterned dress she wore set off her rosy complexion and lovely brown eyes.

"Can anything ever be normal again? After this week?" Jill said, her voice edgy and her face pale. Morgan noticed a tremor in her hand as she clutched her wine glass.

"I think eventually this whole experience will fade away. Time heals all wounds," Georgie said. She turned and smiled at Rex. He squeezed her hand.

More silence. More tension.

Finally, Brad spoke. "You guys might as well know. I'm going into rehab tomorrow afternoon. I've checked myself into the New Beginnings Ranch. I'm going to turn my life around." His hands were shaking, and he had tears in his eyes. Morgan wondered if he was in withdrawal or just plain emotional. He poured himself another glass of red wine.

"That's great," Lars said.

"Yeah, good for you," Jenny echoed.

Rex chuckled and shook his head. Morgan prayed he would keep his mouth shut and not make some snide comment about Brad and his inheritance.

The waitress interrupted by delivering the food. They all kept quiet as she placed the dishes on the table. The guys dug into their burgers and the girls passed the small plates around.

"How about you?" Georgie asked Carter. She glanced ever so briefly at Morgan.

He picked up a fry. "I'm on my way back to UCLA in the morning. I've got a research project that's been on hold this week. I've got to get back in the saddle."

"We're on our way to L.A. tomorrow, too," Rex said.

"What flight?" Carter asked.

"Georgie and I are on the ten o'clock, out of Panama City Beach." He took a large bite of his hamburger, wolfing it down.

"What about you, Mindy?" Carter asked.

"Oh, I'm out of Destin, later."

"Me too. Maybe we could share a ride," Carter said.

Mindy nodded and smiled. She reached over and speared a golden scallop.

Brad poured himself another glass of wine.

Morgan helped herself to a slice of the flatbread. "What's going to happen to Victoria's website?"

"Mindy, Georgie and I have been talking. We're going to keep it going. In spite of Tory's death, she has millions of followers. Right, Mindy?" Rex said.

"Yes, I've been working with the staff. This week we've been recycling posts from the last few years that got the most traffic." Mindy blushed. Morgan stared at her. She hadn't really noticed Mindy earlier, on the drive here. The girl had taken off her glasses and her hairstyle was different. Rather than a messy ponytail, she wore her heavy brown hair loose and full around her face. She was striking.

"Georgie will have to step up and become a little more aggressive, a little more demanding, a little more narcissistic. We're counting on her to keep the Victoria mystique going," Rex said.

Georgie nodded. "I think the three of us will bring a new vibe to the site."

"So, you think you don't even need Tory?" Brad said, his voice slurred. He grabbed the table edge and pushed himself upright. His voice rose as he kept talking, until he was practically shouting. "Maybe the three of you never thought you needed her? Maybe you were using her for your own fame and glory? Maybe you three got rid of her?" Abruptly, he pitched headlong into the table. Glasses shattered, food spattered across the floor, and Brad lay inert.

Chapter 48
Thursday Night

The guys managed to load Brad into the van. He'd revived and was talking incoherently but managed to stumble to a seat. Back at the resort, Lars and Carter helped him up to his room and dumped him in bed.

The girls asked Rex to accompany them to their rooms even though security had been ramped up. There was a policeman in the lobby as well as security staff on both floors where the wedding party resided. Dax had insisted on stationing a guard outside Morgan's apartment as well.

When Carter came back down, Morgan was waiting for him in the lobby. "Did you get Brad settled?"

"Yeah, he's out like a light. Let me go upstairs with you to make sure you're safe."

As they walked towards the elevator, a tall African-American policewoman came forward. She was whippet-thin with the bearing of an Ethiopian queen. Her body was lean and muscular, her expression intense. "Are you Morgan Lytton?"

"Yes, I am."

"I'm going to guard you tonight. We'll go up in the elevator together. Then I'll check your apartment and make sure no one is in there. I'll spend the night in the hallway." She delivered these words with little inflection.

"Thank you, Ms. ..."

"Officer Hanley." The woman turned to Carter. "I'll take care of Ms. Lytton."

Carter had been dismissed. She could see in his face that he knew it. "I'll see you in the morning. I'm glad you'll be safe," he said. Then he turned away and pulled out his phone. Immediately he became engrossed in his messages.

Morgan felt as though she'd been dismissed as well. Disappointed, she followed the officer to the elevator.

On the way up, neither one of them spoke. Upstairs, Morgan walked down the hall behind Officer Hanley. The woman's hand hovered near the big gun at her hip. She stopped outside Morgan's apartment. "You live here, Ms. Lytton, right?"

Morgan nodded. The policewoman looked up and down the hallway. "Does anyone else live up here?"

"Currently, these suites are empty." Morgan punched in the code and reached for the doorknob. Officer Hanley pushed by her and went inside first, her gun on the ready. Morgan followed her in and switched on the lights. The woman locked the door behind them and then began her search. She looked briefly around the wide living room and walked quickly to the kitchen clicking on the lights. She peered into the pantry. Then she crossed the living room and went into the bedroom. Morgan could hear her opening closets and inspecting the bathroom. Morgan looked into the bedroom and watched as the officer knelt down and then lay down to look under the bed. Satisfied that no one was lurking underneath, she rose to her feet in one smooth movement. This gal was one big muscle.

"Doesn't look like anyone's here," Morgan said.

Officer Hanley harrumphed. Back in the living room, she pulled back the curtains and opened the door out to the patio. She looked around and gazed up at the roof line. Then she went to the railing and looked down. When she came back in, she shut the patio door and locked it. Then she closed the curtains completely. "I'll be outside in the hallway."

"Thank you, officer," Morgan said as the woman strode to the door.

"Lock up behind me," she said. Then she turned and flashed the tiniest smile. "You'll be safe, honey."

Morgan did feel safe. She fell asleep instantly, but at three AM she awoke as if a bomb had gone off. Her brain had kept working as she slept, and now she thought she knew who had killed Victoria and why. But she needed to check for sure.

She walked through the living room to the entryway. She knocked gently on the door, pulled back the locks and opened it. Officer Hanley jumped to her feet and grabbed her gun. Her cell phone clattered to the ground.

"Is something wrong?" She looked over Morgan's shoulder into the apartment.

"No, nothing's wrong. I wanted to check if you were here."

Officer Hanley relaxed and shoved her gun back in its holster. "Well, you can relax. I'm here." She reached down and picked up her phone.

"Okay, thanks," Morgan murmured. She felt a little foolish as she shut the door.

In the living room, she picked up her laptop and went back to her bedroom, quietly closing the door behind her. She made sure the curtains to the balcony were fully closed. Then she got back in bed, piled the pillows behind her and opened her laptop. She was feeling a little afraid but also exhilarated. After logging in, she clicked on the photo icon, then on the Palmer-Hughes wedding album. She scrolled down through the hundreds of pictures until she came to the final photos. It was the third picture of everyone on the dais. Victoria's face was turned slightly to the right. The half profile-shot displayed the strong line of her jaw and her straight nose. Brad was on Victoria's left. Mindy was on the other side.

Morgan sucked in her breath and let it out slowly. Mindy was looking to the right as well. Her strong jaw line and straight nose mimicked Victoria's. You could place one on top of the other; they were carbon copies.

That night at Wild Olives, Mindy's resemblance to Victoria had struck Morgan's inner consciousness. Not until she was asleep did her brain put it all together.

"Wow," she said. Then she got to work researching Minerva Fairchild. She had skimmed over some of the information before the wedding. Now she studied it in earnest. Mindy had been born on July 11, 1990 in Kinfield, Missouri to a Ms. Linda Fairchild, father unknown.

She googled Victoria Palmer. Victoria was born on July 11, 1990 as well. She'd been adopted by Robert and Norma Lee Palmer six months later. Morgan remembered when Brad said he won big at the roulette table by placing his bets on seven and eleven, Victoria's birthday.

So, Mindy was born on the same day as Tory. Morgan would bet all the tea in China that Victoria's parents were Big Bob Palmer and Linda Fairchild. Victoria and Mindy were twins.

Morgan was perspiring. Her gaze swept the room, looking into the dark corners. She got up and turned on the overhead light and the three lamps. Then she locked the bedroom door.

Back in bed she continued to research Mindy. There was stuff about her connection to Victoria as her virtual media manager. Mindy's degree was in chemistry and computer programming. In the few pictures Morgan could find, Mindy had on those glasses and sported the messy ponytail. Often, she wore a hoodie that partially obscured her face. She'd been hiding her identity for a long, long time. Why?

Morgan closed her eyes, thinking. Could Mindy have killed her twin sister? Josh? Her father? Would she go after Morgan? Her heart beat faster. She took deep breaths to calm down. She was safe. Mindy didn't know Morgan was on to her. Officer Hanley was outside her door. Nothing to worry about.

Morgan went back to her computer. She googled Linda Fairchild and scrolled down the page. There were a lot of hits, but one site caught her attention—an obituary in the Kinfield, Missouri *Register*. Morgan read through the obit quickly, gobbling up the words. Linda Fairchild, age forty-six, had died suddenly of a heart attack on May tenth…only three months ago. The article reported that Linda would be remembered by her daughter Minerva and her fellow employees at the bakery in the Kinfield Walmart. There were no other family members listed. The accompanying picture showed a pretty, dark-haired woman.

Morgan massaged her temples and took deep breaths. She didn't need a migraine right now. If she was a betting person, she would bet dollars to donuts that Mindy had killed her mother, too.

Something had happened in the spring that had sent Mindy over the edge. Morgan was sure of it. But there was no proof! Mindy had managed to commit a series of crimes leaving no clues.

Should she text Dax? Not now, it was the middle of the night. She would contact him first thing in the morning. She shut her laptop and pushed it to the side. Then she lay down and closed her eyes, leaving all the lights on.

Chapter 49
Friday Morning

In spite of her fear, Morgan managed to sleep until eight AM. She opened her eyes a crack and realized the ceiling lights were beaming down on her. She closed her eyes quickly and took a moment to recall why she'd left the lights on. A wave of angst washed over her. Mindy. She had to contact Dax immediately. She reached for her phone and called him, but there was no answer. Then she asked Siri for the number at the police station and called the desk. The man who answered said Sheriff Simmons was in a meeting, but he would take a message. Morgan left her name and number, but no details, and rang off. A few seconds later, she tapped out a text: *Need to talk to you ASAP*.

Having done all she could for now, Morgan got up and left the bedroom. She pulled back the curtains in the living room and opened the sliding glass doors. She couldn't live with everything closed up tight. It was a perfect sunny day. Morgan made a mug of coffee, and then went to the front door and opened it. A young, blond officer seated in a folding chair jumped to his feet. "Good morning, ma'am."

"I thought Officer Hanley might still be here."

"No, ma'am. I'm Officer Richards."

She managed a smile for him. "Well, Officer Richards would you like a cup of coffee? I could bring it out here."

"I'd be much obliged. Cream and sugar."

"It'll have to be milk."

"Fine by me."

Morgan went back inside and prepared the mug of coffee, then took it out to the young officer. As she went back inside and shut the door, her phone rang. She rushed into the bedroom and picked up.

"Hey, baby girl." It was her dad. He sounded unnaturally cheerful.

"Hey, Dad."

"I hear the Palmer-Hughes wedding party is leaving and the police have pulled out. Now the Magnolia can get back into action."

For a minute, Morgan felt a pang of sadness. Was Carter gone already? They hadn't even said goodbye. "I don't know if they're all gone yet, Dad. I'm upstairs."

"I talked to Hans. He tells me he's hired a new concierge and reservations are coming in. I think we've weathered the storm."

"Yes, I suppose we have," Morgan said, without much enthusiasm.

"I'm down at the new Magnolia in Malibu. This place is heaven. The hotel, spa, pools, beach…it's perfect."

"Sounds great." Morgan wondered if she ran downstairs now, would she catch Carter before he left?

"I was thinking you should come out here. This place will be the new, exclusive, destination-wedding locale."

"Hmm."

A touch of annoyance entered his voice. "Morgan, think about it. I'm not joking. You're a California girl. Come back here. We'll find someone to take over the Emerald Coast Magnolia."

"I don't know, Dad. I'll think about it. I better go. We've got people arriving for a wedding this weekend."

"Okay, we'll talk soon. Bye."

"Bye." Morgan put down the phone. California? What was he thinking? Right now, she felt as though her world had been turned upside down. She longed to get back to her regular routine.

She ate a quick breakfast and dressed in a cool lime sheath, pearls, pearl earrings and white pumps. She twisted her hair into a French chignon and applied make-up with care. Now she looked like the elegant Magnolia wedding planner. It was like a costume for a well-rehearsed play. Maybe, if she pretended hard enough, her world would turn right side up again.

211

Out in the hall, Officer Richards was waiting. "I'm supposed to follow you around, today." He folded up his chair and leaned it against the wall.

"You're going to have a pretty boring day," Morgan said as they made their way down the hall and waited by the elevator. "I'll be spending most of it in my office."

Downstairs, a couple were checking in at the front desk. The new desk clerk was there with Lionel, learning the ropes. Morgan walked over, followed by Officer Richards. She said good morning to the guests checking in and then asked Lionel to step to the end of the counter. "How's it going?" she asked, gesturing to the new employee.

Lionel rolled his eyes, keeping his voice low. "This guy has the right attitude but is a slow learner. It's going to take a while for him to get the hang of it. He keeps asking me these inane questions."

"Patience is a virtue," Morgan whispered back. Then in a normal tone, she said, "Has everyone checked out from the Palmer wedding?"

"I think so. Let me check." He went to the computer, then came back. "Yeah, they're all gone. What a relief. The cops are gone too."

"And…ah…Mindy Fairchild?" Morgan asked.

"Yes, she left with Carter Perry. They shared a ride to the airport."

A wave of disappointment flooded over her. Carter was gone. She would probably never hear from him again. It was like a shipboard romance…here today, gone tomorrow.

She glanced up. Lionel was looking at her. "Are you all right?"

"Yes, I'm fine."

"Were you friends with Ms. Fairchild?"

Another wave broke over her, relief this time. If Mindy was gone, she had nothing to worry about. Any investigation would be in Dax's hands. "No, I just wondered. Gosh, I better get to work." She turned away and went down the hall to her office, her police bodyguard following behind.

Itzel was there, busy on the computer. She took in Officer Richards' presence with a wide-eyed glance but didn't comment.

"Hey, boss. Looks like things are back to normal. The wedding this weekend will be a breeze. Everything seems to be on schedule."

"That's great. Did Lilly Whitehouse call, by any chance? I know she's staying at her parents' house until the wedding."

"Yes, she wondered if you could come over there at five. They're having a cocktail party and she wants to introduce you to everyone."

Lilly Whitehouse was the antithesis of Victoria Palmer. She was sweet, kind, thoughtful and attractive...not gorgeous. Thomas Grant, her husband-to-be, was tall, thin and unpretentious. He had a prominent Adams apple and wonderfully kind eyes. Morgan liked them both. She knew the hundred or so attendees at the wedding would be equally charming. The Whitehouse cottage was one of the bigger houses in Magnolia. The family was quietly wealthy, not *nouveau riche.* They did everything in a subdued style. The morning wedding followed by a champagne brunch would be an elegant affair.

"I'll give Lilly a buzz. I've got her number," Morgan said. As she turned to go into her office, she noticed Officer Richards. She'd almost forgotten about him. "Listen, I don't think I need you anymore. I mean, the danger is no longer here. Whoever murdered Victoria Palmer has left the resort."

Richards looked dismayed. "I'm supposed to stay with you, ma'am, until the sheriff tells me differently."

Morgan shrugged. "At least go out in the lobby. I'd prefer you didn't sit in my office."

He nodded toward the inner door. "Let me look in there and make sure it's safe."

Morgan sighed. "All right. Come in."

The room was a mess. The forensic team had left fingerprint powder on the desk, conference table and chairs. All her desk drawers were open, and the furniture had been moved around. Itzel came up behind them. "Oh, gosh. We better get housekeeping in here to clean up."

While the housekeeping staff performed its magic, Morgan waited in the outer office, working on her phone and discussing details with Itzel. Officer Richards sat on a chair in the hall, protecting Morgan from absolutely nothing.

At lunchtime, she brought Officer Richards down to the kitchen. They sat on stools at a stainless-steel table with all the bustle around them. Morgan had a seafood salad and Richards ate a ham and cheese sandwich. His gaze followed the sous-chefs and line cooks as they hustled around the busy kitchen.

"I never knew all this went on in a hotel kitchen. It's got to be an exhausting job," Richards said in amazement.

"Yes, it is." Morgan didn't mention that sitting on a chair outside her office all morning was the total opposite.

After lunch, she went back to work, and her trusty bodyguard sat down in his chair again. Morgan texted and left more messages for Dax. She also called Claire to see if she knew what was going on with her fiancé.

"No clue, Morgan. He hasn't texted me all day. They must be busy with something big, or he's in a bunch of meetings. If I hear from him, I'll tell him to call."

"Okay, I really need to talk to him."

After she rang off, Morgan leaned back in her desk chair and gazed out at the Gulf, twirling a pencil in her fingers. The truth was she not only wanted Dax to call her; she also wanted Carter to call. He was on his way to California, never to be heard from again. Grady was gone, Carter was gone, and she needed to move on. Maybe she'd put out a video on Match.com and meet someone new. But she'd always avoided those dating sites. She sighed, put down the pencil and went back to her computer.

Chapter 50
Friday Afternoon

At four-thirty, Morgan decided to go upstairs and freshen up before the cocktail party. She put her desk in order and went into the outer office, carefully locking the door behind her. This was something she didn't normally do, but after being vandalized, it seemed necessary. Itzel had gone home early. The outer office was empty. Officer Richards was not in his chair. She looked down the hall and saw him kibitzing with the Magnolia security detail. Fine. She was getting tired of him following her around like a puppy dog. She would just run upstairs, change and pick him up on the way back down. He could walk over to the Whitehouse cottage with her.

In the lobby, Morgan waved at Lionel and headed for the elevator. A very pregnant woman, a frazzled father and three little kids were waiting at the resort's main entrance. The kids were running around and dive bombing onto the plush sofas and chairs. Morgan recognized the woman as Lilly Whitehouse's sister, Josephine. She was supposed to be matron-of-honor. There had been some fear that the new baby might arrive too early. Considering Josephine's physique, it looked as though the baby could pop out any minute.

Morgan went over and introduced herself and admired the children who were spinning around a pillar like whirling dervishes. Once the family had exited the lobby, Morgan walked to the elevator. An attractive man dressed in a Navy uniform held the door with his arm as she entered. He had several little ribbons on his pocket; undoubtedly a high-ranking officer. "Pretty hot out there," he said.

His eyes swept over her. "That's the Emerald Coast for you in summer," Morgan said, smiling.

"Are you here for the wedding?"

She noticed he wasn't wearing a wedding ring. "Yes and no. I work here."

As he got off at the third floor, he said, "I hope to see you around."

"Right," Morgan said as the doors shut. He was probably here for the Whitehouse wedding. *Here today, gone tomorrow.*

***

As she stepped into the hallway upstairs, she thought she heard the whoosh of a door closing, maybe from the stairwell. She looked in that direction. No one. Who could have been up here? Once a week, someone from the housekeeping staff cleaned her apartment. Not on Fridays, though. She walked down the hall. It seemed especially quiet. At her door, she entered the code and went inside. The first thing she noticed was the wind billowing the curtain by the patio door. The glass door itself was slightly open. She remembered opening it wide that morning, but she usually shut it before going downstairs, so the air conditioning could do its magic. Had she left it partially open like this? She didn't remember. She'd been thinking about Mindy and the conversation with her dad, so who knew what she'd done. She walked over to the door, pulled it shut and locked it.

In the kitchen, she poured a glass of ice water and took a long drink, gazing out the window at the waves below. She felt tired and a little down. She got this way sometimes after a wedding. This blue funk usually righted itself after a good night's sleep.

A knock at the front door broke her reverie. *Ah-ha, Officer Richards tracked me down.* She walked quickly over and pulled the door open. Then she froze. "Mindy? What are you doing here?"

"You know what I'm doing here." Mindy said, her voice low and tense. Her hair hung around her face and her eyes were luminous in the dark hallway.

"I thought you left with Carter this morning." Morgan said it in a chirpy voice while her heart raced.

"Don't bullshit me." Mindy pushed her way into the foyer. Suddenly she seemed larger and more powerful, like a super-heroine.

216

"What are you doing here?" Morgan repeated with more bravado than she felt.

"Don't act so innocent!" Mindy screeched. She slammed the door, then rushed forward and rammed into Morgan, sending her sprawling on her back. The glass of water flew across the room and smashed into a thousand shards. Morgan's head hit the marble floor. She saw stars and tried to raise her head, but she didn't have the strength. She groaned in pain.

Mindy stood over her. "Get up!"

Morgan tried to sit up, but her head was spinning. She lay back down, closing her eyes.

"Get up, I said," Mindy hissed. She kicked Morgan in the ribs.

Painfully, Morgan pushed herself over and tried to get on all fours, but she collapsed like a rag doll. Her limbs felt like jelly.

Mindy reached down and pulled her by the hair towards the sofa. Morgan bit back a scream. The girl was amazingly strong. "I want you up and listening to me," Mindy said, yanking on Morgan's hair. The back of her head throbbed with fresh, excruciating pain.

Morgan grabbed the edge of the white sofa with her right arm and tried to pull herself up. Mindy yanked her into a sitting position. Morgan tried to focus on Mindy's face. Dazed, she imagined the girl's head surrounded by an aura of sizzling red hatred.

"I told you to stop playing detective. But you wouldn't listen."

Morgan tried to speak clearly. "I din'nt…"

"Last night at dinner you were studying me. I saw the look in your eyes. You recognized me."

Morgan tried to shake her head, but it was too painful. "I din'nt see…"

Mindy bent over and slapped her hard. Morgan's head snapped to the side. Mindy's breath was hot and rancid. "Last night you googled me. I was watching. You researched me and my mother."

Morgan's fuzzy brain tried to process what she was saying. How did Mindy watch her? Had she been in the bedroom last night? No, that wasn't possible. The policewoman had searched…

"You don't get it, do you? I hacked into your laptop when you left it in your office."

Morgan closed her eyes. Mindy slapped her again. "Open your eyes."

Morgan obeyed.

"What do you need to know? That I killed my sister Victoria? Yes, I did. She stole everything from me. All these years, I had to grovel at her feet like an obedient slave while she paraded around like a fucking princess." Her voice quivered with uncontrolled fury.

Morgan could focus her eyes now. She fought to control her fear. She needed to keep Mindy talking. "Josh..." she managed to whisper.

"He guessed right away. The idiot. He wanted to meet and talk about it...talk about it...like I wanted to *talk*. He had to die, or he would have gone to the police. When he came around that massive bougainvillea, I killed him before he could start blabbing in my face. When I think about it, he helped perpetuate the lie. He knew Tory and I were related but he didn't do anything." Mindy's face was red with rage. She bent over and slapped Morgan again, back and forth, back and forth. Morgan's face was on fire and a spike of pain shot through her skull.

"I'll tell you the story because you're going to be dead soon. You're going to commit suicide by diving off that balcony." She nodded toward the patio door. "Everyone will think it's because of that boyfriend of yours." She laughed diabolically.

Morgan nodded her head ever so slightly and groaned.

"I'm controlling everything now. It's me. I'm in charge," Mindy shouted in demonic glee. "Everyone will admire me. Everyone will envy me. Princess Victoria is dead. Long live Queen Minerva." She fumbled in her pocket and brought out a small container that resembled a black pen. She snapped open the case and extracted a syringe.

Morgan screamed and tried to sit up. Mindy lunged at her, but Morgan rolled away.

Then the world exploded as the patio glass door shattered into a million pieces.

As Mindy shot a swift glance over her shoulder, Morgan tried to stand. On the periphery of her consciousness, she sensed someone barreling through the broken door and sprinting across the room. Mindy turned back around, her eyes hard and empty. As she tried again to plunge the syringe into Morgan's arm, it was knocked from her hand and went skittering across the marble floor.

"Fuck!" Mindy pushed Morgan away, fell to her knees and crawled towards the syringe.

Dax's foot came down on Mindy's outstretched wrist. Then he was on top of her, pinning her to the floor. Another officer moved into Morgan's line of sight, pulled out a set of handcuffs, and cuffed Mindy's wrists behind her back.

Slowly, Morgan pulled herself up and fell back against the sofa pillows. She was breathing hard and tears streamed down her cheeks.

Dax looked up at her. "Are you, all right?"

She shuddered. "Yes…yes, I'm all right."

Chapter 51
Sunday Evening

Morgan, Claire, Dax and Carter were sitting outside The Wine Bar restaurant in Watercolor, a pretty town along 30A. Friday night they'd taken Morgan to the hospital in an ambulance, where she was treated for concussion, cuts and bruises. Now she was feeling a lot better, although the back of her head felt sore if she touched it. Her wavy, blond hair hung down her back. It hurt too much to pin it up.

That morning, Morgan had taken second fiddle at the Whitehouse wedding. Itzel ran the show and the wedding and reception went off without a hitch...except for Josephine's holy terrors. One child fell into the lake, another pulled down a rose trellis, and the third swiped a handful of frosting off the wedding cake. As the brunch drew to a close, Josephine clutched her stomach, and her husband hustled her onto a golf cart and out to a waiting car. The baby girl was born two hours later. They named her Morgan.

Tonight, Morgan felt a mixture of pleasure and relief. Claire and Dax sat close together, their hands entwined. Claire's diamond glittered in the lamp light. Morgan snuck a look at Carter. He smiled at her and she smiled back. She felt incredibly happy right then.

They had just finished Wine Bar salads followed by a shared tomato Florentine pizza. Carter had chosen a smooth and fruity wine to go with it. They were on their second bottle.

"Tell us everything," Claire said. "We want to know why this girl...what's her name again...Cindy? Why she killed all those people."

"Her name is Minerva, better known as Mindy." Dax gestured towards Carter. "We owe a debt of gratitude to Carter, here. He's the one who put me on to her."

Morgan reached over and squeezed Carter's hand. He held it and didn't let go.

"Carter told me to go back and get the lab to compare Victoria Palmer's DNA with Mindy's. The DNA matched. Turns out they were fraternal twin sisters."

"How did you get Mindy's DNA?" Morgan asked.

"We took a water glass from her room. It provided her DNA and her fingerprints."

Morgan squeezed Carter's hand again.

Dax continued. "The girls were born to Linda Fairchild and Robert Palmer. Linda was an exotic dancer with whom Big Bob had a short affair. When the twins were born, he took Victoria to live with him and left Mindy with her mother. He continued to support them and later provided a scholarship for Mindy to go to college at Talbot where her twin sister was enrolled."

Morgan looked at Carter. "What made you think they were related?"

"I thought about the fact that Mindy and Tory were lab partners with Josh at Talbot. Tory was dead. Josh was dead. I wondered if there was some connection. When you came down to breakfast on Thursday and mentioned your research about the destruction of the lab, Mindy looked as though she'd seen a ghost. It didn't register right away, but later I got suspicious about her reaction."

Claire's brow furrowed. "I don't get it."

"Let me explain," Dax said. "Tory, Mindy and Josh were together in a DNA lab experiment at Talbot, during their freshman year. Apparently, Tory and Josh realized that Mindy and Tory had the same genome. Probably out of jealousy, Tory set the lab on fire and destroyed the evidence. Later, she confronted her father. He admitted the affair and that Mindy was his daughter and Victoria's sister."

Morgan frowned. "So all those years when Tory treated Mindy as her servant and fixer, she knew Mindy was her sister?"

"That's right."

"Gosh, that was kind of twisted," Claire said.

Dax went on. "After college, Mindy continued to work for Tory. Picture this: Mindy was in L.A. managing Tory's website and the other social media with a team of people. She was on call 24/7 and

221

was working in some warehouse. Meanwhile, Tory and Georgie flew around the world, ate expensive meals, wore luxurious clothes, stayed in exotic hotels and hung out with handsome men.

"I'll bet she was majorly jealous," Claire said.

Morgan nodded in agreement. "There's some quote about 'our envy of others devours us most of all.' Probably Mindy's envy was eating her up."

"Right," Dax said. "This past spring, there was a blow-up. Tory got enraged at a major screwup on the website and lit into Mindy, who fought back for the first time." He took a sip of wine. "Their quarrel went from bad to worse. Finally, Tory told Mindy they were twin sisters and explained about the discovery of their shared DNA. She claimed Mindy was the ugly duckling their father never wanted. She laughed at her and berated her. Mindy confessed she decided then and there to kill Tory before the wedding."

"What about her mother? Didn't she ever tell Mindy the truth?" Claire asked.

"After Victoria's outburst, Mindy went home and confronted her mother, who admitted the truth. Mindy had a difficult childhood. Her mom drank and was into drugs. She was in and out of rehab facilities and Mindy was sent to foster homes."

"So, while Tory lived a life of luxury, Mindy was living a life of misery. No wonder she was jealous," Morgan said.

Dax nodded. "Not long after her mother confirmed the story of her birth, Mindy obtained R27 on the Dark Web and killed her. That was just a few months ago."

Claire let out a breath. "Wow, truly a cold-blooded murderer."

Morgan shivered and grasped Carter's hand more tightly. Mindy's venom was all too recent in her mind.

Dax continued. "When they got to the Magnolia Resort for the wedding, Mindy tried to drown Tory, but she pushed the wrong person underwater."

Morgan turned to Carter. "That's when you saved Georgie. I remember the girls were all wearing pink swim caps to protect their hair from the salt water. Mindy picked the wrong capped head."

Carter nodded. "She also tried to get into Victoria's room one night, but Brad was there, so she was foiled again. Apparently, she had the hypodermic ready at various times, but wasn't able to get to Victoria. Then at the reception, she finally managed it. We studied the third to last picture of the Talbot gang on the dais. Mindy's face wasn't visible, but on high resolution, we could see the flare of her dress behind Tory."

"How did you learn all the details of Mindy stalking Victoria?" Claire asked.

Dax ran his hand through his hair. "When we got her into the interrogation room, she sang like a canary. She wouldn't stop, like she was proud of it all. You know, I think she's always been a very lonely, pent-up person. I imagine her lawyer will have her evaluated by a psychiatrist. She's definitely got mental problems."

They went quiet. Morgan thought about Mindy's unhappy life and felt sorry for her, but then she remembered Josh. She took a sip of wine. "What about Josh? What happened with him?"

Dax sat back in his chair and stretched, his arms over his head. Then he sat forward again. "Josh contacted Mindy after the meeting when I told the wedding party how Victoria died. He had his suspicions. Mindy asked him to meet her near Magnolia Park. She ambushed and shot him, then pulled his body into the bushes. She managed to rush back and arrive on time to have lunch with Rex and Jill."

"What about the gun?" Carter asked.

"It was registered to Victoria. Mindy got into her room sometime after the wedding and managed to open the safe and take out the gun. Of course, the code, Victoria chose was the date of their mutual birthday."

"Poor Josh," Morgan said. "He must not have realized who he was up against. He probably hoped to talk sense to her."

Dax sipped more wine. "Here's something else. Remember Rodriguez and I did the timeline for the afternoon Josh died?"

Morgan nodded.

"Mindy told us she'd seen Josh leave the hotel at twelve o'clock. But that wasn't true. When we interrogated Katarina Petrov, we

223

learned Mindy couldn't have seen him because just before twelve, a waiter dropped a tray of drinks and they were cleaning up the area. Katarina remembered it because she was waiting for someone to relieve her for lunch and the lobby was empty for several minutes. When I called Mindy on it, she admitted she'd made up the Josh sighting to make her story seem more credible."

Morgan cocked her head. "What about Katarina? I nearly forgot about her with everything that's been going on."

"She'll be tried for attempted murder. I would think they won't be too hard on her. It really depends on how good a lawyer she gets."

Carter leaned back in his chair and crossed his arms. "Okay we've reviewed three murders, what about the fourth one?"

"Big Bob? Mindy knew you'd been to see Mr. Palmer at the hospital and that you'd visited his wife, Norma Lee. She was psycho by then, or maybe she felt invincible. She'd already successfully killed three people. The only other person who knew the full story and who would suspect her as a murderer was her father. That night, she snuck into the hospital through the emergency room, wearing a blond wig in case anyone spotted her. Upstairs, she found her father sleeping and plunged the syringe into the back of his arm, thinking no one would see it. Thank goodness that young resident was so observant."

"How did she get to the hospital? Did she take an Uber?" Morgan asked.

"No, she knew we could trace a taxi or Uber car. When she killed Josh, she cleaned out his pockets. She took his keys and his phone. The night she killed Big Bob, she left the resort by a side door and walked to the resident parking area. She found Josh's car and drove it out of the lot with the lights off. On the way back, she left it in the Sunny Sands parking lot a mile from the Magnolia. We recovered it yesterday afternoon."

Morgan shivered. "I saw the car when I was coming up the drive that night. She almost ran me over. In retrospect, maybe she thought I could see her in the car and that was another reason she went after me."

Claire looked at Morgan. "The main thing is you're safe now, Morgan. Mindy is in jail and you'll never have to see her again."

Dax rubbed his eyes and yawned. "I feel as though I've been up forever."

"You have," Claire said. "We better go home and put you to bed."

"I've got more questions," Morgan said.

Dax grinned. "Talk to Carter. He knows just about everything."

They all stood up. Claire and Morgan hugged, and Carter and Dax shook hands. "Thanks again, Carter, for all your help," Dax said.

Carter smiled. "I hope we can all get together again, under happier circumstances."

Chapter 52
Sunday Night

As Carter drove his rental back to the Magnolia resort, Morgan asked him what happened when he left with Mindy on Friday morning.

"She was pretty hyper, talking a mile a minute. She really wasn't herself."

"Yes, she was normally pretty controlled," Morgan agreed.

"I'd seen how she looked at you Thursday night. If looks could kill and all that…I was worried about your safety, even though Dax had put a security detail on you." Carter looked over at her in the dark car. He brushed her cheek with his knuckles. She smiled at him and clasped his hand.

"Back to Mindy. At the airport, we checked in together. Then, right before we were set to board the plane, she disappeared into the restroom. She went in with her hoodie and came out wearing a blond wig and a red blouse. I had my eyes on my phone, but I was watching the restroom entrance. I photographed her as she exited. She glanced over at me briefly, but I kept my eyes averted. When she disappeared, I texted Dax that she hadn't boarded the plane. He had undercover cops on the lookout for her. She took a taxi to Seaside but escaped their surveillance in the crowd of tourists. Apparently, some tourist gave her a ride to the Sunny Sands."

"At that point, you and Dax were sure she would go after me?" Morgan began to perspire. "Why didn't you tell me? I was an unsuspecting guinea pig."

"We weren't sure of anything. Dax didn't want to scare you and he thought you were safe with your personal bodyguard."

"Right, my personal bodyguard. I thought I could sneak upstairs without him. That was pretty stupid." Her lower lip quivered.

Carter squeezed her hand. Then he continued, "Anyway, while Mindy was being unsuccessfully followed, Dax and another officer entered your apartment. They set up listening devices and hid on the balcony, leaving the door slightly ajar. But when you returned to your room, you slammed the door shut. They couldn't sneak back in without breaking the glass. And they knew Mindy was in the vicinity.

"Oh, right. I did shut the door," Morgan said, feeling guilty.

"So, they were out on the balcony listening to your conversation with Mindy. Once they heard Mindy admit to killing four people, they tried to get in…"

"…which they couldn't, so they smashed the door with the metal patio chairs." Morgan shivered at the memory of those last few moments before Dax crashed into her apartment.

They were quiet as they drove down 30A. In Seaside, families were out strolling, eating ice cream and enjoying the evening. After a while, Morgan said, "In spite of everything, I feel sorry for Mindy. How did she feel at her sister's grandiose wedding, where her dad didn't even acknowledge her presence? Ultimately, he bore the guilt for everything that happened."

"In a way, you're right. And he died for it."

***

When Morgan and Carter got back to the Magnolia, Renaldo drove them over to the resort in a golf cart. He made small talk and they responded. All the way, they sat close together, hand in hand. In the lobby, they made an unspoken decision and headed for the elevator. Upstairs, they entered her apartment and started kissing. Morgan's pent-up need for him matched his for her. Between kisses, caresses and moans, they made their way to the bedroom, leaving a trail of clothes across the living room floor.

Their lovemaking was passionate and tender, fueled by the excitement of newness and discovery. Later, they lay in each other's arms, spent. Morgan sighed with contentment, snuggling in closer.

"Morgan?"

"Yes."

"I want you to come out to California. We have to be together."

She giggled. "We barely know each other."

227

"I know all I need to know. You're strong, resilient, passionate, beautiful, determined, intelligent and utterly charming." He punctuated each adjective with a kiss.

"Let's see, I think you're kind, brilliant, handsome, determined and utterly charming. And I just learned you are wonderfully passionate." She wrapped her arms around his neck and pressed her body along the length of his. Desire flooded over her, and they made love again, slower and more deliberately.

As they lay wrapped in each other's arms afterward, Morgan said, "Maybe I could move to California." She was thinking of the new Magnolia resort in Malibu.

"We could get married right away," Carter said.

Morgan laughed. "Let's see…kind, passionate, intelligent…and utterly crazy."

"Yes, utterly crazy for you."

Dear Readers,

Envy on 30A takes place along the Emerald Coast and most of the towns, restaurants and shops actually exist. However, the Magnolia Resort and Spa is a figment of my imagination.

I consulted with Cheryl Walton, the Wedding Planner, at the Watercolor Resort. She was kind enough to discuss her exciting, creative and sometimes difficult job with me. Thank you, Cheryl.

I also want to thank my editor, Diane Piron-Gelman, for her detailed edit, continued support and excellent advice.

Thank you also to my talented artist, Meg Dolan, who has designed my eye-catching book covers.

Enjoy the Sunshine,

Deborah Rine

Made in the USA
Columbia, SC
16 June 2023